MW00531790

What We Hope For

Kirsten Usé

What We Hope For

Copyright © 2021 Kirsten Usé
Cover images from Canva

All rights reserved. No part of this book may be reproduced, distributed, or transmitted in any form or by any means, including photocopy, recording, scanning, or other electronic or mechanical methods, except for brief quotations in critical reviews or articles, without the prior written consent of the publisher.

Publishers Note: This novel is a work of fiction. Names, characters, places, and incidents are either products of the author's imagination or used fictitiously. Any similarity to people, living or dead, is purely coincidental.

Print ISBN: 978-0-578-95268-0

Printed in the United States of America

www.kirstenuseauthor.com

To my sisters, Kasey and Kylie
In following your own dreams,
you've inspired me to follow mine.

ONE

All Brila Landry had asked of her friends was to let her have one day alone. It didn't seem like too much to ask, yet she found herself explaining once again. "I'm not going anywhere tomorrow until my parents drag me to supper. And I'm still trying to get out of that too." She used her shoulder to pin the cell phone to her ear as she searched for the condo key on a crowded key ring.

"What are you going to do?" her friend, Shanna Garza, pressed. "Stay in your bed all day and avoid all contact with the outside world?"

"That's the plan." She closed the door, kicked off her tennis shoes, and pulled her sweatshirt over her head, dropping it on the floor.

"You have every right to want some time to yourself, but you can't shut everyone out, especially those of us who love you and are just trying to help."

"I can if I want to. All I'm asking is for this one day."

"Then what happens in November? What happens next year? And what if you dig yourself into such a hole tomorrow that you can't get out of it in time for work Monday? I'm not so sure you're in the right headspace to go down that road again."

"Is that a challenge?" Brila knew it was an overreaction as the words spouted from her mouth. Her competitive spirit and stubbornness had aided her in many ways, but they also tended to turn insignificant comments into unnecessary debates.

"It's not a challenge. I'm just saying it's not good for you to be alone all day. At the very least, come to lunch with me. You can have the rest of the day to yourself."

Brila flipped through her mail, tearing the credit card promotion and extended vehicle warranty offer in half before dropping them in the garbage. Given the situation, she thought Shanna would be a little more understanding. "I don't need a babysitter. I'll be fine."

"Yeah, I know. You can take care of yourself." Shanna hardly let her finish. "I'm just trying to be supportive."

"Leaving me alone all day like I've asked would be supportive." She glanced around the room and sighed. "I know you mean well, but I need to do this my way."

A rare silence hung between them. Brila checked the screen to verify the call hadn't been dropped. Shanna answered as she returned the phone to her ear. "Fine. Since you're shoving me out of your life tomorrow, what are you doing tonight?"

She rolled her eyes. "Don't be so dramatic. D.T.'s coming over later. I'll text him to see if he's up for a night out. Vinny's at seven?"

Shanna's bubbly voice returned. "That was easier than I thought. Sounds like a plan."

"We have nothing else to do, and if it'll get you off my back, all the better. I'll let you know what he says."

Brila sank into her couch as she texted her boyfriend, D.T. Bishop, about their dinner plans. Her temporary joy of escaping Shanna's attempts to coddle her was crushed as the reality of the next day set in.

It'd been nearly four months since her sister, Angelle, had died in a tragic car accident. An accident that could have been avoided if Brila hadn't pulled her sister into her drama.

Managing through that heartache had been filled with suffocating pain. Each holiday and event that arrived on the calendar brought with it a new kind of hell. The next day would have been Angelle's twenty-sixth birthday. Another day Brila didn't know how she would survive.

She had celebrated each of her sister's previous twenty-five birthdays with her. Starting at the age of five, when Angelle turned two, Brila had picked out a special present for her sister and helped her mom decorate the birthday cake each year. She could not fathom the idea that Angelle would not celebrate another birthday. A familiar knot twisted itself in the pit of her stomach. Maybe she shouldn't have agreed to dinner plans.

The buzz of D.T.'s response caused her to jump in her seat. She picked up her phone but stared past it at a random speck in the living room carpet. It took her another minute to focus on his message. He'd be there in thirty minutes for dinner with their friends.

Her screen went black. She blinked a couple of times before pushing herself up to change out of her leggings, tank top, and sports bra. Brila should have been scrambling to get her sister a last-minute gift or scheming some little surprise, not getting ready for a night out with her friends. She just needed to hold it together for a few more hours—just long enough to get through supper and back to her condo. She had the night and the whole next day to fall apart. Would the pain expanding inside her stay contained until then?

Brila and D.T. made their way to the booth, where Shanna and her husband, Tony, were seated.

Shanna and Tony were Brila's standard of the perfect couple, rivaling only her parents. They had been introduced by their mutual friend, Cameron, seven years earlier. Their connection had been instantaneous, as if they had known each other their entire lives. Tony would do anything for Shanna, and she adored him with her whole heart. They were both wonderful individually but somehow the best version of themselves just by being with one another.

At first, Brila had been afraid that she'd be replaced by Tony in Shanna's life, but Shanna made sure to not sacrifice their quality time. Tony became like a brother to her. He had even offered a room to her when Shanna decided to move out of the apartment she and Brila had shared to buy a house with him. Despite her fear of living alone, she'd decided to keep the apartment and let them have their own space.

Shanna sat near the wall. She looked like a stereotypical Texas pageant queen. Brila had always been jealous of her height and curves. What she wouldn't give to not feel like a walking wooden plank. Shanna's curly blonde hair, blue eyes, and bright red lipstick were a sharp contrast next to Tony's dark hair and tanned skin, a product of his Hispanic heritage.

"Sorry we're late," Brila said and slid along the bench to sit across from Shanna.

"No problem. We just ordered drinks." Shanna flashed a smile that had been perfected by braces fifteen years earlier and then continued studying the menu. "Are we doing the usual or trying something new?"

The four of them looked at one another for a moment before D.T. spoke up. "Same pizzas, new apps?"

The others shrugged and nodded in agreement.

"Fried pickles?" D.T. suggested.

Shanna scrunched her face. "I won't eat them, but I guess we could get those and something else. Jalapeño poppers?"

"Sounds good to me," Brila chimed in, and Tony echoed her agreement.

The waitress returned with Shanna and Tony's drinks and took the remaining drink and food orders.

Brila stumbled through her drink request as she eyed the glass of water sitting in front of her friend. As Tony mentioned a basketball game to D.T., she saw her opportunity and lightly kicked her friend's leg.

Shanna scrunched her nose, pulling her attention from her husband. "What the hell?" she whispered across the table.

Brila leaned in and mouthed the words, "Are you pregnant?"

Shanna glanced to her right to make sure the guys were still unaware of their side conversation. "I wish," she whispered. "I'm just doing whatever I can to help the process. At this point, I'd try just about anything. Besides, I have work in the morning."

For as long as Brila could remember, her friend only wanted to be a mother. She and Tony had started trying to conceive a month before their wedding. Shanna had reasoned that no one would have questioned the timing at that point. Of course, it hadn't been that easy. In fact, it had taken thirteen months before she first conceived. Since then, they had endured five miscarriages in four years.

Brila couldn't stand to watch Shanna's hope and determination be crushed by the relentless heartbreak.

"It's going to work out." She reached across the table and squeezed her friend's hand. "If there's one thing I know, it's that you're meant to be a mother."

Catching Tony's glance out the corner of her eye, she returned her hand to her lap as the waitress arrived with their drinks.

"So now that you're out of your place, have you changed your mind about tomorrow?" Shanna asked, no longer whispering.

"Not even a little bit." Brila picked up her pint glass and drank nearly a quarter of her beer as Shanna's glare pierced through her. "You should be happy I'm here now."

The basketball conversation died out, and D.T. joined in. "What's going on tomorrow?"

Brila widened her eyes and shifted her weight. She had hoped to avoid the topic altogether. Did she really have to remind her boyfriend that the next day was her sister's birthday? A day she wanted to simultaneously last forever and cease to exist.

"No, I know what tomorrow is," he scrambled, "but what are y'all planning?"

"Didn't you know? She has very important plans to stay in her bed all day and can't even be bothered to meet me for lunch." Shanna's eyes pinned Brila to the bench. "Hell, I'll even bring it to you. I just don't think you should be alone all day."

"Wait. You're really staying home all day?" D.T. looked at her. "I didn't think you really meant that."

Brila stared blankly at him and looked across the table. "I'm going to get through tomorrow however I can. If that means I spend the entire day in bed listening to sad songs and looking at old pictures, so be it. I appreciate everyone's concern, but I have to do this my way." The tears clinging to the base of her eyelashes threatened to ruin her plan to make it through supper without a breakdown.

"We're not criticizing you, babe." D.T. pulled her into his chest.

"If you want to stay in bed, you stay in bed." Tony smiled lightly. Why was he the only one who seemed to get it?

"We support you in whatever you do," Shanna spoke softly. "We just don't want you to have to go through this alone. We're all here for you."

"I know you are. I just need y'all to trust me. I'll be okay."

D.T. kissed the top of her head and unwrapped his arm from her shoulders so she could sit up.

Brila sighed in relief at seeing the waitress approaching with their first round of food. She took a deep breath, swallowing the lump in her throat. "Besides, my parents are still forcing supper on me, so at some point, I'll have to face the outside world." After another long drink, she piled fried pickles onto her plate.

Maybe she would make it to the safety of her condo unscathed after all. She'd just need to fake a stomach ache to ensure D.T. would return to his place rather than staying the night. For the time being, she gave thanks that her friends were more worried about eating than continuing to discuss her plans for the next day.

TWO

Brila felt around the nightstand until she found her phone, which had been vibrating on and off for the past hour. She pulled it under the covers, as the screen illuminated her makeshift fort with its list of notifications: 9:11 a.m., Sunday, March 8. Two missed calls. One voicemail. Six text messages.

Apparently, her friends and family had not taken her "I want to be left alone" requests seriously. What she wouldn't give for one of those notifications to have been from Angelle. She swiped her thumb across the screen to clear them and then placed the phone face down next to her.

They each meant well. Still, why couldn't she be allotted at least a few hours of solitude? She placed both hands over her face, pulling at the corners of her eyes. If she could make herself believe it was just another day, maybe she'd escape with minimal heartache. Just a day of self-care. A day to disconnect from the world and refocus on herself. She'd been working hard and had dedicated plenty of time to others. She deserved a day to herself.

No. That wasn't fair to Angelle. Her beautiful spirit needed to be remembered and celebrated. Pretending it was a random vacation day may have made it easier to get through it, but Brila wouldn't have been able to forgive herself if she didn't dedicate time to her sister's memory.

The cover fort grew stuffy. Brila peaked her head out to breathe in the cooler air and slid her phone up toward her face. She began scrolling through her pictures and stopped when she arrived at pictures from Angelle's twenty-fifth birthday. Her sister's golden brown eyes stared back at her. They'd shared the same eyes, the same wavy dark brown hair, and their mom's upturned nose. When they were young, they had often been mistaken for twins. In middle school, Brila had been appalled to be considered the same age as someone three years her junior. As they grew older, though, it morphed into a compliment. Her sister's beauty and ability to spread joy through any room with the sound of her laughter could not be replicated.

Tears slid down Brila's cheeks as she watched the video of her sister wearing a black sombrero and a wide grin while the El Ranchero staff sang "Felìz Cumpleaños" to her. Groaning, she pulled the covers back over her head and dropped her phone on the mattress.

It wasn't fair. Angelle should've been sending pictures of her students' homemade cards and asking for suggestions on where to eat that evening for their family outing, a tradition they'd had since they were kids. It was her day to celebrate. Without her there to do so, did that make it just another day? Impossible. To Brila, March eighth would never be just another day.

"Why?" her cries filled the room. "Why'd you take her from me?" Her shoulders shook as she sobbed. She wailed. She screamed. She slammed her fist against the mattress.

Angelle had been in her second year of teaching sixth grade. What kind of rare spirit had the patience or the desire to teach middle school? She'd had her whole life ahead of her and so much left to give. How could it have been her time to leave this world? Brila couldn't stand to hear that sentiment.

A vibration from her phone momentarily silenced her cries. She picked it up to find another message from Shanna. Pulling the bottom of her oversized t-shirt up to dry her cheeks, she read the text.

I'm not going to stop

Sighing, Brila unlocked her phone and read Shanna's three previous messages.

Good morning beautiful
This too shall pass
Get up and do something

She snorted a short laugh, shook her head, then responded.

I'm awake and moving. Will you stop now?

Anticipating a lengthy conversation with Shanna, she listened to the voicemail from her mom and then read the text messages from D.T. and each of her parents. She replied to all three of them, letting them know she was awake and okay. When Shanna still hadn't replied two minutes later, she threw the covers off, swung her feet over the edge of the bed, and pushed herself upright.

She shuffled into the bathroom, catching her reflection in the mirror. She examined her red, puffy eyes before undressing and starting the shower. Standing in the porcelain tub, she closed her eyes and let the scorching water cascade over her. A conversation she'd had with Angelle on her last birthday replayed in her mind.

"A quarter of your life, gone," Brila had teased. "What are you going to do now?"

Angelle laughed. "I'm going to make the most of the next quarter, and I'll worry about the other two later."

"Okay, Miss Know-It-All. What about me? What should I be doing with the next quarter of my life or what's left of it?"

Angelle held her chin, considering her answer. "You need to figure out what your purpose is. Find what's going to make you happy and do that."

Brila raised an eyebrow and cocked her head to the side. "You think I'm unhappy?"

Angelle's smile faded. "You could be happier. I just don't know what's going to get you there."

Brila may have been older, but her wise-beyond-her-years sister offered her guidance more often than the other way around. She trusted her advice and valued her opinion more than any other.

Angelle had known she wanted to be a teacher since childhood. She had set goals her whole life and crafted detailed plans on how to achieve each one. Yet, she never stressed when things went awry. Instead, she refocused and adjusted her plans to fit whatever new situation fell at her feet.

Conversely, Brila had no plans and no long-term goals. While working in the admissions office during her senior year of college, she'd helped revamp the school's social media marketing strategy, which earned her a full-time position after graduation on the newly-created team. At first, it had been exciting to get paid to post on social media all day, but after seven years, she'd begun to wonder if it was the career she wanted.

The vibration of her phone jolted her eyes open. She rubbed her hands over her face, sighed, then grabbed the bottle of body wash. Assuming Shanna had finally responded, she didn't have much time before she'd be bombarded with more alerts.

After drying off and wrapping the towel around her body, she picked up her phone to find a notification from her dad rather than Shanna.

Where do you want to go for supper tonight?

A lump grew in her throat. Why did she have to make this decision? She wasn't even sure she agreed with continuing the birthday tradition. She typed and deleted three different responses, finally deciding to leave out the anger and sarcasm.

I don't know.

A sudden tightness clamped down within her chest. She brushed her teeth and pulled on the first set of clean clothes she could find— a long-sleeved t-shirt and leggings. Breathing became a chore as she pulled her hair into a high ponytail. Forcing her feet into a pair of tennis shoes, she scrambled toward the living room. The silence and emptiness were suffocating. Her eyes darted around the kitchen until she located her keys and purse. Scooping them up, she escaped through the front door, slamming it behind her. She ran down the flight of stairs from her second-story condo, nearly tripping as she stepped into the parking lot.

Once inside her car, she gripped the steering wheel with both hands and took a deep breath to push away the tears welling in her eyes. "Get it together," she muttered as she stared at the brick wall in front of her. It took another three deep breaths before she could move her hand to the gear shift and reverse out of her parking spot.

So much for staying in bed all day. Maybe Shanna had been right about not being alone. Was it possible to not be with anyone and still not be alone? As much as she wanted to avoid where she was headed, it seemed to be the only option.

Fifteen minutes later, Brila pulled into an empty parking lot and parked at the far end. She sighed as she stepped out of her car and made her way to the cemetery entrance. She had the location memorized. Third row from the back, twelfth headstone from the parking lot. She sat and ran her fingers along the etching of Angelle's name as tears rolled down her cheeks and slid off her jaw line.

"Happy birthday," she whispered. "You're supposed to be here, and you're not, and it's not okay. And now Dad wants me to pick where we eat tonight. What the hell is he thinking? None of this is okay. I need you here." She groaned at a vibration from her phone. "And everyone wants to tell me what I should be doing and how I should be feeling today. I can't stand it!" She slumped down into the fetal position on the hard ground. "I'm the big sister. I was supposed to protect you. But I was selfish, and I needed you that night. And I need you here, but you're not, and I don't know what to do."

Her phone continued to buzz, this time a call. "Just leave me alone!" She tossed it toward the plot on her left.

"I'm sorry I dragged you into my mess that night. If I'd just waited 'til the morning. If I'd gone to you instead, you'd still be here. You'd be joking about getting old and deciding which damn restaurant we're going to tonight. Why'd you have to leave me? I can't do this without you." She gripped the grass beneath her as her body shook with each sob.

"I thought I'd find you here."

She lifted her head to find Shanna walking toward her. "Why?" She could hardly force out the word as she pushed herself up.

Shanna bent to pick up the phone before reaching Angelle's headstone. "Fine. I went to your place first and when I saw your car missing, I took a lucky guess." She set down her green cloth grocery bag and laid out a blanket before sitting. She held out the phone. "Come on."

Brila dragged herself onto the blanket, grabbed her phone, and set it face down next to her knee. "You were supposed to leave me alone today."

"You've known me long enough to know I wasn't going to do that." She wrapped her arm around Brila's shoulders and pulled her into her body. "So if you're out here, I take it the morning hasn't been so great."

Brila gently shook her head, tears spilling onto her cheeks again. "I don't know when this is supposed to get easier." Her voice cracked through the lump in her throat.

She secretly feared that day. Living with the pain of her sister's death was difficult enough, but the idea that one day life without Angelle would feel normal sounded like a nightmare. The possibility of going an entire day without thinking of her sister was incomprehensible.

"It'll happen, but for now, you only need to focus on today. And it's lunchtime, so let's focus on that." She grabbed the bag and began to empty its contents. "I brought chicken Caesar wraps from Johnny's."

"You just couldn't help yourself." Brila let a slight smile pull at the corner of her lips.

"I don't know why you're surprised. Honestly, you should've seen this coming." She reached back into the bag. "And I brought dessert because chocolate is good for the soul."

Brila stared at the little white box. "Cupcakes? Are you serious?"

"You love cupcakes."

"Are we going to sing 'Happy Birthday' and make wishes for her too?"

Shanna's eyes grew wide. "Jesus, they're not birthday cupcakes. It's just dessert. And they're your favorite."

"I don't do cupcakes anymore. That was Angelle's thing."

Her sister had loved to bake and often recruited Brila to help measure ingredients and decorate. Over the years, many of her favorite memories had come from baking with Angelle, which made them some of the most difficult now.

Shanna's cheeks turned pink as she returned the box to her bag. "I'm sorry. I really didn't think it would upset you."

Brila exhaled slowly as she watched Shanna pick at her food. "It's not your fault." She paused to take a bite of her wrap. "They do look good. Why don't you take them home and surprise Tony?"

"He already complains that he's gaining weight because I feed him too much." She chuckled. "But I'm sure that won't stop him from eating half the box."

They continued eating as Shanna talked about the three babies born during her shift that morning. She was meant to be a labor-and-delivery nurse as much as she was meant to be a mother. She cared for each baby with the same amount of love and attention as the parents. However, each month that passed without a child of her own weighed heavily on her heart. Brila had seen it slowly chip away at her friend's optimism and hopeful spirit.

Once they were finished, they stood up and folded the blanket together. Shanna picked up her bag and started for the parking lot but paused when Brila didn't budge. "Are you coming or staying?"

Brila thought for a moment. "Just give me a couple minutes." She waited until Shanna walked beyond earshot before turning to Angelle's headstone. "I love you," she whispered and ran her fingers along her sister's name. She closed her eyes and dropped her head, breathing in the cool, spring air. A gust whirled around her. If only it had been her sister's arms wrapped around her instead.

Shanna was waiting behind her car when she reached the parking lot. "Do you want me to come back with you?"

Brila shook her head and forced a smile. "I'll be all right. Thanks for tracking me down."

"You knew there's no way I'd let you spend the entire day alone."

"It wouldn't have been the entire day. I still have supper with my parents tonight. But I appreciate it anyway." If Shanna ever got tired of looking out for Brila, she didn't show it.

They'd known each other since high school when Brila's family had moved from Louisiana to Texas for her dad's job. She had been the first to befriend her, and the two had been inseparable ever since. Still, there were many times when she doubted she deserved a friend as kindhearted and selfless as Shanna.

They hugged before getting in their separate vehicles and driving in opposite directions.

On the drive home, Brila cranked up the radio, hoping the upbeat music would push all other thoughts out of her mind. A few minutes of normalcy. A brief moment in time when her only concerns were watching the road and singing off-key.

After pulling into her parking space, she walked at a snail's pace toward her condo, anticipating the silence, emptiness, and thoughts that awaited her inside. If Shanna had come with her, she could have kept herself distracted for a couple of hours. She probably could have convinced her to stay until she had to meet her parents, but it was too late for that now. At least this way, she didn't have to worry about dragging anyone else into her misery.

She headed straight for the living room and turned on the TV to fill the space. After pushing her shoes off and tossing them toward the front door, she dropped her belongings on the kitchen counter. Rummaging through the pantry then the fridge for something sweet, she settled on a pint of cookie dough ice cream. She grabbed a spoon and began eating from the container, her elbows resting on the counter. After eating about half the contents, she put the ice cream away and tossed the spoon in the sink.

She lay on the couch and pulled the mint green fleece blanket Angelle had given her as a birthday gift up to her chin. She rolled to her side so that she faced the back of the couch. As her eyes grew heavy, a text message alert jolted them open. She felt around the floor until her hand located her phone as it chimed again.

The messages were from D.T.

Where we going tonight?
Want me to pick you up or just meet y'all there?

Now she had two people waiting on a decision for their dinner location. She didn't know if her mom had invited him, or if he just assumed he was going because he had the year before. The thought of going out to eat with the three of them was exhausting.

I don't know yet. I'll text you later.

She set her phone back on the floor and rolled over. At least if she could sleep, she could escape the reality of the day for an hour or two. Her phone buzzed again, but assuming D.T. had replied with an "okay," she ignored it and allowed herself to drift off.

She had just begun to dream about lying on a beach when a phone call woke her. Groaning, she reached for the phone. "Hello?"

Her dad's voice bellowed on the other end. "Why aren't you answering my texts?"

"I was trying to sleep." She felt her patience wearing thin. What couldn't wait until that evening?

"Have you decided where we're going tonight?"

"No. Haven't really thought about it. Why do I have to pick anyway?"

"Your mom suggested that you decide. You know better than us where Angelle would have wanted to go."

"So is this what we're going to do now? Go out to her favorite places each year, like she's still around to celebrate? What if they all close down? What if —"

"Dammit, Brila." Her dad's voice was hushed but stern. "You're not the only one who's hurting. Yes, you lost your sister, but we also lost a child. We don't know what we're doing. We're struggling to get through this just as much as you are. Stop being selfish and pick a restaurant like your mom asked you to."

Her heart pounded as the silence lingered between them. "Let's just go to El Ranchero again. It was her favorite."

"Is Daniel coming?" His voice softened.

"Yeah. We'll meet you there at 6:30."

"Okay. I love you."

"Love you too." She clung to her phone and pulled her knees to her chest as tears welled in her eyes.

The last time her dad had raised his voice at her was when he caught her sneaking out of the house the summer before her senior year of high school. His words sat on her chest. He was right, after all. She had spent more time finding ways to avoid dinner and her parents altogether than concerning herself with how they were dealing with their own pain.

Drying her face with the blanket, she texted their plans to D.T. and asked him to pick her up at six. Then she texted Shanna.

> I must be the worst friend ever. I could've at
> least asked how you were doing today.

Shanna was like a third daughter in their family, and she always saw to it that Angelle had been included in her and Brila's activities. Being an only child, she had treated Angelle as her own sister.

Oh please. Don't worry about that

I miss her terribly but I'm trying to focus on the
good memories we had
Like when I spent hours trying to get her hair
right for prom
And I keep praying that you and your family can
find some peace in y'all hearts
She touched so many lives. I guess we all need to
find that peace

Brila thought about all of Angelle's friends, coworkers, and students.

She tossed the blanket to the other side of the couch and pushed herself up. She ran her fingers along her eyebrows and rubbed her hands over her face before twisting and stretching. She rolled out her yoga mat in the middle of the living room and scrolled through videos on her TV until she settled on a thirty-minute power yoga session.

Following the progression of positions, she pushed out the thoughts of worry and sadness. It took a few minutes longer than normal to choose a phrase to meditate on, but she finally settled on "I have healing and peace in my heart." She repeated this with every other breath. When the session ended, she sat, eyes closed, in the middle of the mat and, for the first time that day, embraced the silence.

Five minutes later, she opened her eyes and looked down at the small sweat marks on her shirt. Did she really need to shower again? It was just supper with family. In public. Sighing, she rolled up her yoga mat and headed toward the bathroom.

The soapy water against her skin soothed her, but when she stepped out of the shower, she couldn't cool off. She wrapped the towel around her body, walked out to her bedroom, and sat on her bed. She closed her eyes and lay back, letting the cooler air combat the beads of sweat that had started to gather on her forehead and chest. A moment later, a knock on the front door jolted her upright.

THREE

Brila rewrapped the towel around her body as she shuffled toward the living room. She opened the door to find D.T. on the other side. "What are you doing here? Did you take off early?"

He scrunched his eyebrows as he walked in. "What are you talking about? Why aren't you ready to go?"

Brila spun to look at the microwave: 5:58 p.m. "Son of a ... " She ran back to the bathroom to apply foundation and mascara.

D.T. called down the hallway as he followed behind her. "You did say six o'clock, right? Is everything okay?"

She leaned back to speak through the doorway without taking her eyes off the mirror. "I sat down for a minute after I showered to cool off, and I guess I fell asleep."

"Do you need to call your parents?" He rested his forearm against the bedroom door frame.

"No." She checked the time on her phone as she scurried to her closet.

"You could just stay like that." He smirked.

She peered at him, jumping as she pulled her jeans over her hips. "Now's not the time." She returned to the closet and reemerged a minute later with one shoe on. "Okay, let's go." She leaned down and slid on the other shoe.

On the drive across town, Brila hoped they wouldn't get stuck in traffic. Her dad's words from earlier echoed in her mind. The last thing she wanted to do was upset her parents again. She turned to D.T., studying the stubble along his jaw line. "How was your day?"

"Other than Shanna texting at the crack of dawn to see if I knew how you were doing? I went to the gym and did some rock climbing. How about you?" He glanced at her, and she stared blankly back. He shifted his focus between her and the road. "I meant, did everyone leave you alone like you wanted?"

"Not really, but it's okay. I know it just means there are good people who care about me."

"So now I'm the jerk that actually left you alone when I should've been with you?"

She met his storm-cloud gray eyes. "Not at all. You gave me the space I needed, but you're still here for me now."

He reached over and squeezed her hand. "I'm here for whatever you need."

"Can you keep me from ruining this dinner?"

"No problem." He chuckled as they pulled into the parking lot.

He may have taken it as a joke, but the knot twisting in her gut signaled that she may need saving by the end of the night.

As they entered the restaurant, Brila's parents were seated in the waiting area to the left. They stood as she approached, and the three of them embraced. Her mom, Lyla, let out a soft cry. They each sniffled, reeling in their emotions as they parted.

D.T. shook her father's hand and then bent down to hug Lyla. "How are you doing, ma'am?"

"Oh, you know, I could be better. But I'm glad we're all together now."

Brila turned away and cringed at her words. They weren't all together. Angelle wasn't there. She was never going to be there again. Had her mom already conceded to this new definition of "all together"? She pulled at her eyes, although they were already dry, then turned back to the others as the hostess waved a handful of menus for them to follow her.

After they were seated, D.T. broke the silence. "So, how did y'all spend your day? Hopefully not in bed the whole time like this one?" He pointed his thumb toward Brila.

Brila's cheeks burned as her dad's eyes narrowed. "I didn't stay in bed all day. I planned to. I wanted to. But I got up. I went to the cemetery. Shanna found me there and brought me lunch. I exercised. I showered. I was semi-productive."

D.T. twirled the rolled-up silverware in his hands. "And you forgot to mention this on the way over?"

"You just asked if people left me alone. I didn't know you wanted a play-by-play."

An unsettling silence hung over the table until Brila's dad, Brian, cleared his throat. "To answer your question, Daniel, we took flowers to Angelle in the morning. Then we went through some old photo albums, recounting the day she was born and some of her childhood birthdays."

The waitress approached and introduced herself. "Are y'all here for a special occasion tonight?"

"We're celebrating our daughter's birthday," Lyla answered.

The waitress smiled at Brila, whose eyes grew wide as she shook her head. "Not me."

The young girl scrunched her eyebrows as she studied the full table of four. "Oh, do you need me to get you another chair?"

Brila exhaled loudly. "No one's coming. She died four months ago."

"Oh. I'm sorry," she paused, staring at her notepad like it might hold an appropriate response. "What can I get y'all to drink?"

After they ordered, Lyla glared across the table. "What was that about?"

"Me? Why'd you even bring it up? It's none of her business. She was prepared to bring out an extra seat, the sombrero, and the whole singing crew. Is that what you wanted?"

D.T. nudged her hand with his, but she pulled away. She didn't want him to save the moment. She wanted to blow the whole thing up.

"I didn't want to lie and say we were here for nothing, but I guess I should've." Lyla looked to her husband with tears in her eyes then back to Brila. "I'm still trying to figure out how we handle this."

Brila sighed as she caught D.T.'s eyes begging her to stop before she looked across the table at the two people who didn't need any more pain in their lives. "I guess we all are. Sorry for being so pissy."

Her mom smiled tight-lipped and sniffled. "You're allowed to be upset. We just have to figure this out together."

"All right, you two." Brian wrapped his arm around Lyla. "Let's try to be a little less depressing." He turned his attention to D.T. "Daniel, have any plans for the week? Any work trips coming up?"

D.T. let go of the silverware and straightened his back. "No, sir. I have a trip in a few weeks but nothing 'til then. We might take the kayaks out next weekend if it's warm enough. Otherwise, not much going on. Whatever Brila wants to do is good with me." He smiled at her and then back at Brian.

Brila continually wavered between awe and worry at his ability to conjure up the right answer in any situation. Part of her reveled in the rare occasions when he misstepped.

"Janae's shower," she said under her breath.

"That's next weekend?" D.T. was incapable of whispering.

"What's next weekend?" Lyla asked.

"Remember Cameron's sister, Janae? She's getting married next month, and her bridal shower is next weekend."

"I'm still not sure why you're so involved." D.T. shifted in his seat. "I didn't even know Cam had a sister 'til he told you and Shanna about the engagement. Now suddenly you have to attend every little event for her wedding. And why you but not Shanna?"

"She was friends with Angelle. Not best friends but still pretty close. I guess she feels like having me there is like having her there. It's just a couple of hours Saturday afternoon. We can still get out on the water. And this is the last event I have to attend. I'm just asking you to go to the wedding. We don't have to stay all night, but we need to go for a little while."

Lyla chimed in before D.T. could protest. "I think it's nice that you get to be there for her."

Brila exhaled in relief as the waitress returned with their drinks, putting an end to their conversation.

Cameron had been the second person to welcome her with open arms when her family had moved to Texas. She had been paired up with him in biology class and discovered they lived on the same street. Although he and Shanna hadn't been good friends prior to her arrival, Brila soon became the link that made the three of them inseparable for the remainder of high school. While Angelle and Janae hadn't formed quite as tight of a bond, they'd also become friends. The five of them would cram into Cameron's car before and after school each day until Brila got her driver's license the following year.

Angelle's glaring absence picked at Brila's heart as she watched her parents and D.T. order their food. She swallowed hard to force the lump down her throat and fight back the tears welling in her eyes. She scanned her mind for something—anything that would take her mind off why they were there. "Basketball," she blurted out. She searched the three sets of eyes staring back at her. "Houston. Aren't they doing really well this year?" She had no interest in basketball, and her only knowledge of the team's progress that season had come from D.T.'s comments to her and their friends.

D.T. smirked as if he understood her intent. "They're all right, but they'll have to work on their three-pointers if they want to make the playoffs this year."

"And they need to stay healthy," Brian directed his response to D.T.

As the two men delved into the details of the team's strengths, weaknesses, and remaining schedule, Brila looked across the table at her mom, whose eyes were glimmering with a film of tears that threatened to spill over at any moment. Brila silently begged her not to mention Angelle. Then a safe topic of conversation popped into her mind. "How are classes going this semester?"

Lyla was the head of the mathematics department at Southern College, where Brila also worked. Her mom had dedicated most of her adult life to education, either her own or of others. Her face lifted a bit, and she sat up straighter. "It's a good group. Our department's largest freshman class in years, many of them double majoring in engineering or business."

Brila nodded as she lifted her margarita glass to her mouth. Math, engineering, and education. These things defined the other members of her family. "I don't know how you do it. All those equations never made sense to me. And I sure wouldn't want to put up with college kids."

"No, college is the best. The math majors are actually interested in the classes. And for everyone else just trying to get their requirements, it's their problem if they don't care and fail."

Brila nearly choked on her drink.

"Don't get me wrong. I want everyone to do well, and I'd love for everyone to love math as much as I do. But the truth is, you're not going to reach everyone. I've learned over the years that sometimes it's best to just let them be. There's no use stressing over students that don't want to be helped." She smiled and relaxed against the back of her seat. "Your sister would've been a great professor, but as much as I tried to convince her, she was happy teaching middle school. God knows why."

"It's what she'd always wanted to do. She belonged in the middle-school classroom like you belong teaching math at Southern and Dad belongs engineering robotics at Newford."

"Like you belong running the social media platforms for Southern?" Lyla raised her eyebrows.

Brila continued to drain her margarita. "The point is, she was where she was meant to be. I know how much you wanted to have her on campus, but it wouldn't have worked out like you'd wanted."

"I suppose you're right."

They listened in on the men's conversation for a minute or two until the waitress returned with their food. Brila slurped the remaining drops from her glass and held it up to request another. Her shoulders relaxed as she enjoyed the silence that fell over the table as everyone dug into their meals. Another emotional breakdown threatened to erupt, but she swallowed it down with a bite of her burrito. It could wait until she got home.

FOUR

A month later, Brila stared at the open schedule on her computer screen as she mentally scanned the dresses hanging in her closet. Not formal enough. Too short. Too summery. She sighed. Nothing seemed right for Janae's wedding the following evening. Maybe she could pop into a couple of stores on her way home.

She refocused on the social media posts that needed to be finalized and scheduled for the weekend.

After graduating with her communications degree and starting her full-time job as a social media coordinator for Southern College, Brila thought she had it made. She'd enjoyed creating posts and interacting with prospective students, alumni, and others through the various platforms. And she was good at what she did. Over the years, she had gained the respect of her colleagues and had become the go-to person for other departments when they needed help with their accounts.

At the sound of a prospective student touring the campus, she wheeled her chair to the doorway of her office to sneak a peek at the young man and his parents. She tilted her head, stretching to hear their review.

"The dorms were good, and I like all the food choices."

She laughe   for
visiting high s

"The depa
there were a l

A typical

Brila rolle
admissions lobby
comments from high
exposure to their question
more straightforward. Still
always brought a smile
College wasn't the
picking up the c
the next four
his home.

As the far   te
office, Brila p   nter
station to catch   ve fun
seeing the school t   udents and their
families every day."

"It does keep my love of   fresh, but the travel can
wear on you, especially if you have some of the more distant
territories."

Brila hadn't considered the high school visits and college fairs
that were part of the recruiting process. "I suppose I can see that.
But how cool is it that you get to spread the word about Southern all
over the country and continually impact the diversity of the student
population?"

Darcy chuckled. "Yeah, I guess you're right. But you do know
your social media posts can literally reach anyone around the world,
right? These days, the digital team has just as much, if not more
influence on recruiting as the rest of us."

Brila considered this, turning the printout between her fingers. "Maybe so. Still, there's something special about the personal interaction you get."

Before she got a response, Brila's boss approached. "Ready for our meeting?"

Brila looked at the clock hanging next to the conference room and realized she was four minutes late for her monthly one-on-one session. "Sorry, Mitch. I lost track of time. Let me grab a notebook."

"You shouldn't need one." He began walking toward his office as she followed. "I don't want to keep you too long, especially on a Friday afternoon."

"I have a few posts left to clean up and schedule for the weekend before I leave anyway."

"No need to stay late. I'm sure whatever you schedule will be more than enough." He shifted his weight in the oversized office chair and sipped coffee out of his travel mug.

Certain that fresh coffee hadn't been made since lunch, she looked at his desk and fought the urge to gag at the thought of his lukewarm, stale coffee.

It seemed fitting for him. As appreciative as Brila was to him for being open to her ideas when she'd been a student and for offering her a full-time job, she'd found him to be rather stale. He seemed to do just enough to get by, had a dry sense of humor, and rarely spoke his mind on anything that demanded he take sides.

"Before I get into what I have, is there anything you wanted to talk about?" Mitch leaned forward.

"Well," she paused for a moment, "I was wondering if it'd be possible to do some job-shadowing with one of the admin counselors." With no immediate refusal, she continued. "I mean, I'm happy with my job. I just thought it'd be interesting to learn more about what they do."

"Hmmm." He shifted again and rubbed the back of his neck.

She laughed to herself, fascinated by the range of priorities for visiting high school juniors and seniors.

"The department head was very helpful, and it sounded like there were a lot of activities to get involved in."

A typical parent response.

Brila rolled back to her computer; the conversation in the admissions lobby dulled to a murmur. Reading and responding to comments from high school students online gave her some unique exposure to their questions and interests. They were often bolder and more straightforward. Still, witnessing their experience in person always brought a smile to her face. While she knew Southern College wasn't the right fit for everyone, she'd become keen on picking up the cues hinting that someone had found their home for the next four years. This visitor didn't seem convinced this would be his home.

As the family followed their admissions counselor into a private office, Brila printed one of her schedules and hurried to the printer station to catch Darcy, another counselor. "Y'all must have fun seeing the school through the eyes of high school students and their families every day."

"It does keep my love of our school fresh, but the travel can wear on you, especially if you have some of the more distant territories."

Brila hadn't considered the high school visits and college fairs that were part of the recruiting process. "I suppose I can see that. But how cool is it that you get to spread the word about Southern all over the country and continually impact the diversity of the student population?"

Darcy chuckled. "Yeah, I guess you're right. But you do know your social media posts can literally reach anyone around the world, right? These days, the digital team has just as much, if not more influence on recruiting as the rest of us."

Brila considered this, turning the printout between her fingers. "Maybe so. Still, there's something special about the personal interaction you get."

Before she got a response, Brila's boss approached. "Ready for our meeting?"

Brila looked at the clock hanging next to the conference room and realized she was four minutes late for her monthly one-on-one session. "Sorry, Mitch. I lost track of time. Let me grab a notebook."

"You shouldn't need one." He began walking toward his office as she followed. "I don't want to keep you too long, especially on a Friday afternoon."

"I have a few posts left to clean up and schedule for the weekend before I leave anyway."

"No need to stay late. I'm sure whatever you schedule will be more than enough." He shifted his weight in the oversized office chair and sipped coffee out of his travel mug.

Certain that fresh coffee hadn't been made since lunch, she looked at his desk and fought the urge to gag at the thought of his lukewarm, stale coffee.

It seemed fitting for him. As appreciative as Brila was to him for being open to her ideas when she'd been a student and for offering her a full-time job, she'd found him to be rather stale. He seemed to do just enough to get by, had a dry sense of humor, and rarely spoke his mind on anything that demanded he take sides.

"Before I get into what I have, is there anything you wanted to talk about?" Mitch leaned forward.

"Well," she paused for a moment, "I was wondering if it'd be possible to do some job-shadowing with one of the admin counselors." With no immediate refusal, she continued. "I mean, I'm happy with my job. I just thought it'd be interesting to learn more about what they do."

"Hmmm." He shifted again and rubbed the back of his neck.

Brila's heart beat faster. "I don't need to if it's a problem. I just thought it might be interesting."

"I understand." His eyes shifted, seemingly unable to settle on a single spot. "It's just that there's some news I need to share with you."

She picked at her fingernails. "What is it?"

"As you know, the school is facing some significant budget cuts for the upcoming year. And while we all hoped they'd be able to close the gap, it doesn't seem—"

Brila's stomach started tying itself in knots. She tried to read his eyes as they darted around the room while he regurgitated information on the school's financial situation.

"—and our department has to absorb two positions." He took a deep breath and another sip of old coffee. "We have been asked to eliminate an academic advisor and a digital media position."

She held her breath for a moment and then exhaled slowly. Why would they cut in the one area that has been growing? Maybe there was no other choice. Now she'd have more responsibilities. No wonder he'd been twitchy when she mentioned job shadowing.

"And the directors have advised that we let go of the person in each of those positions with the least amount of time with the school."

She didn't have to do the math. Everyone in the department had been there when she had come on her own high school visit. "So you're telling me I no longer have a job just because I'm the youngest one here? You know I work harder and put out better content than anyone in this entire school."

"It's not based on age," he said quickly, like an English teacher catching her on a technicality. "It's years of service. You still have your job through the end of the academic year. And the school is willing to work with you to find another position that may come available through regular turnover. You're an excellent employee, and I'd personally hate to see us lose you."

"Then why are you letting this happen? You know I'm the most qualified person you have." The words caught in her throat.

He peered out of his large window into the lobby. "These decisions are made by people well above me. I can't just tell them no or dictate what should happen. It's not that simple."

"You can't stand up for me? Or tell them I'm the best person for this position? Or that your social media presence is going to suffer without me?"

"That's not how this stuff works. I'm sorry you're caught in the middle, but we'll find you something. I know there are other departments with openings coming up."

"Then why can't they take the cut?"

"Some of them are, but they have multiple people leaving or retiring. We can't lose all of those positions in one area. It'd be like admissions losing half the counselors and advisors."

"Whatever you say." She swallowed hard so the words she wanted to say wouldn't spew out. "Are there any other bombs you need to drop on me this afternoon?"

"I'm going to set up time next week for us to discuss this more and look at some opportunities that may be available for you."

She could hardly look at him as he rested his folded hands on the desk between them. As if he was doing her a favor. Any department would be lucky to have her.

This couldn't be possible. What was the point of working so hard to get the boot simply for being the most recent person hired? She pushed herself out of the chair and trudged back to her desk.

Punching in her password, she glared at the posting schedule on her screen. She slumped in her chair and debated whether she should push the submit button and walk away. The small clock in the bottom right-hand corner of the screen read 3:11 p.m. She sighed and shimmied in her seat until she was upright once again. She'd call it a day after one quick review and a glance at the interactions.

On the drive home, she cranked up the music three levels higher than normal and danced in her seat. She sang off-key, replacing the lyrics she didn't know with whichever words fell out of her mouth, and drummed on the steering wheel.

Inside her condo, however, the weight of heavy silence greeted her. She scrambled to start a playlist from her phone but didn't act quick enough. The reality of her impending job loss crept back into her mind. She collapsed on the couch as tears streamed down her face.

"It makes no sense," she grumbled.

Just because she had shown interest in something else didn't mean she was ready to leave her job altogether, especially without it being on her own terms. She couldn't decide what would be worse—being placed in a position she didn't want or being forced to leave entirely. She had made such progress not only in her own development but in the innovation she had brought to the school's social media presence. Did all of that mean nothing simply because she was the youngest person in the office? If anything, her age benefited her knowledge of the platforms.

Suddenly, she felt a need for others to share in this anger. She sent out a string of text messages to her parents, D.T., and Shanna. She began typing Angelle's name but froze as reality punched her in the gut.

"I need you here," she whispered through her sobs. That was the problem. She needed her sister too often. Her dependency had led to Angelle's accident and death. She'd created this problem for herself, and that evoked an even deeper heartache within her. She tipped to her side, falling face down onto the cushions. "I should've told you to stay home. I should've just left you alone. I'm so sorry!"

Her phone chimed with responses to the news she'd shared. She silenced it and set it on the floor.

"What am I supposed to do now?" She rolled over and looked at the ceiling, wishing her sister could show up with her perfect guidance.

Did she really want to stay employed by the school that was so quick to dismiss her? Including her time as a student, she'd dedicated eleven years to them, and this was how they treated her? On the other hand, that opportunity meant she wouldn't have to create a résumé or interview for a job—skills she never had to practice or refine.

Angelle's advice to do what made her happy echoed in her mind. Brila scoffed. Like she could magically make that happen. Not everyone could be so lucky as to recognize their dream job as a child and actually fulfill it in early adulthood—or at all.

How was she supposed to know what made her happy enough to make an entire career out of it? Sure, she enjoyed her time with family and friends. She liked to exercise and be outdoors. She liked kayaking and hiking with D.T. All those things were fine, but that's not what her sister had meant. She still enjoyed creating social media posts and engaging with others, but it felt like something was missing. Shouldn't the discovery of her purpose come with some great "aha" moment and elicit ecstatic joy? She certainly didn't have either of those.

She groaned at the vibrations on the floor. Scooping up the phone, she read through the notifications. D.T. was coming over. Shanna was shocked and wanted to know what her next move would be.

The phone buzzed with a call before she could read the rest. "Hey, Mom."

"Why didn't you come see me after you found out?"

"I had to get out of there. Did you know this was happening?"

"Like most, I'd heard there were going to be cuts and that admissions could be one of the departments affected, but I had no idea it would be you. What'd they tell you?'

"He droned on about budget cuts and said our group and the advisers were the ones affected. He also said that the guidance was to cut the people with the fewest years of employment. So I'm getting screwed because I'm young." She shuffled to the kitchen, opened the door to her small pantry, and stared inside.

"Did they offer any placements or give you recommendations for another school in the area?"

"He said something about finding an open position with another department, but I don't know. I'm not sure I want to stick around just to go through this all again the next time there are cuts. You're lucky you don't have to deal with this."

"Oh, honey, I've had my share of bouncing around. You know Southern isn't the only school I've taught at. I never felt safe until I received tenure. Academics is a tough field. I know it's a difficult situation, but it's going to work itself out."

"Thanks, Mom." She twisted her head after hearing a knock at the door. "D.T.'s here. I better let you go."

"Okay. I love you."

"Love you too." She ended the call as she opened the door.

D.T. leaned in to kiss her forehead and then held up a six-pack of beer. "Tell me what happened." He opened a bottle and handed it to her on his way to the kitchen. He grabbed one for himself and pointed it toward the open pantry door. "Planning to cook something?"

"Do you really think I was going to cook?" She grinned, taking a sip. "I don't know. I was just looking. And there's really not much more to tell about the whole thing."

"Do you get to finish the school year?"

"Yeah, I still have a job through May. Maybe through the summer. But I don't know if I want to stick around that long. Why should I keep working for them after what they just did to me?"

"Well, you can't just quit and not have a job."

For as adventurous as D.T. was, his views on things like work and financial responsibility were quite straight-laced. After nearly two years together, she still found it both admirable and annoying. "I know, but I also don't feel any loyalty to a school that was so quick to drop me."

D.T. settled on the couch and pulled her into him, wrapping his powerful arms around her. "That's fair. I'll see if I can find anything you might be interested in."

"That's the other problem." She turned to look up to him. "I don't really know what I'm interested in. I lucked out with this job. I don't know if I still want to do digital marketing, but I also don't know what else I'd do."

He squeezed her until her cheeks forced her eyes closed, then he released her so she could sit up. "I'm sure you'll figure it out. We can start with something easy. What do you want to eat?"

"I'm done thinking for the day. Just pick something." She took another long drink before she laid her head back on his chest. "Oh and, while you're at it, can you pick out a dress for me to wear tomorrow?"

"If we don't go, you won't have to worry about it."

She looked up at him and smiled. "Nice try."

FIVE

Brila smiled in admiration as she watched the bride dance with her father. It was one of her favorite moments at weddings. She had expected to be planning her own wedding by this point in her life but if she'd learned anything in the past six months, it was that things rarely went as planned.

"How long are we staying?" D.T. whispered, jolting her out of the trance.

"The reception just started. Try to enjoy yourself." She smoothed the navy floral dress she'd bought that morning as her gaze returned to the dance floor.

D.T. sighed before finishing his beer.

Brila studied the tightness in his jaw as he stood to make his way to the bar. She knew he wasn't a fan of weddings, but it was clear that being at one full of strangers was bordering on misery for him.

Shanna slid into the seat next to her. "I'm so exhausted. I don't think we're going to make it to the end."

Brila looked around as Tony joined them. "Don't tell D.T. that. He's been wanting to go since we walked in this place. If y'all go, there's no way he's going to stick around."

Shanna yawned, holding her forehead.

"Is everything okay?"

"Work was pretty busy today. I'll be fine after I get a little sleep." She sat up and smiled.

D.T. returned to the table, taking the seat on the other side of Brila. He turned to Shanna and Tony. "So how long are y'all staying?"

They exchanged looks around the table before Tony answered. "I'm hoping to get some cake."

"And we have to watch Brila fight for the bouquet." Shanna grinned.

Brila groaned and buried her face in her hands. That was by far her least favorite part of a wedding. At this point in her life, the only people joining her in this outdated ritual were one other woman her age, teenagers, and divorcée relatives of the couple. "I'm not doing it!"

"If we go now, you can miss the whole thing." D.T. chimed in.

Brila rolled her eyes and tried to choose the lesser of two evils. "How about we stick around for cake, whether or not that means we also see the bouquet toss."

She caught Shanna's knowing glance. They'd both been to enough weddings to know the toss would come well before the cake. Yet, she was willing to risk the five minutes of embarrassment to stay longer. Not only did she enjoy catching up with people she hadn't seen since high school, but she also loved weddings. And since she and D.T. rarely discussed their future beyond the upcoming week, it was going to be a while before she would get to enjoy her own.

As she stood, Janae approached the table. "Thanks so much for coming!" She hugged Brila and the others, ending with D.T. "I'm sorry, I don't believe we've met."

"This is my boyfriend, D.T. He actually works with Cameron."

"We work at the same place. I wouldn't say we work together." He lifted the beer bottle to his lips.

"Oh. Well, I hope y'all have fun. Brila, I'll see you out there in a little bit." Janae grinned as she glided toward the next table to thank them for attending.

Brila made her way to the bar, hoping to escape further discussion of the bouquet toss. Who decided to carry on that stupid tradition anyway? Who would want to humiliate their unmarried friends? And who wants to fight over some flowers to prove they'll be the next one married? She would not have it at her wedding. She probably wouldn't have any single friends left by that point anyway.

"I thought I saw you and D.T. at the ceremony." Cameron approached and hugged her. He leaned on the bar to her left and brought himself closer to eye level with her. "I'm glad you could make it."

He had already removed his suit jacket. Brila admired the deep purple of his tie, which matched the bridesmaids' dresses. The white shirt shone like his smile against his dark skin. He was always well dressed, but his groomsmen outfit suited his lean body perfectly.

"Of course. I wouldn't miss it. Although, I'm not sure how long we're going to stay." She nodded toward the table. "The crew is fixing to leave already."

"No, you have to stay and dance. I need someone out there with me. They'll change their minds once things pick up." He traded his empty glass to the bartender in exchange for a new one.

"I think the consensus is we're leaving after cake."

"So you're saying I need to hide the cake." His brown eyes squinted as he smiled.

"Yeah, something like that."

They both laughed as Cameron walked with Brila back to the table. He shook hands with D.T. and Tony and then bent down to hug Shanna. "So rumor has it y'all are ready to bail."

All eyes turned to Brila as she hid behind the drink she sipped. "Well, it's true," she shot back.

"No date tonight, Cam?" D.T. interjected.

"Between my groomsman duties and having all my family here, I figured it was best to do this one solo."

Shanna chimed in. "Do you have your eye on anyone here?"

Cameron scanned the room, shaking his head. "Most people are family or Janae's friends. And there's something weird about hitting on my brother-in-law's friends. No matter how cute his best man is."

D.T. pulled his beer bottle from his lips. "So it's back to men again? How are we supposed to know who to set you up with when you keep going back and forth?"

"I'm just looking for a decent person who likes to have fun and has a little ambition to accomplish something in their life."

"Seems pretty reasonable to me." Brila glared at D.T. He could be so insensitive.

Cameron's smile returned. "I'm not looking to be set up anyway. But maybe I'll play matchmaker for someone new tonight."

He had introduced Shanna and Tony at his college roommate's wedding seven years earlier and had introduced Brila and D.T. at a separate wedding.

Two years earlier, Cameron had begged Brila to attend his coworker's wedding with him. "I need someone I can trust around all these work people," he had told her. She reluctantly agreed but regretted it as she sat at the table, watching a reception hall full of strangers laugh, embrace, and retell stories that made no sense to her. While Cameron tried to explain and include her in the conversations, she did her best to enjoy her favorite moments of any wedding, like the father-daughter dance.

As she approached the bar to replace her drink, unwilling to be empty-handed, she noticed a tall, handsome man in front of her laughing with three other groomsmen. His arms looked as if they would bust through his shirt if he moved the wrong way.

When he turned, his wide smile sent a flutter through her chest. His eyes met hers as he ran a hand through his sandy blonde hair. Lost in that moment, a tight-lipped smile forced itself on her face. Immediately regretting it, she cursed herself for being so awkward as she waited for her vodka and lemonade.

Cameron approached and followed her gaze to find the man who still held her attention. She sipped her drink as it slid across the bar and then looked at her friend. "Is it time to go yet?"

"We haven't even shown off our mad dance skills yet." His own bright smile eased her. "Besides, I want to introduce to you someone first."

Brila groaned and rolled her eyes. "Why?"

"Just come with me." He pulled her away from the bar, like a toddler being pulled away from their favorite toy before bedtime.

Her eyes grew wide as they approached the bulging-arm man and his fellow groomsmen. She lifted her glass and took a slow drink, scanning the room to avoid making eye contact. Cameron shook hands and exchanged small talk with the group of large men. He matched them in height, but his slender frame paled in comparison to these guys who must have spent most of their free time in the gym. He nudged her shoulder with his elbow. She glanced up at him before daring to look around the circle of unfamiliar faces while he introduced her.

D.T. stood directly across from her, flashing his perfect smile. "You don't look too excited to be here."

"Oh, you know, just doing a favor for a friend." She shot Cameron a look.

"And I am forever in your debt." He bowed with a smirk.

Her eyes stayed laser-focused on him while he continued, afraid to meet the gray eyes across from her.

"D.T. is a real outdoorsy guy. Goes hiking and kayaking and all that stuff you always talk about doing."

She felt her cheeks flush.

"Maybe we can get out on the river sometime." That smile slipped behind the beer bottle he brought to his lips.

"Sure." She tucked a strand of brown hair behind her ear and turned to Cameron, as she silently pleaded for him to end the awkward encounter.

"Okay, we'll go if you want."

She stole another glance at D.T. as they walked away. "I still have this drink to finish. Maybe we can stay for a dance or two."

A week later, she'd received a text from an unknown number. D.T. had tracked down Cameron at work and asked for her number. They'd gone kayaking the following weekend and had been dating ever since.

Now at a wedding he desperately wanted to leave, D.T. twisted his mouth. "How many single friends do you have left? Who's hooking you up?"

Cameron chuckled. "That's about the last thing I need." He looked at his sister and new brother-in-law and then turned to Brila. "Did D.T. tell you there's an opening in the HR group at Halltown? It might not be exactly what you want, but it'd be a steady job and good pay."

"I told her, man." D.T. answered for her. "She doesn't want to work over there."

Brila furrowed her brow. "I said I don't know if I want to just take the first job offered to me. I was considering new career opportunities before this happened. Maybe now's the time to figure out what I actually want to do with my life and go after that instead of lucking into another job."

"That's fair." Shanna smiled. "You should find something that makes you happy."

"But you also need to find a job before you lose the one you have." D.T. fired back.

"I have a few months. I'm sure I'll find something before then." A sense of freedom washed over her as she considered the opportunity she'd been given.

Then Shanna's words echoed in her mind. The same words Angelle had spoken to her a year earlier. Her smile faded and her heart raced. Sure, it was common advice. It wasn't crazy for both her sister and friend to want her to be happy. Yet the words "find something that makes you happy" reverberated through her bones.

"Is everything okay?" Cameron leaned down until he was eye level with her. "You look like you've seen a ghost."

Brila looked up to see the rest of the table staring at her. "I just need a minute," she barely whispered as she stood and rushed toward the restroom.

She shoved the door open and ducked into the last stall. Twisting her head around to scan her surroundings, she found no surface she was willing to rest against. She should've escaped through the front doors. Tucking her wristlet under her arm, she dropped her face into her hands and breathed deeply to gain control of her pounding heartbeat.

As her eyes closed, Angelle's face appeared. Her beautiful smile. Her glistening eyes. Brila let out a whimper as tears fell into the palms of her hands. She ripped off a wad of toilet paper to dry her eyes and wrapped her arms around herself. What she wouldn't give to have Angelle holding her up instead.

At the sound of the door opening, she inhaled slowly and dabbed her cheeks.

"Brila?" Shanna called out. "Are you in here?"

"I'm back here." She exhaled and opened the stall door.

"What's going on?"

Her friend's concerned look indicated she wouldn't be able to lie her way out of this one. "Just an Angelle memory. I really thought I was doing better about holding it together when that happened, but this one caught me off guard. It felt so intense."

"I get that." Shanna handed her a tissue from her purse. "That happens to me sometimes but with babies."

Brila approached the mirror to inspect any potential damage to her makeup. Thankful for waterproof mascara, she turned to her friend. "I just wish it'd get easier."

"Me too." The two smiled and hugged. "But maybe she was looking out for you."

She pulled back and raised an eyebrow. "Why would you say that?"

"They were getting ready for the bouquet toss when I came in here. And judging by the music, they'll be done and on to the garter toss by the time we get out of here."

Brila chuckled. "Sounds like good timing." She looked in the mirror again, and then she threw away the tissues. "I thought you were going to tell me you're pregnant."

"Well, since you mentioned it ..." Shanna grinned from ear to ear.

Brila's eyes widened and her mouth dropped open. "Shut up! Are you serious?"

"We just went to the doctor Thursday to confirm. It's super early. It's only been three weeks. You cannot tell Tony I told you. We promised we wouldn't say anything until the second trimester. And *la familia* would kill me if they knew we told anyone before them."

Shanna's attempts to speak Spanish always made Brila smile. Tony's family never excluded her from conversations. In fact, they were mindful to speak English in her presence. Still, she made it her mission to learn their native language.

"You can't pull that off." Brila grinned.

Shanna's shoulders slumped. "Why not?"

"Forget it." Brila wrapped her arms around her. "I'm so happy for you. And I promise not to say anything." She leaned down to talk to her friend's stomach. "You should know, I'm going to be your favorite aunt. We'll go on lots of fun adventures and drive your parents crazy."

"You know that's just my normal stomach fat at this point. And he can't hear this early in his development."

"He?"

Shanna shrugged. "I don't know. I just feel like it's a boy."

"Antonio Junior. Baby A.J." Brila smiled.

"Don't do that. Don't jinx it. No names yet. And besides, Tony's already a junior."

"Really? So can I call him T.J. for Tony Junior instead?"

Shanna stared at her.

"Fine. This whole conversation never happened." She watched the smile return to Shanna's face. "Now let's go make sure D.T. didn't run away."

SIX

Brila sat in her parked car Monday morning, gathering the courage to walk into work. Rumors and pity certainly awaited her inside that building. Maybe if she closed her eyes and wished hard enough, the events of the past Friday would become nothing but a bad dream. She glanced at the clock on the illuminated dashboard screen: 8:11 a.m. Sighing, she pushed the door open and forced herself to face reality.

Before she could turn on her computer, Darcy was in her office. "I heard the news after you left Friday. I'm so sorry!" She stared at her with large puppy-dog eyes.

What was she waiting for? An outburst? A breakdown? Inside information? Brila refused to give her any of those things. "Thanks."

Darcy sank into the seat across from her and rested her elbows on the desk. "I was shocked. I can't imagine how you felt. Were you pissed? I know I would be."

"I can't say I was excited about it." Brila chose her words carefully. "But I knew there were cuts coming, and there's not much I can do. It'll work itself out." She forced a smile and turned back to her computer, hoping Darcy would get the hint.

"Do you think?" She didn't move any closer to the door. "I hope for your sake it does. I just don't know how they can promise to find something for everyone. I mean, if the whole point is to cut budgets, they're not going to achieve anything by keeping everyone."

Brila shrugged at the echo of her own concerns. "Well, either it works out here or somewhere else. It has to, right?"

"I guess you're right." Darcy peered over her shoulder into the lobby. "I should get back out there. I have a family coming in soon. I just wanted to make sure you were okay."

Brila waited for Darcy to leave. When that didn't happen, she replied, "Yep, I'm okay."

Darcy nodded and finally walked out to talk with the administrator.

A minute later, Brila glanced up to be met by their stares, which they quickly diverted. With a knot twisting in her stomach, she reached for her coffee mug but came up empty-handed. She must have left it on the kitchen counter. The coffee maker in the lobby was surrounded by five of her coworkers catching up on the weekend's activities before everyone settled in for the morning. The coffee shop in the student union was inconvenient but the only other option. She watched as one of the counselors pulled out her phone to share a video of her baby and seized the opportunity to escape.

As she waited for her coffee in the union, she hoped everyone would be out of the lobby by the time she returned.

"Looks like great minds think alike."

Brila cringed but fixed her face before turning to face Mitch. "Great minds would've kept me around." She looked back at the counter, praying her order would appear.

"Fair enough," he stepped closer and lowered his voice. "I did try, for the record, even if you don't believe me. They wanted to use a fair process across the board. It's just the way it had to be."

She reached for her cup as the student worker called out her name. "That's because no one had the balls to stand up and say it isn't right. No one had the courage to point out the obvious fact that this flawed process is going to hurt the school. Not only are you losing talented, dedicated employees but you're burning bridges with alumni. And I don't just mean me." She brushed past him and left the union.

Halfway back to the admissions office, Mitch called her name as he jogged up behind her. "You know this is far above me. I'm not the one making budget cuts or deciding which departments have to take those cuts. I'm not sure why you're taking it all out on me."

She stopped and looked into his eyes for the first time since he'd given her the news. "Because I don't work with the dean, the president, or the directors. I work with you. You know me. You know the work I do, the improvements I've made to our entire group, and how greatly they've benefited the school. You know damn well that I deserve to be here more than anyone in that office." She pointed down the hall. "I don't expect the board to care about me. But you, I expected you to fight for me. And you can tell me all you want that you did, but the fact that I'm still leaving tells me you didn't fight hard enough." She sighed. "Now if you'll excuse me, I have work to do in an office that is bound to gossip about me for the next two months. I'm super excited to get to it." She rolled her eyes and walked away.

Taking a deep breath, Brila stepped inside the admissions office, relieved to see just the administrator. As the door closed, however, Darcy suddenly appeared and followed her to her desk. "There you are. I was looking ..."

"I have a lot of work to get done today. And I really don't want to talk about the layoffs anymore. Besides, didn't you have a family coming in?" Brila shot her a quick look and then closed the door before she could sneak in behind her.

The end of the day couldn't come soon enough. She glanced at the clock to find only an hour had passed. She groaned. Exactly an hour had passed. Come to think of it, she'd seen the eleventh minute quite often lately. Weird. She smiled as she remembered how Angelle would make a wish whenever she'd seen 11:11 on the clock. This didn't count as a wishing moment, though if it did, she'd wish this whole thing would go away. Taking a long sip of coffee, she began compiling the data from her weekend posts.

Brila was wrapping up responses to the last post when there was a knock on her door.

"I think we need to talk." Mitch closed the door and sat across from her.

"I'm not sure there's anything left to say. And you know Mondays are always busy for me." She took a second to look from her monitor to him. "Unless you're here to tell me I have to leave now."

"Of course not." His voice lowered. "You know, if someone in the department was to retire, we'd be able to keep you as their backfill."

She ran through a mental list of the admissions staff. "No one's considering retirement this year."

"Not right now, but maybe someone could be talked into it."

She shook her head, realizing who he meant. Was he serious? "I'm not going to beg someone to retire early just so I can have a job. Especially when they depend on their job."

"Don't we all depend on our jobs? Don't you depend on yours?"

"Well, yeah, but—"

"And didn't you say you were the best employee, the most deserving to stay here?"

"Don't twist my words to make me out to be the bad guy." Brila's cheeks burned.

"I'm not trying to make anyone the bad guy here. I'm just giving you an opportunity to stay if you so choose." He stood, placed his hand on the door handle, and turned back. "Think about it."

As he walked to his office, Brila calculated her savings and how long she could afford to be unemployed. It wasn't much. She didn't want to deal with the gossip or the pity for another two months, but where else was she going to go?

She loved Southern. It was hard to imagine leaving. But was she willing to talk someone into early retirement so she could stay? Could she see herself working in a different department—if that was actually an option? It felt like a no-win situation.

Sighing in exasperation, she returned to her work. She'd have to deal with it all, but if she could just focus on her tasks for the day, she could momentarily forget the stress weighing on her shoulders.

That evening, Brila headed straight from work to the yoga studio. After quickly changing her clothes in the tiny restroom stall, she rolled out her mat in the middle of the room. While the afternoon had been quieter than the morning, finally being away from work comforted her.

She'd first gone to a yoga class during her junior year of college when her roommate had begged her to go. She'd fallen in love with it at that first class. She enjoyed pushing her body to stretch further and grow stronger. She found solace in the peaceful studio, and she loved the idea of meditation, although she found it difficult to keep her mind quiet long enough to do it properly.

As she pressed the palms of her hands together in front of her chest for prayer pose, she began to relax. Her boss and coworkers, the stares, and the whispers slowly faded away. Hinging at the hips with her hands and feet on the ground, she pressed her chest toward her legs into downward dog. She closed her eyes and breathed deeply. Tomorrow would be better. She reassured herself through that pose and the next. The right opportunity would arise. She found a new affirmation to repeat with every other pose and help her focus. Throughout the session, she remained concentrated on her own voice. The instructor's directions were a mere distant calling.

Before she knew it, the instructor was asking for them to sit cross-legged on the mat for guided meditation.

Since Angelle's birthday, she had tried harder to focus during these sessions. While she wasn't particularly religious or spiritual, she did prescribe to the idea that each person had a specific purpose or calling in life. It had been Angelle's advice a year earlier for her to find her own purpose. Now the opportunity to figure it out had been thrust into her lap as she had to begin searching for a new job.

Throughout the meditation, she focused on finding her purpose. She asked for guidance, a sign—anything to help lead her in the right direction. She tried to envision her dream job, but all she saw was an empty room. Suddenly, it was illuminated by a bright white number eleven. Her eyes shot open as the instructor announced the end of the session. She crawled on her knees to roll up her mat, breathing deeply to slow the pounding in her chest. Was that how meditation was supposed to work? Did she stop too early? Would she be able to get it back to figure out what it meant?

The instructor's voice grew as she stood. "And if anyone is interested, a new session for yoga teacher training starts in May. I have information by the door, and it's on the website. You can let me know if you have any questions."

Brila froze. A studio was an empty room. She loved yoga and it made her happy. Was this the opportunity she had been hoping for? She felt a flutter in her stomach as she approached Anna, the instructor. "Can you tell me more about this training?"

"It's a two hundred-hour program. Once completed, you would be a registered yoga teacher. You learn everything from the history and philosophy of yoga to teaching techniques and how to guide meditation."

Brila tried to do the math in her head, but it wasn't working out. "Two hundred hours?"

"It's Friday night and all day Saturday and Sunday for ten weeks. Plus the week before, we have you come in for paperwork, physicals, and that sort of thing. So eleven weeks total."

Her eyes widened. Eleven weeks. This had to be what her vision was about—if that's what it was. Could it really be that simple? "Great! I'll check it out." Brila smiled and scurried toward the table by the door to pick up the information packet. She hugged the packet to her chest, feeling a weight lift off it, as she walked out.

SEVEN

"So you're not going to work all summer?" D.T. stared across the table in his small kitchen. For the three days since Brila had told him about the yoga teacher training program, he'd been full of questions.

"I told you I'm working through May. I'm sure I can find something to get me through August if I need to, but I don't think I do. I have enough saved up to cover my bills for about three months."

"And what about the weekends? We're just not going to see each other for the next four months now?"

She stared back at him to keep from rolling her eyes. "I'll be gone Friday, but I'll be free Saturday and Sunday nights. And I'll be free on weeknights like I am now." She took a bite of her baked chicken, giving him time to realize he was overreacting. When he didn't respond, she continued with a new suggestion. "I did find out last night there's an immersion class that starts at the end of this month."

"Does that mean you'd be gone for more days?" He raised an eyebrow.

"Not really. It'd be ten hours a day, Monday through Friday, but it's four weeks." She waited again for a response that never came. Her mind wrapped around her words, and she surprised herself. "I hadn't really considered it, but that might actually make more sense.

I'd have to stop working earlier than I planned, but I'd only have to cover one month of bills with my savings. Then I can start working in a studio sooner, and I wouldn't have to give up my nights and weekends."

"Of course that's the better choice. You're just realizing that now?" D.T. scoffed and shook his head.

"I guess I just got so excited about the original program, I didn't really give much thought to this option when I heard about it." She paused. "But do you really think it's okay for me to leave Southern this early? We were just talking about me working through the summer."

He considered it. "Any word of openings in other departments?" She shook her head.

She'd reached out to financial aid, the alumni office, and the student resource team. None had openings in their departments nor had heard of others on campus. When she'd asked Mitch about it, he'd promised to ask around and then asked if she'd talked to her coworker about retirement. After brief consideration, she couldn't bring herself to do it.

"Are you really going to give up on Southern that easily?" D.T.'s eyes held hers.

Her jaw tensed. "I'm not giving up. I'm running out of options. Now I have this opportunity to do something that I could really enjoy. Why not take it before I end up with nothing?"

"I guess." D.T. took another bite. "Do you pay any less for the shorter session?"

"It's still the same amount of time, so it's the same cost."

"At least you'd be going at normal hours, not taking up nights and weekends."

"Don't you think I should do whatever it takes, even if it means giving up my weekends for a few months?"

"Not if you don't have to."

"Maybe so." She took her dishes to the sink. "I just thought you'd be happier for me. I found something I'm excited about and even set out a plan before committing to anything."

D.T. twisted in his seat to look at her. "I'm happy for you. I just want to make sure you have it all figured out so it doesn't go south."

Brila dropped her fork in the sink as she turned on the water. "There's nothing to worry about. I know it's going to work out." A lack of confidence in her own words churned in her stomach.

As strong as she felt she had received a sign to follow this new career path, the idea of leaving Southern was still terrifying. What if it was just a coincidence? What if it didn't work out? What if there was a way for her to stay at Southern?

Still, a small voice in her said she had to try. She'd committed herself to finding a purpose in life that made her happy, if not for herself, to honor Angelle.

After they finished cleaning up in the kitchen, they retreated to the oversized black leather couch. Brila picked up her phone as D.T. turned on a basketball game. She leaned against his arm, looking up at the TV from time to time.

In the early days of their relationship, she had pretended to be interested in every game he watched. Over time, though, her apathy for anything other than baseball seeped through. It was nice not to have to keep up the facade, and he didn't seem to mind. They could have ended their night together after dinner. They could have fought about one not caring about the other's interests. Instead, they were comfortable sharing in each other's company, in their unspoken agreement to be together while doing their own thing.

Brila had scanned through each of her social media accounts and scrolled through a handful of online shops. Bored with her phone, she set it next to her and decided to watch the remainder of the game. She reviewed the score as a timeout was called: Denver one-eleven, Houston one-ten, with one minute, eleven seconds left. "You've got to be kidding me," she mumbled under her breath.

"I know." D.T. glanced at her. "Houston should be killing them. They need to get it together and finish the game." He pulled her closer.

"That's a lot of elevens on the screen."

His head tilted to the side. "What?"

How could she explain something she didn't understand herself? "Nothing. You're right; it shouldn't be this close."

She leaned back into him. The game would be over soon enough, and she would head home after that. While some nights she thought it'd be easier to stay and get ready for work at his place, tonight she was thankful to be going home to address this eleven thing without D.T. questioning her.

She stretched and sat up while D.T. clapped his hands as Houston regained their lead and held on to win one-fifteen to one-twelve. She smiled at his enthusiasm, waiting for a commercial break to kiss him goodnight.

No sooner had the door closed behind her that she began searching for answers. Why was the number eleven showing up again? She scrolled through the results as she got into her car. A barrage of words jumped out at her: 'angel number,' 'divine,' 'power,' 'master,' 'message,' 'curse.'

She dropped the phone in the cup holder and started the ignition. Was it really more than a coincidence? What was an angel number? Was there really validity behind anything that popped up in the search results? How could it be a curse? Her mind reeled the entire drive home.

Brila yawned, checking the time on her phone as she opened the door to her condo: 10:30 p.m. She needed to shower and get to bed so she wouldn't struggle to stay awake at work the next morning. She stood frozen in her kitchen. There had to be an answer for this strange occurrence, and she had to get to the bottom of it. She wouldn't be able to sleep until she did.

Reopening the search results, she clicked the first link. She read about angel numbers and how the number eleven was meant to be a message, inspiration, and guidance related to finding one's purpose. A warmth flowed through her body, and a smile pushed on her cheeks. It made perfect sense. Of course that's what had been happening. That's why she'd seen the eleven right before learning about the yoga teacher training program and again, earlier, when she'd started second-guessing herself. This was the confirmation she needed. She closed out of the search and headed toward the bathroom, glad she finally had an answer to this nonsense.

While eating lunch on the outdoor patio of a bistro the next day, Brila told Shanna about her decision to leave work earlier than planned and start training to become a yoga instructor. She was also excited to share her latest discovery. "Have you ever felt like you've been given a sign—like you just know you're supposed to do something?"

Shanna nodded in agreement, but her eyes gave away her concern.

"Lately I've been seeing the number eleven everywhere. Random places and times. Like when I'm meditating, on the clock, and last night it was in the score of the game D.T. was watching. Anyway, I looked it up, and it turns out it's an angel number, which is basically a sign from above that you're on the right path to realizing your purpose. So, I must be on the right track." She leaned back in her chair, smiling into the sun as she took a sip of water. "It just feels really good."

"You know I love you," Shanna's smile faded as she ran her fingers through her blonde curls, "but you're crazy. First of all, why would seeing a number mean anything? How are you going to let that decide what you're supposed to be doing? And do you really think teaching yoga is a sustainable career? What happens when it's no longer trendy, and you have no one taking classes from you? What happens when you get old, and your body can't do it anymore?"

"I just poured my heart out to you, telling you how excited I am, and you're going to knock me down like that?" Brila set down her glass. "All I've heard for the past week is I need to find something that makes me happy. Angelle said the same words a year ago. I think yoga could do just that, and you call me crazy. Would you like to tell me what's going to make me happy if it's not this?"

"You're not crazy. I shouldn't have said that. And, yes, it's great you found something you're excited about." She took a deep breath. "It just feels like maybe you jumped on this opportunity without really thinking it all the way through. And isn't that what you said you didn't want to do with that Halltown job D.T. and Cam mentioned?"

"I didn't want to just fall into another job offer. This isn't something I lucked into. I know it's a little out of the box, but it feels right. And now with this little sign from above, I know I'm making the right choice."

Shanna held her gaze. "How can you be so sure it's not just a coincidence?"

Brila thought for a moment. "At first, I thought that's all it was, but it just felt different. Almost as if something was forcing me to notice that number. I can't explain it. I mean, how many times in my life have I probably seen an eleven on the clock or in a score, or anywhere else and never paid attention? Why am I just noticing now? It has to mean something."

"But what if it doesn't? Maybe you noticed it once, and now you're more aware of it. What if what you saw while meditating wasn't even the number eleven? Two straight lines could be so many different things."

"I don't get it. You're always so supportive. I want to do this for myself." She swallowed hard. "I want to do this for Angelle. Why are you so hell-bent on ruining this for me?"

Shanna frowned. "I don't want to ruin it. And I'll always support you. I just don't want to see you get hurt or end up worse off. Losing your job is already hard enough. I'd hate to see things fall apart even further."

"Now you sound like D.T."

"Oh, good Lord!" Her eyebrows raised. "Don't tell me that! I take it all back. Whatever you say, I believe you. Everything is going to work out."

Brila laughed. "There's the Shanna I know and love." She lifted her fork, leaned over the table, and whispered, "So how's the pregnancy going?"

"The morning sickness is miserable, and I swear I fall asleep at eight every night. I'm not supposed to be this tired yet, but apparently, it's normal for some."

"Sounds terrible."

"No, it's great!"

Brila scrunched her face.

Shanna chuckled. "Sure, I'm not feeling great, but that's part of pregnancy. I'll suffer through it all because having a baby will be worth it."

The love and joy shining in Shanna's eyes touched Brila's heart. She beamed with excitement for her friend. "Do you really think you'll be able to keep this secret for another two months?"

"It'll be hard, but I'm going to try." She paused as the waitress refilled their water glasses. "But I ended up telling Tony that I told you."

Brila rolled her eyes. "Of course you did."

"You know I can't keep anything from him. Besides, I'd rather just tell him than have it accidentally come up later."

"You don't think I can keep this a secret?"

Shanna raised an eyebrow. "I think you can keep quiet to most people, but you're going to slip up one night when we're all together."

"Well, I'm not going to say anything, even to Tony, just to prove you wrong."

"That'd actually be wonderful. Thanks."

They both laughed as they continued eating. It wasn't always easy to fit it into their schedules, but Brila loved that Shanna held her to their Friday lunch dates. It'd be easy to let a few weeks slip by without seeing one another, but their face-to-face discussions always energized her. And that was something she needed in her life, probably now more than ever.

EIGHT

That first week following the budget cut announcement had been painful. Many coworkers dropped in to express their sympathy and vow to let Brila know of any job opportunities, but it all seemed to be for their own benefit. Most didn't speak to her again after offering their initial words of comfort.

Once she gave her two weeks' notice, she might as well have left that very day as most coworkers went about their days without acknowledging her. Even Darcy stopped coming by to pry out information about her feelings and plans. Although it was a little lonely, Brila was somewhat relieved to no longer have others worry about her. She enjoyed the peace and continued doing her work.

Now she counted down the final hours of her last day. She had scheduled her weekend posts before turning over all of her templates and plans to the remaining coordinators. Soft murmurs echoed from the other offices. It was a rare quiet day—perfect for letting the mind wander when it didn't have much else to do.

She smiled and folded her arms as she leaned back in her chair, reflecting on the past seven years. Her first day as a student worker. The nerves she had fought off to present her restructure proposal to Mitch. Receiving her full-time job offer. The high school students that had visited because of something she had posted. Working on the same campus as her mom. She had so many fond memories to take with her. As excited as she was to start her yoga training and follow this new path, it was still a bittersweet day.

A knock on her door jolted her upright.

"Do you have a minute?" Darcy poked her head inside the doorway. "I need you to look at something for me."

Brila sighed. "Don't you want someone who will actually be here next week to help you out?"

"I'd rather have you do it. Come on. Just this one last favor before you go."

"Fine." She pushed herself out of her chair. She didn't have much else to do anyway.

Brila listened to Darcy ramble on about her weekend plans to visit Galveston, as they walked to the back room.

As they turned the corner, the rest of the admissions department greeted them with big, goofy grins. She surveyed the room through squinted eyes. "What the hell's going on?"

Glances were exchanged, but all eyes eventually landed on Mitch. Judging by his hesitation and the shuffling of his feet, he wasn't prepared to provide an explanation. Maybe this hadn't been his idea, and he was just going along with it.

He turned a bright shade of pink. "Well, I know this isn't exactly what you had wanted. I wish there had been a way for us to keep you here, but it seems you have found a new path to pursue. You've contributed so much over the past six years."

Brila felt like the air had been sucked out of the room as someone near Mitch whispered to him.

"Excuse me. Seven years. I guess it's true. Time does fly when you're having fun." He rubbed his arm as he chuckled at his own joke. "You'll be greatly missed. We hope one day the road leads you back to the Southern family. And as a little thank-you for your time here, we got you this basket of Southern swag and a cookie cake." He motioned to the table in the middle of the room. He leaned in to grab a plate but stopped when he realized the attention had turned to Brila.

She cleared her throat and smiled. "What can I say? I thought we'd all be together a lot longer than this. I'm quickly learning that I can't always control what happens, but I know it all happens for a reason. So, while I'm sad to be leaving a place I've enjoyed so much, I'm grateful I met some good people and have learned so much. Thanks to each of you." She paused to look at all the faces she had grown accustomed to seeing day in and out. She found it hard to believe she'd never see most of them again. She faked a cough to combat the tears threatening to spill over. "All right, I think that's enough talking. Let's cut into that cookie cake."

After being handed a plate, she made her way around the room to thank each of her coworkers individually. She may not have been close with all of them, but a bond had been made nonetheless. A by-product of working together for that many years. Slipping out quietly may have been easier, but getting to say goodbye to each of them warmed her heart and gave her closure she didn't realize she needed.

Mitch stepped next to her as she dropped her plate in the trash can. "Sorry I messed up your years of service. I guess I forgot to count your time as a student worker."

"The seven years doesn't include my senior year." Brila started toward the middle table as he followed. "Seems like something you could've checked before coming in here."

"Okay, I messed up." He shifted his weight. "This situation is tough enough. Can we try to end on a good note?"

She exhaled deeply. "I suppose."

"So yoga. That should be a fun adventure until you find something a little more steady."

"What's that mean?"

His eyes searched the room. "Well, my sister taught yoga part-time for years. She was always bouncing around and picking up random classes. It just didn't seem like something sustainable."

"There's a difference between doing it on the side for fun and making it a career, which is what I plan to do." She stopped herself before she got into her desire to do something she loved in honor of Angelle. She didn't owe him an explanation. "I should get back to my desk. I'll see you around, Mitch." She slid the gift basket into her arms and walked out of the back room.

She placed the basket inside the paper box that held every personal item her office had accumulated over the years. Sinking into her chair, she turned to the computer monitor and stared at the screen for a minute. There was nothing left for her to do. The weekend posts were complete. She'd said her goodbyes. Why sit around and drag out her last day?

She called IT to give them the go-ahead to pick up her hardware as she shut down her computer and then called human resources. They had given her a list of things to do before she left, but it was nowhere to be found. It probably got thrown away when she'd cleared out her desk that morning. They reminded her to turn in her parking pass to security and stop by HR to complete an exit survey.

The conversations from the backroom drew closer as everyone returned to their afternoon routines. Brila slung her purse over her shoulder, picked up the box containing her possessions, and hurried through the lobby. She heard someone call her name as she shifted her belongings under one arm and opened the department door with the other. There was no turning back, no hesitation. She was around the corner before the door had time to close.

She placed the box in the backseat of her car, and as she closed the door, her phone began to ring. She looked at the screen for a moment and scrunched her face. "Hey, Mom. Is everything okay?"

"Are you leaving already?"

Brila whirled around but didn't recognize anyone nearby. "I was just putting my things in the car before heading to HR. Why?"

"Oh, good." Lyla exhaled. "Someone reported to HR that you had walked out. They were concerned and asked me to get a hold of you."

Brila sighed. "I just talked to them five minutes ago. Did they really think I was running away?"

"I don't know. But why don't you stop by when you're done? We can go grab ice cream in the café."

She turned and began walking toward the HR office. "I'm not too hungry. We just had cookie cake."

"Then just stop by my office for a few minutes."

She hesitated but finally agreed. It was going to be weird not working at the same place as her mom. The least she could do was visit one more time. And her office was much more secluded than the café.

Brila arrived in the math department twenty minutes later.

Dr. Lyla Landry. She stared at the nameplate until a student opened the door and stepped out of her mom's office. Brila slid past him, closing the door. She sighed and slumped into a chair opposite her mom. "Well, that was a waste of time. A bunch of useless questions from HR and a rundown from security about my new parking rights. Or lack thereof. Which reminds me, I probably shouldn't stay too long."

Lyla pressed her lips together as if she was holding back her initial word choice. "I'm so sorry you have to go through this."

"Oh, Mom. Don't worry about me. It's all going to work out."

"I know. You always end up on your feet." She paused. "I'm still allowed to be upset for you."

"And worried about me?" Brila pressed.

"I know you believe this yoga training is the right thing. And it certainly sounds exciting. But what if it doesn't work out the way you expect it to? How many more yoga instructors does Houston really need?"

Brila scrunched her eyebrows. "I don't know, but there's clearly some sort of a demand if they're pushing for people to do the training."

"I'll have to trust you on this one. You know we support whatever you want to do."

Brila walked around the oversized desk to hug her. "Thank you." She checked the clock. "I really should go. Getting a parking ticket from this place is the last thing I need today. I'll come by this weekend. Maybe we can do Sunday brunch?"

"That would be great. I know your dad would love to see you." Lyla squeezed her daughter's hand as Brila pulled toward the door.

She finally freed her hand and smiled. Her mom's nameplate caught her attention again on her way out. Her heart pounded quicker for a few beats. Lyla had dedicated years of work and sacrifice to earning her degrees and advancing her career. She had been a role model for both of her daughters throughout their childhood. Brila hoped one day she'd realize her own dreams and do something meaningful like her parents and sister had.

NINE

That following Monday, Brila walked into her first yoga teacher training class. Entering the softly lit studio, she sat on the dark wood floor and examined the contents of her bag, just as she had done three times before leaving the house ten minutes earlier than necessary. The cream-colored walls, the set of wooden chairs near the entrance, and even the light scent of lavender were reminiscent of her regular studio. She sighed with a slight smile as a petite woman approached.

"Welcome! I'm Heidi." She extended her hand and smiled, accentuating the wrinkles around her eyes. She looked around the otherwise empty room. "We should have a few others joining us shortly. So tell me, what are your plans once you receive your certificate?"

Brila hesitated, her eyes locking on a set of bamboo paintings hung on the side wall. "I guess I'm going to try to find a studio to teach at. Isn't that what everyone does?"

"Not necessarily." Heidi sat cross-legged next to her. "Program participants range from people looking to do personal instruction to gym owners looking to offer something new. Where do you work?"

She rubbed her arm. "Well, I was recently let go due to cutbacks at Southern College."

"Ah, so you have time to do your training now while you look for another job. Perfect timing." Heidi turned as four other students entered the studio. She popped up to greet them. "Speaking of perfect timing ... Welcome!"

Look for another job? That was certainly not on Brila's to-do list. She had assumed there'd be openings at the studio she attended, and she'd be able to teach her own classes immediately. What if that weren't the case? Would she have to find another studio? Could she teach at multiple studios on different days? There were plenty of people making a living as yoga instructors, right? Why would she have to work a second job?

After the last three students arrived, Heidi called the group together and began handing out papers and books.

Brila's mind continued to swirl around Heidi's words. She thought she had everything figured out. Would she need extra training? Did she need to open her own studio or become a personal trainer? The questions and uncertainty were suffocating.

Heidi reviewed their schedule and introduced another instructor, but Brila barely heard a word. As the other students started to roll out their mats, she numbly followed suit.

Brila inhaled deeply and stretched her hands to the ceiling as they started their first sequence. Her worries slid from her mind as she tuned in to Heidi's instructions. Everything around her began to melt away. With each new position, her body felt stronger. Things weren't as cut and dry as she'd thought, but a sense of belonging washed over her. For the moment, that's all that mattered.

By the second week of the training program, Brila was beaming with pride over the progress she had made. Her flexibility had improved. She was more confident in her ability to help others properly execute the poses and transition through sequences. Even the history of yoga practices and the technical details, which she had decided would be a waste of time, was fascinating. What she enjoyed the most, however, were the meditation exercises.

During their Tuesday class, she closed her eyes as their meditation session began.

"Today we are going to work on finding our inner peace." Heidi led the guided session with a soft, calming tone. "Sit up nice and tall. Elongate your spine as you inhale. Allow your breath to fill your lungs and expand into your belly. Exhale slowly, letting go of all your concerns. As thoughts enter your mind, allow them to pass as you continue to focus on your breathing."

Brila's breathing slowed, and her body grew heavy as she relaxed each part of her body from her face to her toes. Her vision behind closed eyes flooded with a bright light, as if a spotlight pointed directly at her. Everything around her faded. Even Heidi's voice sounded faint and distant.

"Feel your body connect with the energy of the universe, from the base of your spine to the top of your head. As your breath becomes more controlled, I want you to repeat this quietly to yourself. 'I cannot control my circumstances, but I can control my choices.' Repeat this again with each breath."

Suddenly, the bright light faded to dark. Twisted red metal appeared. Angelle's mangled car. A door shut out that image. Southern's Admissions Office door. She was left standing in a deserted hallway. "I cannot control my circumstances, but I can control my choices," Brila whispered as she squeezed her eyes tighter. She shook the image from her mind and refocused on her breathing.

"You control your choices." Heidi began again, her words soft, rising and falling with each breath. "You choose how you feel. You choose how long you remain in those feelings. You choose your actions. And you choose how you will react to the circumstances that are out of your control."

Brila sat in silence, the bright light washing over her again for six breaths before Heidi continued.

"What does success look like for you? Imagine yourself in your success. Where are you? What's around you? Who is with you?"

Brila tried to picture herself leading a yoga class in her own studio. As the image came into focus, it was immediately replaced by Angelle's smile. It morphed into a memory of the two of them sitting at the large island in their parents' kitchen. It was one of their regular Sunday family brunches while they were both in college. They joked about who would have a higher GPA that semester as they picked crumb-sized bites from the cooling cinnamon rolls.

She held her breath for an extra second, trying to dismiss the memory. Again, she let the image of herself teaching yoga form in her mind. It was fuzzy and continued to fade back to the bright light. Her muscles began to tighten as she tried to bring it back.

Thankfully, Heidi moved on. "Now focus again on your energy streaming from the base of your spine to the top of your head. Let go of what you cannot control. Continue your breathing, as you feel the space around you slowly start to return. When you are ready, open your eyes."

Brila pried one eye open then the other. She stretched both arms above her, leaning to one side then the next. Letting go of her circumstances was not her strong suit. Being cut off in traffic? Sure, she could let that go. Being insulted or misjudged by a stranger? Annoying, but she could move on. Being betrayed by someone she trusted? That would stick around for a while. Having her sister ripped from her world without a moment's notice? There was no letting go of that. How do you possibly let go of losing the one person who shared your every childhood memory? The one who knew you better than you knew yourself. No, there was no letting go of that.

Heidi held her lower back and pushed her hips forward and shoulders back to stretch as the class slowly rose to their feet. "Let's break for lunch. We'll regroup at twelve-thirty to review sequencing techniques."

The group of eight students scattered throughout the room in search of their personal belongings. Brila usually packed a lunch from home, as most of the other students did. However, she had forgotten to go to the grocery store over the weekend and the night before, leaving her with nothing but leftover pizza, and that hardly seemed appropriate to eat in the middle of yoga training. She plucked her phone and wallet from her bag and headed toward the café at the end of the block.

After ordering a spring mix salad, she scanned the dining area of mismatched furniture before selecting a small table along the right wall. She unlocked her phone and sipped on her cucumber and lemon-infused water. She started a grocery list to ensure she'd have lunch for the rest of the week and then texted D.T. to see whether or not he planned to stop by that evening.

During the first week of training, she had been so exhausted, she'd either fallen asleep right after supper or in the middle of a conversation with D.T. She was finally starting to regain her energy and owed him a night that didn't end with her crawling into bed at eight o'clock.

Setting the phone down, she looked around the room, but nothing held her attention. In just two and a half weeks, her training would be complete. It was nice to focus on the training, but she needed to put some effort into finding class openings at studios. Assisting or filling in for classes here and there was not going to pay the bills. Even though she had enough money saved up to cover payments for a few months, she'd feel better if she had a steady income flowing in again. She had placed so much faith in it all working out because it was meant to. Her meditation vision and her gut told her so. What would Angelle tell her to do? She sighed, fighting off the idea of working a second job. This was meant to be a career path, not a side gig. What would she do if that wasn't possible?

She forced a smile as the server arrived with her salad. She checked the time on her phone: 12:11 p.m. She'd have to eat quickly. Bringing the fork to her mouth, she tapped her phone again. The time stared back at her as she chewed, daring her to question it. Always eleven. Why? She kept the phone illuminated until the time changed. Aware of the minute she had wasted, she jabbed her fork into the salad.

At the end of the day, Brila stopped into her regular yoga studio to visit the owner. They were the ones who pushed the training in the first place. They must have been in need of instructors.

"Hey, stranger!" The owner, Callie, stood to hug her as she entered the office. "How are classes going?"

Brila smiled. "They're great. I love it even more than I thought I would."

"Even the history lessons?" Callie raised an eyebrow.

She chuckled. "Surprisingly, yes. I love it all. I have a whole new appreciation for the practice and the instructors."

"Well, we miss seeing you around here."

"I miss coming by, but I couldn't possibly do another session and function after. As much as I love it, my muscles are struggling to keep up." She rubbed her hands along her thighs, giving a light laugh. "But I'm looking forward to coming back once training is done. That's actually why I'm here." She waited for Callie to chime in. When she didn't, Brila continued. "Are you looking to hire instructors?"

"Not really at this time. Our schedule is full, and I don't know of anyone planning to leave."

Brila looked at the floor. "Yeah, I guess that makes sense. But why advertise the training if you're not in need?"

"Oh, it's just something they ask all prior participants to do in their studios and gyms. It's not really based on our needs." There was a short pause. "I can add you to our list of subs, though. And I can look into the possibility of having you assist in some of our larger classes."

"That would be great. I'll take whatever I can get."

"It can be tough." Callie nodded. "It took me months to find just one steady class and probably a year before I was doing multiple classes."

Brila's stomach knotted. "Well, you know I'd rather be here than another studio. Hopefully, I can find something in the meantime."

"I appreciate you coming to me first. I'll see what I can do for you."

Brila sighed as she left. Not only were there no openings, but Callie's experience added to her discouragement. She had a couple more weeks to find a studio with an opening. Or a couple of months if she wanted to stretch her savings.

Would the others in her class be looking to start right away, too? Were they already gym owners or personal trainers? Were they her competition or did they know about opportunities that could help her? If anyone would even be willing to help her. Some of them looked like the type to smile in your face as they stabbed you in the back.

She hadn't discussed plans with any of them. To be honest, she couldn't remember half their names. It dawned on her that she'd spent hardly any time at all getting to know her fellow classmates. As she headed to the grocery store, she resolved to do better.

TEN

Throughout the rest of the week, Brila made the effort to talk with her training classmates. Two were from a wellness center. They were planning to increase their class offerings and would split them with their current instructor. Two others were personal trainers trying to expand their programs. The other three were looking to pick up a class here or there "for fun."

She'd also spent her evenings researching yoga studios around the greater Houston area, contacting ten of them so far, with a total of zero instructor openings.

"I don't get it," she complained to D.T. as he drove toward the restaurant where they were meeting their friends. "Why would all these studios push their teacher training on members when none of them actually have openings?"

D.T. shrugged. "That's why you should stick to business. They don't post jobs that aren't actually open."

"No, they'll just take them away after you've revolutionized their online presence." She crossed her arms and watched the blur of buildings out her window.

"That's not business. That's a government-funded college." He glanced from the road to Brila then back again. "Have you given any thought to the PR job?"

She looked back at him. "I still don't know."

It had been fortunate that D.T.'s company had a second opening in their HR department, and public relations seemed close enough to digital marketing. "What if I do take this job and an instructor opening comes up? I don't want you putting yourself on the line just for me to end up leaving a month later."

"Then don't leave. Yoga won't pay the bills unless you open your own studio. I've been telling you that."

Brila furrowed her brow. "Just because your only concern is earning as much money as possible, doesn't mean that's everyone's goal in life. I want to do something I love, something that has some meaning to it."

She wouldn't give him the satisfaction of being right by admitting she'd had similar concerns. She held out hope that the right opportunities would come, even if they didn't come right away.

"I enjoy what I do." D.T. shrugged his shoulders. "And I make good money. There's nothing wrong with that. Who says you wouldn't love this job? Just give it a try." He smiled and grabbed her hand. "Besides, we could see each other more often. We could even go to lunch together."

She narrowed her eyes, smiling with tight lips. It'd be nice to have a steady job, especially one that allowed her to see D.T. more often. However, something about his offer felt a bit like a diminishing of her own desires.

"Fine. I'll think about it. Even if I apply, that doesn't mean I'll get the job."

"Of course you'll get it." He glanced at her. "I'll make sure of it."

She pulled her hand away. "What's that supposed to mean? You did enough by telling me about the opening. I can hold my own in an interview, if I even get one. I don't want you trying to coerce them into giving me the job." Did he not believe she could get the job on her own merit?

"I meant I'd put in a good word. Let them know how talented you are to be sure you're at the top of the list."

"I appreciate it, as long as it doesn't come off as demanding or desperate." She paused. "Why are you pushing so hard for me to do this anyway?"

"I don't see how this yoga thing is going to work out. I'm glad you love to do it, but it's a hobby, not a career. Halltown is a good company. Good people. It's stable. And there's plenty of opportunities to move around and move up. Why wouldn't I want you to work there?"

Brila folded her arms. "Who says yoga is just a hobby? Plenty of people make it a career. Why not me?"

 D.T. remained silent.

She shifted her weight and softened her tone. "Won't you get tired of having me around all the time?"

"I don't sit near PR," he said, pulling into a parking spot. "Won't even have to see each other if we don't want to."

She unbuckled her seatbelt and rested her forearms on the center console. "I guess that means I'll have to hunt you down when I want to see you."

He took the keys out of the ignition and turned to kiss her. "You won't have to look too hard. You know I can't stay away from that sexy body for long."

"Hey now. If I'm working in HR, I'll have to write you up for those kinds of comments," she said and pulled the door handle.

D.T. walked around his Jeep and wrapped his arm around her waist. "We're off the clock. You can't write me up. Besides, that's not a PR responsibility." He pulled her body into his. She clutched his back as he leaned over and pressed his lips against hers.

Inside the restaurant, Shanna and Tony were seated at a table with four empty seats. "At least we beat Cameron and his date," Brila boasted as she hugged her friends.

"Who is it this time?" D.T. asked, shaking Tony's hand.

"Alex somebody." Brila shrugged as she hung her purse on her chair back. "But not the girl he dated last year."

"I can't keep them all straight." D.T. inched his chair closer to hers.

"No one can." Shanna sipped her water. "But we love him anyway. Maybe one day he'll find the right one." Her voice trailed to a whisper as Cameron approached.

"Okay, you can stop talking about me. I can see it in Shanna's eyes." He made his way around the table to greet everyone. "Alex isn't going to make it. He got called into work."

D.T. leaned over and whispered to Brila, "You could've told me this Alex is a guy."

"It's more fun to keep you on your toes." She grinned, holding his gaze for a moment, and then turned to Cameron. "So how'd you meet this one?"

"We met at the concert a couple of weeks ago. He's got a good sense of humor and a killer smile."

Tony rolled his eyes. "You say that about all of them."

"Well, now you know my type. A fun, decent person with some ambition and a nice smile." Cameron grinned. "I set y'all up. Now it's your turn to find someone for me."

"We've tried. But didn't you tell us a few weeks ago you didn't want to be set up?" Brila had introduced him to plenty of people in the past, hoping he'd find someone with whom he could settle down, but it never worked out. He had such a knack for matching up others; she couldn't understand why it was so hard for him to find a lasting relationship for himself. "Besides, you don't like anyone we pick. You're the matchmaker. Find yourself a match."

Cameron held her gaze. "Believe me, I'm trying."

"Maybe you met the right one but were too picky and let them go," Shanna interjected with a smirk.

"Who?"

"The other Alex was good for you, and you just let her go. Maybe that's why you're attracted to new Alex."

"No. We're not doing that." Cameron narrowed his eyes. "No 'new Alex.' And she had no drive to do anything with her life. She's content bartending and living off her parents' money." He turned to Brila. "Which reminds me, I heard you're coming to work for Halltown."

"Well, it sounds like your source is speaking out of turn again." She glared at D.T.

"It wasn't me." D.T. threw his hands in the air.

"A friend in HR mentioned you were applying for the opening," said Cameron, defending him.

"It's incredible that I've somehow applied or been given the job or whatever other stories are being told when I just gave into the idea of applying about ten minutes ago." She shifted in her seat. "It's not what I want to do, but I guess I need to do something. Maybe I should go bartend with 'old Alex.'"

Cameron cringed. "Seriously, stop."

"I knew you'd apply and, of course, you'll get it. You're perfect for the job." D.T. kissed her temple.

She looked at Shanna. "Am I selling out?"

Tony shook his head as his wife answered. "I wouldn't say selling out. If the yoga jobs aren't there, you have to do something to support yourself. But don't stop looking and getting experience where you can. If that's your dream, you can't give up just because there are obstacles in your way."

"I know, but I'm afraid if I do this, I'll get comfortable and just settle in."

"Like that's a bad thing." D.T. focused intently on Brila. "It's a good company with plenty of potential. Even if PR isn't where you want to be long-term, I bet you find something you enjoy just as much as yoga. Then you can do both. What would be so wrong with that?"

"Nothing's wrong with it. And if that happens, fine. I just don't think it will. I'm not really the corporate type."

"Just apply and do the interview. Then you can decide whether you want to join us or hate us." D.T. grinned and raised his glass to Cameron.

"Yeah, come to the dark side. We have cake. And the life gets sucked out of you so slowly, you won't even notice." Cameron tapped his fingers together in front of his face and let out an exaggerated evil laugh, giving his best villain impression.

Brila stared at him. "Are you saying I shouldn't do it?"

D.T. glared across the table.

"I'm just messing with you. It's a good opportunity. And they're flexible. You'll easily be able to do this and teach yoga at night." Cameron leaned forward, a soft smile pulling at the corners of his lips. "We'd be lucky to have you join the team."

"Thanks." Her shoulders relaxed. "We'll see what happens. I still need to get through the last week of training, and there are still a few studios I haven't contacted yet. Besides, I may not even get the job."

Since when were her friends so invested in her career choices? Did no one believe she could make it as a yoga instructor? She sighed. "Enough about me and this job. I want to hear more about 'new Alex.'"

Cameron put his hands on the table and pushed his chair back. "I will walk out of here if one more person says 'new Alex'!"

"Oh, relax," Brila laughed. "You know we're messing with you. Tell us about him. Like, what does he do that would require him to be called into work on a Friday night."

His eyes shifted around the room as he mumbled, "He's a bartender."

The other four looked at one another, suppressing their laughter. Tony was the first to break. "Come on, man. How can we not call them 'old Alex' and 'new Alex' when they're the same person?"

"Not the same person! He's doing it to put himself through school. He's studying engineering, not freeloading off his parents."

Recognizing his agitation, Brila chimed in. "Fine. They're two very different people. So, what's everyone getting?"

At D.T.'s house that night, Brila continued to wrestle with the idea of working at Halltown. She had been considering other career paths before she was forced out at Southern. Did she really want to take a job so similar to what she had been doing? What if she did find a yoga instructor opening that required more time? She didn't want to hurt D.T.'s reputation by leaving a job right after being hired, but she also wasn't prepared to stay in that position just to satisfy him.

The reality was she needed a job. She was already spending enough free time looking for yoga instructor opportunities. The mere thought of putting additional energy into finding another job was exhausting.

Sighing, she pulled back the covers and crawled into D.T.'s king-sized bed. Her phone illuminated as she placed it on the nightstand. 11:11 p.m. She stared at the screen until it faded to black. Did she just notice the number eleven more often, now that it was stuck in her mind? She resolved to try to find the number two as much as she could over the weekend to see if all that nonsense with the elevens was in her head. Rolling over, she shimmied to the middle of the bed until she was resting on D.T.'s chest.

"When did we get to be so lame?" he whispered. "We used to party all weekend. Now we're in bed at eleven on a Friday night."

"No longer getting drunk, making fools of ourselves, and trying to hook up with strangers doesn't make us lame. It means we're functional adults with better things to do with our lives." She rested her chin on his chest to look up at him as she ran her hand down his thigh. "Why? Is there somewhere else you'd rather be right now?"

His white teeth shone in the glow of the street light outside his bedroom window. "When you put it that way, I'm pretty lucky to be so lame." With one sweeping motion, he pulled her on top of him. She let out a giggle before he pressed his lips against hers.

ELEVEN

Brila's eyes popped open, staring into the darkness of D.T.'s bedroom. She turned her head to find him sleeping with his back to her. Twisting to the other side, she slid her phone off the nightstand. Squinting to block out the glaring light, it took a second to focus and for the time to register in her mind: 1:11 a.m.

A knot wrapped around itself in her stomach. It wasn't just a coincidence. It wasn't something she just happened to notice. Why was she up? She rarely woke in the middle of the night. Why had she grabbed her phone at that moment? She squeezed her eyes shut, trying to recall the dream she'd had before waking. Was she at a party? A carnival? An amusement park? With whom was she laughing? The images escaped her now.

She looked at her phone again and waited until the time changed before she began her search for an explanation. The angel number explanation she had found a month earlier seemed to explain everything, but it didn't make sense now. Her yoga teacher training was nearly complete. She was actively searching for opportunities to pursue it as a career. If she were meant to do it, why hadn't she found the right opportunity yet? And why was she still seeing the number if she had already followed the guidance to find her purpose?

This time, she searched for 'one hundred eleven.' She scanned the results, again finding words like 'angel number,' 'purpose,' and 'power.' Clicking on the first link, she read about the importance of positive thinking and how thoughts manifested into reality. Not satisfied with this answer, she skimmed forward as the article continued to list possible explanations for spotting the number. The third reason caught her attention: *find the strength to leave the past behind.*

If this really were some sort of divine intervention, was it not related to her career change? The only thing in her past that she hadn't let go of was losing Angelle, and she refused to let that go. Sure, she was functioning and doing her best to live a normal life, whatever that actually meant. But she would never forget, and she would never stop wishing she could change everything about that night. Certainly, the angels, God, or whoever was supposedly sending these signs understood that.

Shaking her head, she continued to read. Spiritual awakening. Start something new. Seize new opportunities. It all felt so generalized. Anyone at any point in their life could be made to believe these things applied to them in one way or another. Yawning, she locked her phone and laid it down. Maybe it didn't mean anything after all.

She rolled over to face D.T. so she wouldn't be tempted to restart her investigation. If it were some sort of sign, it should be clearer. What was she supposed to do with a bunch of elevens and explanations that were relevant but not at all helpful?

What if she couldn't figure it out or it really did end up being nothing? Yoga felt like the right path, a journey to something meaningful, but what if it wasn't? Was she wasting her time, heading down a dead-end road? Would she end up stuck at Halltown doing mediocre work?

If only Angelle were still alive. She'd have the perfect advice to help Brila make sense of it all. Oh, how she longed to have one more heart-to-heart with her.

A week later, the yoga training program came to an end. Brila hugged Heidi and the other instructors during their certificate ceremony, thanking each of them. She was relieved the training was complete, but she didn't have much to celebrate. She still hadn't found any openings to teach classes.

Her classmates tried convincing her to grab a bite to eat with them at a bar down the road. As much as she wanted to go, the hiring manager at Halltown had made it clear she wanted to wrap up interviews ahead of Memorial Day weekend.

She walked with them out the door, listening as one of the "just for fun" classmates shared that she'd picked up a morning class.

"Which studio is that at?" Brila asked.

"Yogatopia in Midtown. Have you heard of it?"

All eyes turned to her. "Sounds familiar." Yeah, they told her a week ago they had no openings. She buried her building emotions. "I better get going. Have fun and keep in touch."

She headed toward her car in the opposite direction of the group. Maybe she had been too late, too slow on starting her search. Maybe she didn't know the right people. Or maybe she just didn't make a good enough impression. She continued to push the worries out of her mind and focus on responses to the potential interview questions D.T. had rehearsed with her the night before as she drove.

With her condo en route from the training studio to Halltown, she stopped at home so she didn't have to change at the studio. After rushing up the stairs and pushing through her door, she left a trail of workout clothes from the living room to the shower, where she rinsed off any lingering sweat from the morning session.

She had felt out of place when she arrived at class that morning with a full face of makeup, but she was glad that she only had minor touch-ups to do now. She ran her fingers through her hair with a small amount of gel. While she usually straightened it, she used the natural waves to her advantage that day. Pulling on the burgundy pencil dress and black pumps she had laid out that morning, she scooped up a set of silver teardrop earrings and a black blazer before jogging through her living room and back to her car.

With the temperatures already in the nineties, she worried the heat of summer would be more unbearable than normal. The sun beat down through the windshield. She cranked up the air conditioning, tossed the blazer to the passenger seat, and put on her earrings. She took a deep breath to slow her heart rate as she left the parking lot and continued her route to Halltown.

She smiled at the security guard as he directed her to the main office building around the curved road. The layout of the campus mimicked the company sites where her dad had worked, a welcomed similarity. However, as she neared the main office, she noticed that Halltown had more buildings and covered a larger span of property.

She reached the HR lobby at 2:22 p.m. With the few minutes she had to spare, Brila absentmindedly pushed back her cuticles as she mentally practiced her responses to potential interview questions. Spotting Cameron out of the corner of her eye, she waved her hand, her elbow still resting on her lap.

She stood to hug him as he walked through the door, but he grabbed her arms and stopped her short. His eyes searched the otherwise empty lobby as he stayed a step away. "I didn't know your interview was today. I thought you had training this week."

"We just finished about an hour ago. I ran home to clean up and rushed over here." She glanced past Cameron as a tall, middle-aged woman in a navy pantsuit approached the lobby.

He followed her gaze. "Looks like they're ready for you." He backed toward the door. "Good luck," he whispered as the woman entered the lobby.

Trying to swallow her nerves with a smile, Brila shook the manager's hand through their introductions and then followed her to the conference room, where two other managers were waiting. She had never been in a formal interview. The closest thing to it was when she had a ten-minute conversation with the owner of a sporting goods store before she began working there in high school. She had continued working there part-time throughout college until she was offered her job in the admissions department. As much as she had prided herself on her loyalty, she now wished she'd had a little more experience.

D.T. had preached his confidence into her all week. "You're going to crush it. They'd be lucky to have you," he had told her the night before. She wasn't as certain but let his words echo louder than her doubts as she took her seat at the oversized wooden table.

She left the conference room an hour later, not feeling any more confident than when she went in. Would she be able to find D.T.'s desk on her own? Was she even allowed to walk the halls? It was late, and D.T. had planned to stop at her condo once he was off work anyway. She made her way back to the HR lobby.

As she pushed through the door, D.T. turned, offering comfort in his smile and open arms. "So, will we be carpooling to work?"

She allowed herself to relax against his chest. After a moment, she stepped back and tugged at her dress as she surveyed their surroundings. She didn't need to blow her interview by acting unprofessionally now. "They haven't made their decision yet. I should know something next week. And it would make no sense for us to carpool. We live in opposite directions from here."

"Not if we had more weeknight sleepovers." His grin widened.

Brila's eyes darted around the room. "Stop."

"No one heard me, and everyone here knows we're dating."

"What does that mean? You went around announcing that you got your girlfriend an interview for the PR job?"

He smiled. "No. I mean HR is aware of our relationship."

A part of her wanted to question him further, but she let it go. "Are you done for the day?"

"I have a few things to wrap up. I just wanted to see how it went. I'll let you know when I head out."

Brila turned her head as he bent to kiss her, so that it landed on her cheek rather than her lips. Even if their relationship status was well known in the HR department, public displays of affection in the office seemed inappropriate.

Stepping outside, she was hit by a wall of heat. She hurried to her car, pulling off the blazer as soon as she was out of sight from the office building.

As she navigated her car through the parking lot, she jumped at the sound of her phone vibrating in the cup holder. She pressed the button on her steering wheel to answer the call.

"Any chance you're free this afternoon?" Callie from the yoga studio was on the other end.

Brila hesitated. She and D.T. hadn't made specific plans for the evening. "I'm pretty open. Why?"

"Our four o'clock instructor can't make it. Her assistant is going to fill in, but it's a large class. I know you just finished your training, and it's super-short notice, but is there any chance you'd be able to come help out?"

It would only be an hour, and D.T. was probably working until five anyway. Certainly, he would understand. "Sure, I can do that."

She glanced at the clock and used the car's voice commands to text D.T. to let him know about this opportunity and that she would go to his place after. Her grip tensed on the steering wheel. She mentally located a clean set of workout clothes and tried to remember where she had kicked off her shoes just a couple of hours earlier as she prepared for another quick change. At least this time she wouldn't have to shower.

Brila arrived with an enthusiastic grin on her face ten minutes before the class started. She approached the instructor for the evening to get a feel for the planned sequence.

"Don't worry about that." The woman looked past her as the studio door opened. "Just walk around and help people with their posture."

Brila raised an eyebrow. It wasn't an extraordinary request. Perhaps she was stressed over having to instruct on such short notice. "No problem. I'm happy to help with anything else you need."

"I've been assisting in this class for a year now." Her voice was low but stern. "I don't need you or anyone else getting in the way of this chance to prove I can lead. Just help the people who need help. Otherwise, stay in the back and don't make a sound."

Brila clenched her jaw and shook her head in disbelief. She watched the woman walk around her to greet participants with gentle words and an inviting smile.

Two women she recognized from the five o'clock class arrived a minute later. They nodded at the instructor as they bypassed her and welcomed Brila back to the studio with hugs and chatter about what she had missed over the past month. It was comforting to see some familiar faces.

A glare from across the room burned a hole into her chest. She tried to ignore it as she focused on her friends. "I'm just here to help. The sub has a great session planned." She walked with them to the spots where they rolled out their yoga mats and then retreated to the back of the room.

The fill-in instructor led the class through the series of poses with an exaggerated gentle tone and encouraging words that felt rehearsed. Brila fought to keep her eyes from rolling. It was over the top, as if she was trying to portray some false ideal of a yoga instructor. Who was she trying to impress? It wasn't like Callie was there evaluating her abilities. She looked around the room. Was anyone actually buying this act?

When the session ended, she grabbed her bag and rushed to the door. Getting home to get ready for her evening with D.T. was motivation enough. Not wanting to spend another moment around someone so phony pushed her out the door without a second thought.

The following Tuesday arrived as a cruel slap in the face. Brila had no training to attend, no job to work, and no one to visit. The day before had offered her false comfort. With D.T. off for Memorial Day, they had spent most of it kayaking. Now everyone had returned to their jobs, leaving her on her own.

Her stomach churned as she curled into the fetal position. Her hand flopped onto the nightstand, and her outstretched fingers slid her phone into the bed. 9:10 a.m. She perked up a bit, knowing that it would soon change. Maybe seeing an eleven would be the motivation she needed to get going for the day.

She waited, illuminating the screen every five seconds after it faded to black. The minute seemed to stretch on for five. Huffing her annoyance, she placed the phone back on the nightstand before the time changed. If there was some significance to the elevens, watching the clock until one appeared probably didn't hold the same meaning.

If only Angelle were still alive. She would have been kicking off her summer break. They could've spent the day watching movies or shopping. They could've road-tripped to Galveston and hung out on the beach. It was a trip their family had made numerous times when they were younger. Even when they were still living in Louisiana, they ventured to the Texas beach at the beginning of each summer.

Brila closed her eyes and smiled as the memories flooded her mind like a movie reel playing each trip's highlights. Sandcastles. Jumping in the waves. Packed lunches. Visiting Pleasure Pier. Her first roller coaster ride. All the shirtless boys. But it was the laughter she remembered the most. It didn't matter what had happened that week, that morning, or even on the drive down. When they were in Galveston, nothing could take away their joy.

With the memories still playing in her mind, she turned over and began to drift back to sleep. It felt like twenty seconds had passed before she was jolted awake by the ringing of her phone. She opened one eye to peer at the screen. Not recognizing the number, she set it down and rolled over.

Another thirty seconds passed before there was another short ding. Brila raised an eyebrow. Who left voicemails these days? Her eyes grew heavy. Then it hit her. She sat straight up and scooped her phone off the nightstand. The time on her phone indicated that more than twenty minutes had passed, rather than twenty seconds. She listened to the voicemail and confirmed her guess. It was Kathryn, the hiring manager from Halltown.

She fluttered her eyes and cleared her throat to help wake herself. Her heart rate accelerated. She pressed the number, jumping out of bed as it rang. Just as she was about to hang up, she heard a voice on the other end. She froze at the foot of her bed. "Hi, Kathryn. It's Brila. Sorry I missed your call."

"No problem. Thanks for calling back. We completed our evaluations, and I'm happy to say we'd like to offer you the position."

"That's wonderful news." Brila beamed at the validation of being the best candidate.

"Yes. And like I mentioned last week, we would like to move quickly with this. I am going to email you the offer letter along with some job details. Look it over. If you accept the offer, sign it and send it back to me by the end of the day. If you're available, we'd love to have you start Monday."

Brila's eyes grew wide. It was so soon, but what else did she have to do? "Sure, I can do that."

They exchanged some small talk and pleasantries about working together before the conversation ended.

Was this really what she wanted? She didn't really have much of a choice. She needed the income. She stared off in the direction of her bedroom door before shaking her head back to reality. After texting D.T., she started to text her parents. Before she could finish, a message from Cameron popped up.

Congrats! Rumor has it you received the job
offer. Looking forward to having you here next
week!

Brila grinned and headed toward the bathroom. It was just the boost she needed to do something more than sleep all day.

When she stepped out of the shower, she had a message from D.T.

I just realized I'll be traveling next week. I won't
be there for your first week.

It was probably for the best. If others in the company were already aware of their relationship, it would be nice to get her footing and make some of her own connections before he tried to help. She typed out her response with one hand as she held the towel around her with the other.

We can celebrate this weekend before you
leave.

TWELVE

After Brila returned home from her morning yoga session that Friday, she texted her friends to make dinner plans. She scrunched her eyebrows when she received a text from Tony instead of Shanna.

I don't think we're gonna make it. Shanna's not feeling good.

Brila's stomach knotted.

Not feeling good like the flu or not feeling good like pregnancy problems? When did it start? What's going on?

He was slow to respond.

Pregnancy. Started this morning. At the hospital. I'll let you know.

Brila collapsed onto the edge of the couch, a weight settling on her chest. Each breath grew more difficult to inhale. She gripped the sides of her head and prayed this was a false alarm. Maybe a shower would help her relax. Before she reached the bathroom door, she turned and headed back to the kitchen. Pausing, she looked around. Why was she here? She went back to the bathroom.

The knot in the pit of her stomach twisted tighter. She stared at the wall as water from the showerhead spilled over her shoulders. Shanna deserved better. She was kind and loving—the type of friend people spent their whole lives hoping to find. Motherhood was the only job she had ever wanted. Brila closed her eyes and begged God to make everything right.

Tying a towel around her dripping wet body, she tapped the screen of her phone to verify Tony had not sent any new messages. 11:11 a.m. She'd been in the shower for over thirty minutes. She began to type out a request for an update but deleted it and set her phone down. They didn't need to be bothered.

A warmth expanded in her chest as she realized the time. She tapped her phone again, but the minute had already changed. She had seen few elevens since her middle-of-the-night confrontation with the number. Perhaps it meant she was on the right path and no longer needed guidance. Or maybe she was so far off her path that whatever divine intervention it was had given up on her. Did this reappearance carry meaning with it or was it just a coincidence?

She jumped at the chime of her phone and snatched it off the counter. She placed her hand on her chest and sighed. It was just Cameron responding to her proposed dinner plans. She couldn't tell him anything was wrong with Shanna. They still hadn't announced their pregnancy. And there was still a chance everything would be fine. Her response could wait until she had more information.

The reflection in the mirror staring back at her was tired, worn. She dabbed a light serum around her puffy eyes followed by tinted moisturizer on her face. After slipping into some clean clothes, she shuffled to the kitchen in search of something for lunch. With the refrigerator door open, she scanned the contents without actually looking at any of them. Sending positive vibes across town and willing her friend back to good health, her mind was on Shanna.

The beeping that warned the refrigerator door had been open too long jolted her back to reality. She pulled out the lettuce, cucumbers, green peppers, baked chicken, and hard-boiled eggs, and then she got out of the way for the door to slam closed. There had to be something else she could do to fill her time. Who knew how long they'd be at the hospital, and sitting around waiting for an update was like having teeth pulled without Novocaine.

She ran through a list of activities, dismissing each one, as she fixed and ate her salad. She finally decided to get groceries, not that she wanted to, but it was best to get it done before everyone else crammed into the stores after work and over the weekend.

After returning from the store forty-five minutes later, she was putting food into the pantry when a muffled ringtone called out. She left everything in the center of the third shelf and rushed to dig the phone out of her purse. When she answered, there was only heavy breathing. Her heart pounded. "Tony? What's going on? Talk to me."

"It's gone." His voice was barely audible.

"What do you mean?" A nauseating tightness gripped her stomach.

"The baby. It's gone." There was another long pause, then a loud slap, like a hand against a countertop. "Dammit, Brila! What did we do to deserve this?" his voice cracked. "How many addicts out there have babies? How many careless teenagers, deadbeats, abusive assholes all have kids they don't even want? It's the only thing she wants, and I can't give it to her."

Tears streamed down Brila's cheeks. She tried to swallow the lump lodged in her throat. "It's not fair. You two deserve to be parents more than anyone I know." She shook her head. Nothing she could say would take away his pain. "It's going to happen. It has to.

I don't know why y'all have to suffer like this." They were both silent, except for sniffles and stifled cries. "I'm sorry. I don't know what to say or what to do. Are you back home?"

Tony cleared his throat. "Yeah. Shanna's in bed. The others were hard enough, but I think this one's going to break her. She was certain this was it."

Brila knew exactly what he meant. After her first miscarriage, Shanna had been cautious with each potential pregnancy. This time around, though, she had been more optimistic, making plans from the start. "Do you want me to come by?"

He sighed. "I don't think she wants to see anyone right now. Even me. I'll let you know if that changes. Tomorrow might be better."

She nodded, then verbally agreed. "Go to her. She may want to be alone, but she needs you. And you need her. Let me know if I can do anything. I'll come by in the morning."

Hanging up, she collapsed to the floor, resting her hands and head against the kitchen cabinet as she sobbed. She slammed her hand against the cabinet door. How could this be happening? Her stomach twisted tighter. No one deserved to feel that loss, much less suffer through multiple miscarriages. Why hadn't the doctors figured anything out?

The chime of a text message beckoned. As her tears subsided, she felt around the counter above her head until she found her phone. Cameron was checking in again. Brila sighed. Canceling dinner was now her responsibility.

> Shanna's sick. We'll have to get together another night.

She stared at the message for a few seconds and then added to it.

> Sorry for the late notice.

She then sent a similar text to D.T., as well as an extra note.

> I'm also not feeling great. Think I'll just stay
> home and rest.

She wasn't in any mood to go out or to see anyone, and she wasn't prepared to answer any questions D.T. might ask about the situation.

Placing both hands on the counter, she pulled herself up and found a few remaining items left to put away. She reached for the bags of flour and confectioners' sugar. She had bought them to make cookies for the get-together Shanna had planned to host in a couple of weeks to announce her pregnancy.

Memories of baking with Angelle popped into her mind. From a young age, they had both taken an interest in watching their mom in the kitchen. As they grew older, they became more involved with helping and eventually began baking on their own. Cookies, cake, fudge, brownies. They tried their hands at many things, but cupcakes were their favorite.

Their baking wasn't just reserved for special occasions. They would bake on the weekends when they were bored. Angelle would try new flavors and recipes. Brila would practice new decoration styles.

When Brila moved to the college dorms, it was something they did less often, but that only made it more meaningful. Breakups, big tests, good grades, any heartache, any accomplishment—all of these warranted a special cupcake delivery from one sister to the other.

Brila smiled as tears welled in her eyes again. She was thankful she had opted for no mascara after her shower. She moved from the pantry to the fridge, gathering various items in her arms and piling them on the counter. Finally, she grabbed measuring cups, a rubber scraper, and the standing mixer.

The teasing she'd heard from Angelle for years rang again in her mind as she measured out ingredients. "Is that really what you're doing? You know mine always taste better. I don't know why you don't just listen to me." Her sister's laugh echoed throughout the empty condo until she turned on the mixer. She pulled two muffin tins from the bottom of her bakeware cabinet, then dug behind the storage bags and aluminum foil in her pantry until she found a package of cupcake liners. It's a good thing she hadn't seen them when she threw out the others the day after Angelle's accident.

Suddenly, she froze. Her legs felt like she had run a marathon. Her chest was tight. She gripped the counter but couldn't steady herself. Once again, she found herself on the floor.

Her tear-streaked face fell to her hands and rested on her knees. What was she doing? After vowing to never touch a cupcake again, here she was baking them for Shanna. With the memories of Angelle, she was doing what had been a natural response to someone in need for so many years.

The oven beeped, indicating it was to temperature. She clawed against the cabinets, pulling herself back to her feet. She pushed tears from her cheeks, lined muffin tins, and added the batter. Once they were in the oven, she set the timer on her phone, dragged herself to the living room, and flopped onto the couch.

The night of Angelle's accident replayed in her mind. After talking on the phone for more than an hour, Angelle had decided she'd come over to talk in person. It was late. Brila should've told her to stay home. But she was selfish. She wanted to see her. She needed her to say it would all be okay. She had always relied on her little sister to comfort her. And being the caring, generous person she was, Angelle had always been there for her at the drop of a hat, usually with a dozen cupcakes in tote.

The police said she had been distracted or lost control of the vehicle, crashing into a light pole. Brila knew it was her text message that caused her sister's accident. If she had just left her alone after she didn't answer the first three times, she'd still be alive.

The picture of her sister's vehicle from the newspaper was burned into her mind. She shuddered at the warped pile of red metal and the front-end smashed like an accordion against the splintered windshield, which had been splattered with blood on the driver's side and frosting on the passenger's side.

"I'm so sorry!" she cried out. An ache gripped her chest. If she had one wish, one miracle, one do-over, she'd take back that night. She'd give up everything she had and everything planned for her future to have her sister back.

She checked her timer. Eleven minutes and eleven seconds left. She rolled her eyes and threw up her hands. "What do you want for me?" Shouting through the emptiness of her condo offered as little help as her previous silent pleas. If some specific path or master plan existed for her to follow, she was wandering in a weed-filled ditch. Divine guidance? A special sign? More like self-inflicted frustration.

She pushed herself up and shuffled to the kitchen to rotate the muffin tins. She stood there, staring blankly into the oven for another minute before her growling stomach broke her trance. Even with a kitchen full of food, nothing looked appetizing.

Staggering back and forth between the pantry and the refrigerator, she hopelessly stared into each one as if a meal would make itself if she waited long enough. Finally, she opened a food delivery app on her phone and scrolled through the list of restaurants before settling on a burger joint. She threw her vow to eat healthier out the window. She would regret it in the morning, but she'd deal with it then.

As she waited, she slumped to the floor and watched the cupcakes rise through the oven door window.

The first time she and Angelle had baked together was for their parents' twentieth wedding anniversary. After putting the cake in the oven, they went into the living room to watch a celebrity reality show. They got so caught up in the drama, they forgot about the cake. The scent of burnt batter finally reached them. They looked at one another, shouted "The cake!" at the same time, then jumped up and raced to the kitchen.

Angelle pulled it out of the oven while Brila turned on every fan and vent on the main floor to avoid setting off the smoke detectors. They stood together, staring at the blackened cake cooling on the stovetop. First, they blamed one another for not setting a timer or remembering to check it halfway through the show. Then they burst into laughter. It was an epic failure.

They ran to the local bakery and swapped cakes when they returned. However, between the stench of burnt baked goods and Angelle's inability to keep a straight face, they were caught in the lie as soon as their parents walked through the door. The story would be retold in their family countless times and served as assurance for both sisters to always set a timer while baking.

Brila watched the cupcake tops turn golden. She slid on the oven mitts and pulled the cupcakes out of the oven. As she closed the door, the timer on her phone went off. She smiled. Perfect timing. To make sure, she stuck a toothpick into the center cupcakes of each tin, inspecting each toothpick as she pulled them out to ensure no cake was stuck to them.

Five minutes later, as she was moving the final cupcakes to the cooling racks, a knock on the door announced that her food had arrived. She sat at her counter to eat, running through frosting possibilities in her mind. Decorating had always been her favorite part of baking. White was too plain. Black was too depressing. Blue and pink were obviously not options. She didn't have cocoa powder to make chocolate. She didn't have the energy to think about other flavors. Grabbing a few French fries to eat on the way, she walked to the pantry to verify she still had food coloring. Spotting the box of gel coloring, she reached inside and pulled out a bottle. Yellow. That would work. She set it on the counter, then slid around the corner and back onto her stool.

Later that evening, she whipped up the yellow buttercream frosting and swirled it into large roses on top of each cupcake. She was halfway done when a knock at the door jerked her hand and caused her to smear the frosting. Sighing, she set down the piping bag, wiped her hands on a towel, and went to see who it could possibly be.

Brila's eyes fell to the floor when she opened the door and D.T. walked in.

He walked into the kitchen. "What's all this?" he asked, turning back to her. "Why'd you tell me you were sick when you really just wanted to spend the night playing Betty Crocker?"

"I know. I shouldn't have lied to you. I was just ... I'm dealing with a lot today and needed some alone time. I was planning to just spend the night in bed. This all just sort of happened." She watched him for a moment and then grabbed a butter knife out of the drawer to remove the smeared frosting.

D.T. furrowed his brow and crossed his arms. "Exactly how do you accidentally bake cupcakes?"

Brila bit her bottom lip. It wasn't her place to tell him about Shanna's miscarriage. She didn't want to betray her friend's trust, but she also didn't want to lie to D.T. There was no way to explain what she was going through without telling him the full story. He had known about the other miscarriages, and the odds were good that he'd eventually find out about this one, too. It might as well come from her now.

She explained everything from Tony's messages and calls, to her breakdowns. She told him that she hadn't realized she was baking until she was already in the process. The tears gathered again and a lump lodged in her throat as she told him how the memories of Angelle were taking over her every thought. "It's like no matter how much time passes, no matter how well I think I'm doing, there's always something that puts me back in that hole. I guess I just wanted to do something for Shanna. I know she's suffering. And this is the only thing I know to do when people are hurting." She looked at the cupcakes. "I tried avoiding it. After the accident, I had vowed to never touch another cupcake, but here I am. I know it's crazy, and it doesn't help anything." She turned back to him. "And I'm sorry I lied to you. I just ... I don't know what I'm doing anymore."

D.T. wrapped his arms around her and sighed. "You should've just told me."

She buried her face into his chest. "It wasn't my business to tell. I didn't know what to do."

He kissed the top of her head, leaned back, and tilted her chin up, waiting for her to look at him. "Not that. All you had to say was you were having a bad day."

She smiled softly and leaned back into him. "I'm going to head over there in the morning to be with Shanna."

"Are you staying there all day?"

"I'll stay as long as she wants me to. Why?"

"I thought we could kayak before I have to leave for my trip."

"That would be nice, but I can't say for sure that I can."

"She has Tony. Why would she need you to be with her all day?"

Brila pulled away and looked at the floor "I don't know how to explain it. Sometimes you just need a friend to talk about things. I'm trying to be open with you. I'm going to do what I can so we can go, but I can't guarantee it."

D.T. stepped back. "Whatever you say."

She picked up the piping bag and continued swirling roses onto the cupcakes. He couldn't possibly understand. She would stay with Shanna for as long as necessary. If that meant he'd be upset about not kayaking, so be it.

THIRTEEN

Brila picked up her phone: 6:30 a.m. Sighing, she returned it to the nightstand. She rarely woke up that early for work. It was certainly no time to be up on a Saturday.

She had tossed and turned most of the night, yet she could not will herself back to sleep. Was Shanna getting any rest? Was she still in pain? Did she let Tony in or keep the hurt to herself? They had already suffered so much. If she had a second wish, Brila would give Shanna and Tony as many healthy babies as their hearts desired.

She squeezed the pillow around her head as she closed her eyes and groaned. There had to be something better for her to do with her time. She shuffled to the living room to work through some yoga sequences, but when she reached the couch, she sunk into it and pulled her mint green fleece blanket up to her chin. What was supposed to be a few minutes of checking social media turned into scrolling through a list of streaming movies. Finally, she selected her favorite rom-com. A classic tale of enemies-turned-lovers with the high school jerk who ends up having a soft side. She and Shanna had watched it together at least twenty times. Vowing to exercise later, she fixed a cup of coffee and settled in to enjoy the movie that held so many memories from her own high school days.

As the ending credits rolled, she stretched her arms into the air. It was still too early to send a text message. Even if they were up, she didn't want to intrude on their morning just yet. Instead, she tossed the blanket over the back of the couch and made her way to the bathroom to get ready for the day.

She took a shower and brushed her teeth. She pulled her hair back into a knot and searched her drawers for athletic shorts and a tank top. After mindlessly busying herself around the condo for another ten minutes, she couldn't wait any longer. If they were still sleeping, they could just ignore her. She scrolled past Tony's name in her message list and chose Shanna's name. Tony was like a brother to her. She had no problem talking with him, but she didn't want relayed information. She needed to hear from Shanna.

Are you up yet? I'm coming over.

Ten seconds later, she had a response from Tony.

She's in the bathroom. Come on over.

Brila chuckled and shook her head. They were basically one person at this point. He couldn't even wait for his wife to get out of the bathroom and respond for herself. She gathered her purse, the cupcakes, and a banana to eat on the way.

She stepped onto the front stoop of the two-story gray brick home and rang the doorbell. She admired the large wooden "G," hand-painted in dark red, hanging on their front door. Footsteps on the stairs just past the entryway on the other side of the door grew louder. A moment later, Tony was on the stoop with her.

The dark circles under his bloodshot eyes made him look like he hadn't slept in a week. "She's back in bed." He looked toward the street as he spoke. "I didn't tell her you were coming. I didn't want her trying to get herself together or pick up the house."

A smile pulled at her lips. "Yeah, that's probably for the best." She shifted the cupcake carrier from her right hand to her left. "And how are you doing?"

He forced a weak smile, but tears welled in his eyes. "I have no idea anymore. When she said she was bleeding, I went to the closet and dropped to my knees." The tears spilled onto his cheeks. "Is it me? Am I the problem?" He ran his fingers through his black hair. "She's perfect in every way, and Lord knows she's meant to be a mom. She deserves to be with someone who can give her that."

"Don't say that." Brila placed her free hand on his arm. "You two are perfect, and you deserve to be parents together. She's getting pregnant. It's just a matter of staying pregnant. Did the doctor do more tests?"

He nodded. "But it could still come back with no reason for the miscarriage. At this point, I'd rather it be something so at least we'd know if we can do something about it."

"I can understand that."

Tony wiped the tears from his cheeks and a bead of sweat from his forehead. "We can head in."

She followed him inside and kicked off her sandals.

"She should still be awake." He gestured up the staircase. "I'll let you two be for a while."

Brila gave a soft smile. "Try to rest a little. I don't know how, but things are going to work out."

She knocked on the bedroom door as she opened it. The bed was empty. She set the cupcake carrier on the first nightstand, wishing she had left it in the kitchen.

"Shanna, are you in here?" She walked toward the master bathroom. "Is everything okay?"

The closet door suddenly swung open, nearly hitting Brila.

She jumped back, her hand instinctively clasped against her chest as Shanna stepped out. "What are you doing in there?"

"I peeked out the window when Tony went downstairs and saw it was you. I just wanted to change quick." She smoothed the front of her t-shirt.

Brila rolled her eyes. "You know you didn't have to do that."

"I needed to. I haven't changed yet today."

"You don't need to do anything but rest right now." She held her friend's arm and walked with her to the bed.

After propping up a pillow and helping Shanna settle in, she walked around and crawled up onto the bed. "So do you want to talk about it or would you rather chat about something else?"

"Neither," she huffed lightly, wrapping her arms around her stomach. "I want my baby back." She looked down as tears started to trickle down her face. "Everything was going so well. He was healthy. I was healthy. We were so close to being past that point. We were going to tell everyone in two weeks. Now we either cancel or have a party for no reason. And I don't think I can face people knowing what a wonderful celebration it was supposed to be."

Brila inched closer and linked her arm with Shanna's. "Then you just tell people something came up. They don't need to know if you don't want them to."

"I just hate letting people down."

"I promise you're not letting anyone down."

Shanna sniffled. "Except Tony. He wants this just as bad as I do, and my body keeps rejecting one baby after another. And the worst part is the doctors can't even tell me why. Just tell me why I'm broken!" She leaned into Brila's shoulder.

"Hey. You're not broken. If the doctors can't find anything wrong, maybe it really is a fluke thing." She considered her words. "A really terrible fluke, but if they can't find a cause, that means there's still a chance for you to have a baby."

"Or we keep trying and failing. I don't know how much more of this I can take. It's too hard. Maybe it's just not meant to be."

Brila shook her head. "If there is one thing I know to be true in this world, it's that you are meant to be a mom. Now, I have no idea why the universe has decided to make it so damn hard. It's absolutely heartbreaking to watch you suffer when I know you and Tony deserve to have a child more than anyone. But I guess it's just meant to be part of your story and will make it that much more rewarding once you do finally hold your child in your arms."

Shanna sat up and wiped the tears from her cheeks. "I hope you're right."

Brila hugged her. They held each other in the heavy silence. Words were no longer necessary. She couldn't take the pain away. She couldn't make things better. All she could do was be there.

The sound of Shanna's rumbling stomach alerted Brila. "I almost forgot. I brought you something." She rolled to her side and carefully lifted the carrier to the bed.

Shanna pushed herself up, squinting as she inspected the container. "You baked?"

With her cheeks warming, she nodded and removed the lid.

Wide blue eyes carved a hole in her. "Cupcakes? After all the hell I caught for bringing you cupcakes on Angelle's birthday, that's what you show up with?"

"I know, I know. It just sort of happened." A raised eyebrow reminded Brila of D.T.'s reaction the night before. "I know it sounds crazy. I was putting away groceries, memories of baking with Angelle popped into my head, and I just started mixing up the batter. I was practically done before I realized what had happened. It had been such a natural reaction for so long, I guess it's still embedded somewhere in me."

"So cupcakes weren't just Angelle's thing you went along with. It was your thing together." Shanna picked up one and started to peel back the liner. "I think it's okay for you to carry that on."

"It felt weird. And brought up all sorts of—"

"Whoa! These are amazing. And here I thought Angelle was the baker, and you just decorated." She yelled toward the bedroom door, "Tony, you have to get up here!"

Heavy footsteps rushed up the stairs. Tony pushed through the door with panicked eyes. "What is it, babe? Are you okay?"

Shanna smiled. "I'm fine, but you have to try these cupcakes."

He looked from her to Brila, who shrugged her shoulders. "Don't scare me like that." He watched his wife continue eating before he stepped closer and picked one up. "I'm glad you're eating. Do you want me to make something for lunch?" He hesitated for a moment. "We have burgers I could throw on the grill."

Shanna appeared to consider the suggestion while finishing her cupcake. "I could eat about five of those and be good." Her glowing smile lit up the room, even if it was for just a few seconds. "I suppose we do need to eat, but I don't want you to mess with the grill just for us. We can have sandwiches or whatever's easiest." She turned to Brila. "Unless you want a burger."

"I'm good with whatever you want. I'm really not that hungry right now." She looked at each of them, trying to determine how this would go. Neither wanted to bother the other. She tried to remember if she'd ever seen them fight. They were basically a fairy-tale couple. It warmed her heart and made her want to roll her eyes at the same time.

"I don't mind." Tony peeled back one side of the cupcake wrapper and took a bite. "It's still early. I can start in a while to give y'all some more time together before it'll be ready."

Shanna smiled. "Whatever you say, babe. Thanks." She leaned forward.

Tony walked to her, bent down, and kissed her. "Let me know if you need anything. And you're right. These might be the best cupcakes I've had." He held it up and then took another bite as he left the room.

"Sorry for interrupting." Shanna turned to her. "So you felt weird about making the cupcakes, but it was still your first instinct when you heard from Tony?"

Brila nodded. "After I swore I'd never bake them again."

"Maybe it's something you needed. It's like anything else that reminds you of Angelle. It's going to bring up emotions and be tough, but the more you do it, the more you return to yourself. And, in a way, continuing to bake helps keep her memory alive."

Brila reached a shaky hand toward the cupcakes. "I hadn't thought about it like that." She swallowed the lump growing in her throat. "But I can't get the image of the frosting smeared across her windshield out of my mind. It's just another reminder that if she hadn't been coming to comfort me and if I hadn't kept texting her, she'd still be here."

Shanna tapped her knee. "We've talked about this. You can't blame yourself for her accident. You didn't ask her to come over, and even if you had, there's no way you would've known what was going to happen."

"I know, but if I wouldn't have bothered her with my problem—"

"Stop. You have to stop blaming yourself. All these what-ifs will eat you alive. You have to accept there's nothing you could have done to stop it. We all have problems. We all lean on others. I mean, you're over here right now because you wanted to be here for me." Shanna smiled softly.

Brila pulled the tears from the corners of her eyes. She looked out the window, wishing the sunlight would wash away the pain squeezing her heart. "You're right. I'm here for you, so let's stop talking about me."

"Fine, but you have to promise you won't let her death take away everything you are and everything you once loved."

Brila thought of Angelle's big heart, her drive, and her encouragement. Shanna's words echoed in her mind. She couldn't let herself continue to be a shell of who she once was. After all, it was remembering her sister's determination to do what she loved that had led Brila to complete the yoga teacher training and pursue a new career.

"You're right. There was enough loss that day between her and ..." She'd held onto her secret for over six months. That was the closest she had come to letting it slip. "And there's no need for me to let myself be lost in that day too." Her heart pounded.

Shanna's brows furrowed. "Between Angelle and what now? You never said anything about another loss." She leaned over to make eye contact with Brila, who was staring at the bed. "What are you not telling me?"

If she could trust anyone besides her sister with her secret, it was Shanna. Still, she racked her brain for a way to escape the corner she had just backed herself into.

FOURTEEN

Shanna stared at her, waiting for an answer.

This secret had been hers to carry alone for the past six months. She had hoped that eventually it would fade out of her memory, and no one would ever find out. Yet a part of her was ready to make this confession. "I hadn't been talking to Angelle about a fight with D.T. that night. I mean we had a small fight about something I can't even remember, but that wasn't the reason I was upset. That wasn't the reason Angelle was coming over."

Shanna picked up another cupcake and held it in her lap, eyes still focused on Brila.

"I ..." The truth was caught in her throat. "I'd been to the doctor."

Shanna put the cupcake back. "For what? Were you sick? Are you still sick?"

"No. I'm okay."

"Oh my God! Don't scare me like that!" Shanna's hands clasped over her heart.

"Sorry. I didn't mean for it to sound like that." She hesitated for a moment as she considered how she was going to share this truth she thought she'd take to the grave. "I guess I should back up to the Thursday before. At my annual checkup, I had mentioned that my period was a week late. While I was there, the doctor confirmed I was pregnant." Tears pooled in her eyes as Shanna looked at her like a deer in headlights. "I was so in shock and still trying to process it; I didn't even tell D.T. Then that Monday afternoon, I started cramping and bleeding. I left work to visit the doctor." She paused. "I had just found out I was pregnant, and then I was being told four days later that I had miscarried."

"And you never told me?" Shanna pushed Brila's shoulder as a tear rolled down her cheek. "After all I've been through, and you didn't think you could trust me? I'm the one person who'd understand."

"Of course I could trust you. But you've suffered so much with your own miscarriages. I didn't want you to have to worry about mine too." She hung her head. "Besides, I wasn't trying to get pregnant. I still hadn't decided how I felt about having a baby. It was stupid to be so upset about losing something I barely knew I had, something I didn't even know I wanted."

"Losing a child is hard, no matter when it happens. And I know that because I'm practically an expert. Just look at me." She waited.

Brila's stomach churned as she wished she would have kept her mouth shut. She allowed her eyes to meet Shanna's. Her friend's pain permeated through her. She should've trusted her with this secret six months ago. "You're right. I'm sorry."

Silence wrapped around them for a minute before Shanna spoke again. "So does D.T. know?"

She shook her head. "I was still processing the news myself. I wanted to get my head around it before explaining it to him." Brila thought about how that conversation would have gone. "And I guess I was scared he'd panic and leave me. I planned to tell him when he got back from his trip, but then the accident happened, and that consumed my entire world."

"You should've told me."

"I know." Brila pulled at the corners of her eyes and dabbed her cheeks with the palms of her hands. "Man, this conversation took a hard left. Can we get back to taking care of you and doing what you want?"

"What I need is to feel normal, not like some broken, useless being. What I want is for my friend to feel like she can trust me and not drop bombshells on me."

Brila studied Shanna's face as she sat with her arms folded in front of her chest. "I'm sorry. What more do you want me to say? If I could do it over, I'd tell you right away."

If she'd confided in Shanna instead, Angelle would still be alive. She added it to her list of mistakes she'd made that led to her sister's death as a familiar ache knotted in her chest.

"It's fine." Shanna's telltale phrase. Things were not fine, but she didn't want to discuss it any further.

Brila took the hint as guilt gripped her heart like a vice. "What time is it?" She reached for her phone to answer her own question as they both shimmied back to recline against the pillows lining the headboard.

"A little after eleven." Shanna beat her to it.

"11:11 to be exact," Brila mumbled.

"Not this again." Shanna rolled her eyes. "Since I saw it too, do I also get some cosmic guidance?"

"I'm starting to have a love-hate relationship with it. I was seeing it all the time, then I thought it had stopped, then it started yesterday again. It's like the universe is trying to tell me something, but I don't know what. Every time I think I have it figured out, it no longer makes sense."

Shanna stared at her.

"I know. It's crazy. I can't explain it. I wish I could. It'd make things a lot easier." Shanna's laser focus made her squirm. "And this is why I don't share things. Stop looking at me like you're about to put me in a psych ward."

"I'm not! I just never thought you'd be the type to get wrapped up in spiritual signs and becoming one with the universe."

"You make me sound like some kind of hippie. I don't know what it is, but if you saw the same thing over and over, wouldn't you think it was something more than a coincidence?"

"Maybe. But if it's not consistent, maybe it is just a coincidence, and you're just more aware of it when you do see it. What if you tried to focus on a different number? You'd probably see that more often if you were looking for it."

"I tried that. I spent a weekend looking for twos. And I found some, but the eleven thing kept coming up more than twos. I don't know. I just wish that if it is supposed to mean something, I could figure it out. Clearly, I'm not getting whatever message I'm supposed to be getting."

"Well, maybe you still have work to do. Like you're on a path and, eventually, these signs will lead you there."

"Look at you getting all prophetic. If that's the case, I hope I get there soon because I'm losing my damn mind trying to figure it out."

Shanna laughed. "Fine. Let's forget about it. Hand me another cupcake."

As Brila reached for the cupcakes, her phone chimed. It was a message from D.T.

How are things? When are you coming over?

She sighed.

Probably not 'til later.

Was it so wrong for her to want to spend the day with Shanna instead of D.T.? Sure, he was leaving the next morning for his business trip, but everything in her soul wanted her to stay where she was. They could still have supper together, and she could stay over to see him leave in the morning. They could kayak another time.

"D.T.?" Shanna asked as she bit into the cupcake.

Brila nodded. "That reminds me. He showed up last night in my little frenzy. I ended up telling him the news. So I guess you were right. I couldn't keep your secret."

"I guess you're only able to keep your own secrets."

Damn. She'd messed up again. "I guess I'm not winning any friend awards anytime soon." She forced a smile and let out a nervous laugh.

Shanna showed no emotion. "I think exhaustion is setting in. Can you tell Tony that I'm going to take a nap on your way out?"

Brila froze as the chill in Shanna's words penetrated her veins. She opened her mouth to begin damage control, but the reality of the situation became clear. Shanna had a right to be mad. They could discuss it later. Right now, Shanna deserved a little peace. And Brila deserved to carry her guilt out the door with her.

She left the cupcakes on the nightstand as she walked away. "Get some rest. I'm just a text away if you need anything." Without a response, she slipped out of the room. She'd really messed up this time.

She only wanted to be with her friend, to explain herself, and to heal the pain in her heart. In both their hearts. Instead, she drove back to her condo with plans to curl up on the couch to allow the pain to swallow her up again.

The following Monday, Brila took a deep breath as she pulled open the door to the Halltown office lobby. Her heart pounded as she gave her name to the receptionist, who directed her to a corner, where three other new employees were already seated, waiting for the orientation leader.

It was just training. There was nothing to be nervous about. Other than meeting new people, making a good first impression, attempting to be competent in something she'd never done, and trying to not embarrass herself or D.T.

As expected, he'd been upset when she'd bailed on kayaking Saturday afternoon. She'd forced herself to bring him supper that night so they could spend a couple of hours together, but reconciling their fight was still on her list, along with making things right with Shanna. She could focus on that after the workday ended.

She took another deep breath as the door opened. Her shoulders relaxed and a wide smile raised her cheeks as Cameron approached. She knew he worked in the training department but didn't realize he led new employee training. He had shaved his curly black hair short since she'd last seen him. Throughout high school and college, she had told him to leave it longer but seeing it short now with his button-down shirt and slacks, she decided this look was better. She resisted the urge to jump up and hug her friend.

"Welcome to Halltown. I'm Cam Young. I'll be leading your orientation today. If you'll all come this way, we'll head back to the conference room and get started." He held the door open as everyone stood and filed through.

Brila allowed the others to go ahead of her. As she passed Cameron, she whispered, "Why didn't you tell me you were doing orientation?"

"I didn't know if it was going to be me or my coworker until I came in this morning," he whispered back, allowing the door to close behind them. He walked around the group so he could lead them to the conference room.

She stayed back, adding Cameron to the list of people she didn't want to embarrass. She admired the confidence he exuded, even in his friendly, laid-back demeanor.

Once everyone was seated, Cameron asked each person to introduce themselves and their new position.

"Brila Landry, Public Relations Specialist." She fought back a smile. While it made sense for her to introduce herself to the other new employees, doing so to her close friend was entertaining.

Cameron gave a history and an overview of the company. He walked through various policies, forms, and procedures.

Brila had to remind herself to pay attention multiple times. She found herself in awe over Cameron's presence and delivery. It was hard to believe this was the same person who had done everything in his power to avoid class participation throughout high school and most of college.

Once the three-hour-long meeting ended, her boss, Kathryn, met her in the lobby. They went to her office and proceeded to go through additional orientation, this time specific to the public relations department. Brila wrestled back a yawn. She hadn't started training on her job yet but was already mentally exhausted.

She had hoped to visit with Cameron over lunch, but Kathryn escorted her to the cafeteria along with a few others in the department. She noticed the lunch bags in the women's hands and made a mental note to follow suit going forward. Luckily, the cafeteria had a decent salad bar.

As she joined her department at a table in the middle of the room, she looked around for any familiar faces. She spotted Cameron to the right with a small group, but she didn't see any of D.T.'s coworkers. Were they all traveling this week, or did they not eat in the cafeteria? She couldn't think of a time when D.T. packed a lunch. In fact, she was fairly certain he didn't own a lunch bag.

She and her coworkers were leaving the cafeteria when the sound of her name halted her step. She turned around to find Cameron walking toward her.

"We'll start training when you get back." Her boss smiled and continued down the hall with the group.

"How'd I do this morning?" Cameron raised his eyebrows.

"You did great, Mr. Young." Brila grinned. "I had to keep reminding myself it was you."

He rolled his eyes as they began walking down the hall. "You know I couldn't show any favoritism to you. Sorry if that made it weird."

"No, I understand." She was already D.T.'s girlfriend. While she wasn't going to hide her friendship with Cameron, she also didn't want to make any waves by having a second connection in the company. "So do most people eat down here?"

"I guess so. Most groups go out to eat once or twice a week. Some people eat at their desks. Some always go out."

She assumed D.T. belonged in the last group. "It's a good thing I usually keep salad ingredients on hand. I'll have to make sure I get up early enough to fix my lunch."

"Well, don't worry about that for tomorrow. We can go to the café down the street." He stopped as they reached the training department.

"Isn't that showing favoritism, Mr. Young?" She raised an eyebrow with a smirk.

"I'm not training you anymore. And stop calling me that."

"Okay, Cam."

He scrunched his face. "Since when do you call me Cam?"

"That's how you introduced yourself. I didn't want to make things weird."

"You've always called me Cameron. Why would you stop now?"

She shrugged. "It's work. I don't want to cause any problems." She paused. "Does it bother you that I don't call you Cam like everyone else?"

He smiled. "No. It's our own special thing."

"Good. And it's not my fault. You introduced yourself as Cameron when I first moved to Cedarwood. You should've just said Cam like you did this morning, and we wouldn't be in this mess."

They laughed together. "Well, there's no going back now." He stepped toward his department. "Good luck with training this afternoon."

"Thanks." She watched as he walked away, trying to determine where his desk was but lost him in the sea of cubicles. She shrugged and then continued down the hall, hoping she'd remember how to find Kathryn's office.

FIFTEEN

The following Sunday, Brila was back to baking. A playlist of upbeat pop songs, reminiscent of her high school days, sang out through a Bluetooth speaker as she mixed the cupcake batter. She moved effortlessly and even danced around the kitchen. It had been a long time since she'd baked for a joyous occasion. Not only was D.T. back from his work trip, but his birthday was the next day. She wanted to surprise him with the treats at work, so she had waited until he left for the night before she started baking.

The smell of chocolate seeped out of the oven and filled her condo. Brila prepped her lunches for the week, folded a load of laundry, and then retreated to the couch. Flipping through the channels, a wide grin stretched across her face as she settled on a frosting choice. It was something she hadn't done before, but she was certain she could pull it off. Hopefully, D.T. would appreciate it.

As she returned to the kitchen to begin mixing the frosting, her phone vibrated in her hand. She flipped it up to find Callie's name on the screen before answering.

"How's the job search going?"

The random call and the even more random question caught Brila off guard. "I just started working full-time at Halltown. Still nothing on the yoga front."

"Well, I might be able to change that."

Brila's heart fluttered as Callie continued.

"The instructor for our 6:00 a.m. class has a two-week vacation coming up and just decided after that she wants to take the summer off. I don't know what time you're going into work, but how would you feel about filling in for her while she's out?"

Getting up early wasn't Brila's strong suit. Being awake, alert, and coherent enough to lead a yoga class two days a week was well outside of her comfort zone. Still, it was an opportunity to lead her own class and get her foot in the door. "I don't go in until eight. I could make that work."

"Great! Stop by sometime this week and we'll work through the details."

Brila set her phone on the counter and grabbed the mixing bowl from the drying rack with a smile on her face. It was just a couple of months. She could learn to get up early for a few weeks if it could be the breakthrough she needed to start her yoga career. Unwrapping the butter and dropping it into the bowl, she started planning a sequence for the class.

She paused for a moment and closed her eyes, inhaling slowly. If only Angelle could see her working toward finding her own happiness.

Then it hit her. Discovering purpose in her life, something that brought her joy, wasn't a one-time achievement. That journey could last another day or another sixty years. A smile pulled at the corner of her lips. She may not know the length of her journey, but a sense of pride swelled in her chest knowing that she had at least started down the road, thanks to her sister.

Monday morning, Brila arrived early to take the cupcakes to D.T.'s desk before he came in. She placed the bakery-style cupcake box next to his keyboard. Admiring her surprise for another moment, her shoulders began to relax. Finally, she turned to walk the length of the second floor, down a flight of stairs, and through a row of cubicles until she reached her own desk.

During her first week of work, she had eased into her responsibilities and started to get a feel for what her daily routine would look like. Having Cameron nearby was comforting, especially since her coworkers had been less friendly than she had expected. She worked with five other women. Only one had stopped by to introduce herself and ask Brila about her past work, where she grew up, and other personal details. While she had been invited to join them for lunch each day, they talked around her more often than they talked to her.

After her computer booted up, she sent an email.

I did a little baking over the weekend. Please help yourselves to the cupcakes outside Kathryn's office.

She began scanning her assigned media outlets for weekend updates, waiting to hear the box open.

Twenty minutes later, she received a reply to her email.

I bet they're great, but I'm on a diet. Thanks.

Within a matter of minutes, she received two other replies with a similar message. Brila pursed her lips. She was all for eating healthy, but when someone brought in treats, you ate them.

She refocused on her work only to be interrupted by an instant message from D.T. ten minutes later.

Thanks for the cupcakes. Got anymore? They're already gone.

She smirked. At least someone was enjoying them.

I have some over here. If we don't eat them, they're all yours.
How'd you make the stars like that?

Baker's secret.

She thought of the orange stars she had created surrounded by navy frosting to resemble the Houston Astros logo.

Another message popped up on her screen from one of his coworkers.

How much do you charge for your cupcakes? My son's birthday party is this weekend. My sister's friend was supposed to make a cake, but she just backed out.

She sat back in her chair. Until two weeks ago, baking cupcakes was something she had sworn she'd never do again. If she did continue to bake, it'd be on rare special occasions. And now someone wanted to pay her for it? She stifled a laugh. She wasn't good enough to charge anything.

I just did these for D.T. I don't usually bake and certainly wouldn't make anyone pay for them.
But they were so good. They're much better than anything I could do.

Brila considered it for a moment. It would be good practice, and the woman could clearly see from D.T.'s cupcakes that she wasn't a professional. That didn't seem to bother her. Finally, she agreed to make the cupcakes but insisted on doing it for free.

By eleven, Brila had deemed her attempt at breaking the ice with her coworkers a failure and planned to take the cupcakes to D.T. after lunch. That's when she heard the crinkle of the flimsy window on the box as someone opened it.

"Did you really make these?"

She jumped at Kathryn's voice behind her. "Yeah." She swallowed hard. "I made some for D.T.'s birthday and thought I'd share the extras to say thanks for being so welcoming last week." She gritted her teeth at the lie.

"They're delicious. The frosting is perfect. It all just melts in your mouth. I really should've waited until after lunch. Now I'll want another one." She took another bite.

Brila smiled as she felt her face flush. "Thanks. My sister was always the baker in the family. I guess I just learned from her." She looked to the floor as her chest tightened.

"That's so sweet y'all can do that together."

She should've corrected her to explain that they used to bake together, that her sister had died, and now she was the only one doing the baking. Instead, she held her smile and nodded.

After lunch, the rest of the department gathered around the cabinet. One by one, each of Brila's coworkers grabbed a cupcake. She retreated into her cubicle and listened to their comments.

"They do smell good."

"Does anyone want to split one with me?"

"I remember when I used to bake before I had kids."

Brila sighed as she read her new email messages. She wouldn't have brought them in if she had known it'd be such an ordeal.

"These are really good." One of her coworkers was standing outside her cubicle. "Did you say bake on the side?"

She tried to recall their brief conversation at lunch. "No. I mean, I do it once in a while, but it's not like a hobby or side business or anything."

"Oh, I must've misunderstood. Well, thanks for sharing." She continued on to the next cubicle.

Brila waited thirty minutes before she went to the cabinet to survey the damage. There were still half a dozen left. She decided to leave them and bring any extras to D.T. after work. Maybe someone would dare sneak another one later in the afternoon. She continued toward the hallway to fill her water bottle. As she started back to her desk, Cameron stepped out of the restroom.

"How's the second week going? Ruling with an iron fist yet?"

"Not exactly." She sighed. "It's a tough crowd over there."

He looked down the hall. "Yeah, I've heard that. But how's the work going?"

She shrugged. "It's fine. The social media part of it is pretty similar to what I was doing at Southern. Still learning, but I'll get there." She swung her bottle from one hand to the other. "I brought cupcakes in if you want one."

He hesitated. "Did you make cupcakes or buy them?"

"I made them for D.T.'s birthday and brought in the extras."

"If you made them, I'll definitely take one." They walked together down the hall. "I can't remember the last time I had one of your cupcakes."

She tried to remember when it would have been. "I have no idea." She set her water bottle on the edge of her desk as they passed. "Maybe back in college, but they were probably Angelle's with a little of my flair."

Cameron hummed in agreement as he lifted a cupcake out of the carrier. "Navy and orange. I see what you were after." He smirked and peeled back the wrapper. "Even better than I remember," he said in between bites.

She smiled. "I'm glad you like them. You can take a couple back with you if you want." She lowered her voice. "I think everyone here is afraid of sugar."

"Wait," Kathryn called from her office before appearing in the doorway. "I'd like to take one home for my daughter."

"How about I take two, and you can take the last three home for you and your family?" Cameron took another bite and smiled, creasing the corners of his eyes.

"Sounds fair to me." She smiled back before disappearing into her office. She returned a moment later with two paper plates.

Cameron divvied up the cupcakes, and Brila folded up the box and placed it in the nearby trash can.

"Any time you get the urge to bake, be sure to bring in the goods." Kathryn chuckled before retreating to her desk.

"Now I need to figure out how to hide these so they don't get stolen before I leave today." Cameron walked with Brila back to her desk. "Thanks for the treats." He held up the plate before continuing toward the hall.

As she returned to her desk, she overheard whispering from the next cubicle.

"Who does she think she is? Bringing in treats to get on Kathryn's good side. "

"And how did she even know cupcakes were her favorite? I bet D.T. prepped her on how to get an edge. Must be nice to have your boyfriend hand you a job on a platter."

"Him or Cam. Who knows how many other connections she has. But I'll tell you one thing, if she thinks she's going to come in here and ruin my chances at a promotion, she's got another thing coming."

She sighed, blocking out the rest of their conversation as she unlocked her computer. Is that what they all thought? D.T. helped her apply and may have put in a good word, but he barely knew

Kathryn or anyone in HR for that matter. Who would think he'd have any pull in their decision? And she had no desire to get promoted or get in anyone's way. Maybe she needed to try harder to make that abundantly clear.

Her eyes drifted to the bottom right corner of her screen. It was 1:11 p.m. She leaned back and smiled as the picture of Angelle pinned to her wall caught her eye. Tears welled and a lump got stuck in her throat. She fought back both as warmth filled her chest and stomach.

Brila was raised in a Christian household and held on to most of those beliefs and values. Still, she had never considered herself a spiritual person. With Angelle's passing, she began to question and doubt even more of what she had believed. Yet, at that moment, she felt her sister with her. Maybe all these elevens weren't angel numbers. Maybe it was her sister. Maybe Angelle was her angel. Could it have been as simple as a connection to her sister? No more chasing hidden meanings and undecipherable messages? That would be nice.

Since the accident, she had only felt the loss of her sister. The ache in her heart. The numbing void in her life. The cruelty of a young life cut short. Everything she once knew had been ripped from her that night. And, sure, she wasn't the only one suffering that loss. No parent should have to bury their child. Extended family, friends, students, and coworkers all lost someone they loved. Yet everyone else seemed to be dealing with it better than her.

This was the first time since November that Brila felt Angelle's presence. She had heard people talk about signs from heaven and other symbols they clung to as some sort of reassurance that their loved ones were still with them. It was a nice sentiment, but she had never searched for it in her own life. It had seemed more like grasping at straws. Seeing a bird or a butterfly happens all the time. Who decided that meant a loved one was with you?

But now, overwhelmed with a sense of calm, it was as if Angelle was right in front of her. She wanted to reach out and feel her sister's hand grab hers, reassuring her she wasn't alone. Providing hope that everything would work out. It was just a picture. Just a number on the clock. Yet something in that moment felt so real, so tangible.

Even if the elevens were something else, even if angel numbers and spiritual connections didn't exist, it didn't matter to her. Angelle's presence gave her a sense of peace like nothing she'd ever experienced. She'd do anything to get it back.

She shifted her weight to tuck her right ankle under her left leg. Clearing her throat, she whispered, "I see you. I need you. Don't leave me again."

SIXTEEN

"So we're going to grab food here, right? I really need to get home and bake." Brila and her friends had gathered for happy hour at Shanna's favorite Mexican restaurant. It was Shanna and Tony's first outing since the miscarriage. As much as Brila wanted to support her friend's attempt to inject some sense of normalcy into her life, she also didn't want to be up all night making cupcakes.

To make things worse, Shanna still seemed to be upset at Brila for hiding her own miscarriage from her. Just when their texts would return to their friendly banter, something would spark her disappointment again.

"First you have to bail on our Friday lunches because you decided to take this job all the way across town, and now you want to leave early to go bake? I sure hope this doesn't become a habit." Shanna crossed her arms.

"No one said we had to stop doing lunch on Fridays. It'll just take a little more planning. And we probably can't do it every week. And this cupcake thing is a one-time favor for D.T.'s coworker. She was in a bind. What was I supposed to do? Let her not have treats for her son's party?" Brila looked from Shanna to D.T. to Tony, daring one of them to challenge her.

Shanna didn't miss a beat. "There are plenty of grocery stores and bakeries around town. She could pick up something from any one of them."

Brila turned her attention to the menu as if she would actually order something other than her usual. "Well, it's too late now."

"I think it's nice of you to help out." Tony smiled, but it quickly faded as Shanna narrowed her eyes. "What?" he asked her. "You know how much I'd pay to have those cupcakes at our next family get-together?"

D.T. put his arm around Brila. "I'm glad you're doing something you love again. Hopefully, it works out better than your little yoga instructor phase."

She leaned away from him. "What's that supposed to mean?"

"Oh, come on," he chuckled. "You were dead set on teaching yoga. You're teaching one class, temporarily, and barely talking about it anymore. I don't want to see you get obsessed about this too, only to move on to something else in another month."

"First of all, I haven't given up on yoga." She set down the menu. "The last time I assisted in a class, the sub was a B, so now I'm a little more selective about when I go to class and which opportunities I take. I'll see what happens with this morning class, get more experience, and ease my way into full-time teaching. Second, you're the one that insisted I take this job. Finally, baking is a hobby at best, but it makes me happy. I actually feel connected to Angelle when I'm doing it. And I know that sounds crazy, but it is what it is. I'm not trying to make it a career. The two aren't even comparable." She finished her beer, picked up her purse, then turned to Shanna and Tony. "Thanks for meeting us out. Sorry I can't stay longer, but I really need to get home and start baking. Maybe we can—"

"Really?" D.T. cut her off. "Come on. It was a joke. Sit back down, and let's order food."

"I'll just eat at home." She kept her attention on Shanna and Tony. "Sorry for bailing like this. Maybe we can get together another night this week."

They nodded, as she bolted for the door and prayed D.T. wouldn't follow.

Her heart was pounding as she stomped to her car. Who did he think he was? For as close as they were, sometimes it felt like he didn't know her at all. She was doing this one favor for his coworker. Maybe she'd bake once in a while for family or friends. She wasn't even close to being good enough to actually be considered a professional baker. It'd probably end up being stressful and turn into something she hated anyway—just like D.T. was getting at. She sighed and rolled her eyes.

She was thankful for the drive home. It was long enough to calm down but short enough that she didn't begin to overanalyze. Her phone buzzed with text message notifications. She left it in her purse. Whoever it was could wait.

Inside her condo, she unloaded her belongings on the counter and gathered her baking ingredients. As the batter mixed, an idea for the icing came to her that would fit perfectly with the pool theme of the party. A grin spread across her face. She needed to go to the store to get the final touches for her new plan. She put the cupcakes in the oven and would make the quick trip once they were done.

While waiting, she changed into shorts and a tank top and then slumped onto the couch. Panic knotted her stomach as she realized she hadn't set a timer. She scrunched her nose as she stared at the time on her phone, trying to remember when she had put the cupcakes in the oven. Erring on the side of caution, she set the timer for fifteen minutes.

The text message notifications from earlier were glaring at her. She had no choice but to read them now. She started with Shanna.

Well that escalated quickly
 D.T.'s not leaving. Guess we're all staying to eat
You could've stayed a little longer

She was right. D.T. probably just wanted to protect her. She didn't need to storm out, especially on Shanna.

> I'm sorry. I shouldn't have left. I don't know
> why I let his comments about these things
> get to me. But I should've stayed for you. I
> promise we can do lunch or a girls' day soon.
> Whatever you want to do.

Her stomach growled as she made her way to the kitchen. She groaned back. Nothing looked appetizing in the refrigerator. She checked the timer. Ten minutes left. Making a mental note to also pick up supper, she rotated the muffin tins, then returned to the couch and moved on to D.T.'s messages.

I don't know why you left
It was a joke
Are you still coming over tonight?
Guess you're ignoring me
I'm going out with the guys

Brila rolled her eyes. That's what she got for not having her phone with her all the time. It was probably for the best. Chances are they'd end up rehashing the same argument if she went to his place or he showed up at her door. They could both use the time apart to let it go and start fresh the next day.

She tossed the phone onto the cushion next to her and folded her arms. What if she did want to start baking for others? Who was he to judge what she should or shouldn't do with her time? Not everyone had to fit into his business world.

She scanned the living room as if the silence was judging her. Maybe it had been a harmless joke and she was overreacting. It didn't matter. She was allowed to react the way she did. So what if she took it too personally? It was extremely personal to her. It was an ingrained connection to Angelle, after all. And he knew that.

Retrieving her phone, she decided to get the last word in.

Not ignoring you. Taking care of things. Have fun.

Before she set it down, Shanna's response chimed.

We'll talk tomorrow. Get those cupcakes done.

A weight settled on her chest. Would she ever make things right with Shanna? In keeping her miscarriage a secret from her friend, Brila may have spared her the sorrow of another lost pregnancy, but instead, she lost her trust.

The timer showed five minutes remaining. She decided to check on the cupcakes, knowing they weren't done. She turned on the oven light and crouched to peer through the hazy oven window. Cleaning it over the weekend went on her mental to-do list.

She watched the creamy white tops puff up to be level with the edge of the liners. Stopping the timer on her phone, she committed herself to staying in front of the oven. These cupcakes would not burn.

Just as they began to turn golden yellow, she pulled them out. She searched for her flip-flops, finding them in her bathroom, then returned to the kitchen to move the cupcakes to the cooling racks. With one last scan of the pantry and refrigerator, she finalized her short shopping list.

Brila returned home thirty minutes later with more snack food and cupcake topping ingredients than she had intended to buy. She knew better than to shop when she was hungry, but she didn't have much of a choice. When she had left the restaurant, her craving for Mexican food followed her, so she picked up tacos as well. Drive-thru was not the same as the authentic restaurant, but it was good enough.

After she finished eating, it was time to decorate. She opened a music app on her phone, started a playlist of early 2000s pop music, and began to mix her frosting. As the paddle spun around the mixing bowl, she twisted the cap off the small food coloring bottle. Adding a few drops, she watched the white frosting transform into ocean blue. She turned off the mixer and folded in three more drops so that some areas were darker than others.

She piped the frosting, creating rows of waves with the flick of her wrist as she moved across the cupcakes. Once they were all frosted, she topped each with a bright red Swedish Fish.

When she was done, she popped the two remaining fish into her mouth. With her hands on her hips, she inspected her work. Some were smaller than others. Some had more frosting. None of them looked the same. Still, she had to admit, they were pretty cute. Perfect for an eight-year-old's birthday.

She grabbed her phone, snapped a picture, and sent it to Shanna. Her friend would appreciate her work and, hopefully, be more forgiving of her leaving earlier in the night.

As she turned, the pile of dishes sprawled across the counter knocked the wind out of her sails. She moved everything to the sink and began scrubbing. After every bowl, spatula, pan, and piping bag were settled in the drying rack, she threw the dish towel onto the counter, turned off the lights, and used the glow of her phone screen to illuminate the path to her room.

The sound of her alarm the next morning startled her awake. She stretched as she sat up, waiting for her eyes to adjust. Maybe she could go back to sleep after delivering the cupcakes.

Taking another look at her phone, she squinted at the social media notifications. She hadn't posted anything in the past day. She leaned forward, opened Instagram, then whispered, "What the hell?"

Shanna had shared the picture of her cupcakes with the caption "My friend is more talented than yours."

Brila rolled her eyes as every imperfection became more apparent the longer she stared at the post.

She inhaled slowly and began to scroll through the comments. Of course, no one was honest about the many flaws in her work. It was mostly just empty compliments like "looks great" and "yum." No one had even retorted with pictures of their own friend's talented work. But what caught her off guard were the requests. Birthdays, anniversaries, and even a bridal shower.

Had people suddenly forgotten the convenience of a grocery store bakery? Did they all think supporting a friend-of-a-friend was more important than getting quality baked goods from an actual baker? Sure, the support was nice, but did she want to give up even more of her time to do this for others, especially when the cupcakes wouldn't end up like people expected? Certainly, if she did fill any of these requests, she'd end up as one of those viral fail posts. She didn't want to disappoint anyone or ruin their event. And she wasn't going to do all of that work for free.

She shook her head and snorted as she pushed herself out of bed. She'd have to respond later when she could muster up the courage to tell people no. For the time being, she needed to make herself presentable and get to Halltown, where she had promised to meet D.T.'s coworker.

Brila looked from the clock in her car to the one on her phone screen. Both read 9:35 a.m. Having kids and trying to organize everything for a party likely made it difficult to be on time for anything, but she hoped the wait wouldn't be much longer. She inspected the cupcakes again to ensure they had held up in transit and tried to convince herself they turned out okay.

Seven minutes later, a black SUV pulled up next to her and the woman hopped out. "I'm so sorry. My son didn't want to eat breakfast, then we fought over what he was going to wear today, then I thought I could pick up the balloons on the way over here, but they were so slow."

Brila smiled as she lifted the cupcake box off the passenger side floor mat. "Not a problem. I hope he likes them."

The woman peered into the box. "They're perfect. You really did this last night? That's incredible."

"They're far from perfect." She wrapped her arms around her stomach. "There are all sorts of bumps and holes, and the more I look at them, the less they look like waves."

"Oh, honey, a bunch of eight-year-olds aren't going to notice that. And I wouldn't have either if you hadn't said anything." She slid the box onto the floor of the SUV's backseat. "You're probably your own worst critic. Just don't critique yourself in front of others." She held out some folded-up cash toward Brila. "Here you go."

She shook her head and waved her hand. "I told you I'd do it for free. I'm not a professional. I just wanted to help."

The woman took Brila's hand and placed the money in it. "I know, and I can't thank you enough. This is just to cover the costs of your ingredients. And based on how cute they are, I'm getting a great deal."

"Well, thank you. You definitely don't need to. I had fun making them. I hope your son and his friends enjoy them." She smiled as she retreated to her car, and they drove their separate ways.

Brila stopped at a coffee shop on the way home. While waiting in line, she thought about D.T. He was probably still passed out. Even if he wasn't, he wouldn't be the first to send a text after their argument. She sighed as she reread their last exchange. Asking if he wanted her to bring him breakfast, her thumb hovered over the send button. She finally pushed it a moment later, moving forward with the line.

The two people in front of her placed their orders. She flipped her phone up to illuminate the screen. No response. She scanned the menu boards as if an extra five seconds would change that. The eyes behind her burned pinholes into the back of her head. Giving up, she ordered an iced coffee and two blueberry muffins, just in case.

As she walked toward the door, Cameron walked in. His drowsy eyes widened and a grin spread across his face. "What are you doing here?"

"I had to drop off those cupcakes and decided to pick up some breakfast on the way home." She held up the small brown bag.

"So you're headed out?" He shook his head. "Dumb question. Of course, you are."

"Why? Are you staying?"

"I usually just pick up and go back to my place but figured if you were staying, I could keep you company."

She checked her phone once more for a response that wasn't there. "I don't need to be anywhere. I'll grab a table while you order." She walked toward an empty table, then stopped and turned back. "Oh, and if you like muffins, I have an extra one."

He smiled. "Sounds great. Thanks."

A few minutes later, he sat across from Brila with the same iced coffee, just two sizes larger.

She set her phone face down on the table and slid the second muffin toward him. "Where's 'new Alex'?" Her eyes locked on his, waiting for his reaction.

"There's no 'new Alex' anymore."

Her shoulders fell. After a moment, she wrestled back a smirk and raised her eyebrows. "So now there's an 'old Alex one' and 'old Alex two'?"

"Why are you doing that?"

"Because it's funny to see you get annoyed. Except it's not working today." Her grin faded as she drank her coffee. "What happened?"

He shrugged. "Same as the rest, I suppose. No real connection." He paused for a moment, peeling back the wrapper from his muffin. "So are you taking orders now? Starting a side business?"

She huffed at the idea. "Not even close. Just this one favor."

"Well, that's unfortunate."

She continued to drain her coffee. There was no going back to sleep now. "A couple weeks ago, I wouldn't even taste a cupcake. Hadn't since the accident. I'd say this is good progress. Besides, I don't have what it takes to run my own business."

Cameron eyed the muffin before breaking off a piece. "That doesn't sound like the Brila I know. The one who revolutionized the social media presence of an entire college. The one who takes innocent comments as a personal challenge. You could do anything you want to do. I don't want to hear that you don't have what it takes. But it's good to see you baking again."

Brila smiled and shook her head. "Yeah, okay." Still, she couldn't help but wonder, what if she did have her own bakery someday? One could dream.

SEVENTEEN

D.T. didn't reply until after two o'clock that afternoon.

We doing anything tonight?

As if nothing had happened between them the night before. He likely assumed her text that morning was some sort of apology. Waiting for him to apologize would have been a lost cause.

It wasn't clear if he had finally slept off a hangover, had gotten bored and decided to stop ignoring her, or had simply forgotten about her text until that moment. At this point, it didn't matter. He could have responded at any time and chose not to.

A part of her wanted to make other plans and tell him he was on his own. He never did wrong in his eyes. If she could make him sweat for even a night, it'd be worth it. Then again, he'd probably twist it so she was the one in the wrong. Besides, as much as she wanted to make a point, she just wanted to get back to normal.

Instead of responding, she opened Shanna's post to read through more comments. The notifications had continued to pop up all day. She scrolled through and counted twelve comments either requesting orders or asking about pricing. She shook her head. They were just cupcakes. While she decorated better than the average home baker, she was far from great. The praise was kind but not justified. The idea that anyone would want her to bake for them was absurd.

Closing the app, she texted Shanna.

> I don't know if I should thank you or
> curse you for that post.

She stared at three dots indicating Shanna was typing her response.

> You can thank me
> And you're welcome
> I'm still mad you bailed, but they turned out
> great

Brila smiled. She didn't deserve such a wonderful friend. The small container of leftover blue frosting on the counter caught her eye.

> How about lunch and manicures tomorrow?
> I'll bring you the leftover frosting.

She owed her a lot more than that, but the peace offering was a start.

> Sounds like a plan

Brila laid out a sheet of parchment paper and then assembled the piping bag sitting in the drying rack. Her mouth pulled to the side as designs of flowers, stars, and swirls floated through her mind.

She practiced each of them, using different starting points, directions, and widths. She inspected each, scraped her work off the paper, scooped it back into the piping bag, and did it again. Then she switched to a new tip and started another set of designs.

When she was done, she returned to the comments and responded to each one. The hardest part was answering questions about pricing. She couldn't charge bakery prices, but if she was going to do this, she might as well cover her costs. After a little research, she settled on twenty dollars a dozen. Her smile grew with each order she accepted until she had agreed to do all of them.

Closing out the app, she noticed the time: 3:11 p.m. She stood, looked at the ceiling, and closed her eyes. "I don't know what this is all about, but thank you," she whispered. The thought of Angelle somehow being near sent a warming sensation throughout her body. Everything around her was muted for that moment. The connection to her sister was the only thing that mattered.

She opened her eyes and stared at the time on the screen. She heard her inner voice speaking Angelle's words, telling her to find her purpose and do good for others. It was okay to not have all the answers, okay to not follow others' ideas of success. The final thought came through as Angelle's voice. "I'm okay. I love you. I'm always with you."

Brila's eyes welled with tears that never spilled over.

The minute ticked up to twelve. She blinked rapidly, with the reality of the emptiness of her kitchen washing over her. She had put off D.T.'s message long enough. Of course, he hadn't sent any other messages, so it wasn't like he was all that concerned.

What? You don't want to get hammered with
your friends again?

No, she didn't want to start a new fight.

What do you want to do?

She stared at her new response for a moment, then deleted it as well. She didn't want to keep going back and forth. Instead, she settled on something slightly more definitive.

> You can come over whenever and
> we'll figure something out.

Bright blue frosting resembling grass, lion manes, and furry monsters still sat on the counter. She scraped it back into the container, crumpled up and threw away the parchment paper, and washed the remaining utensils. If she and D.T. were going anywhere, she would need to change out of her yoga clothes.

Two hours later, D.T. knocked on her door. She had started a movie after the first hour had passed with no sign of him. Now the movie was just getting into the heart of the storyline. Sighing, she turned it off and let him in. "So glad you could make it."

He walked past her. "The game went into extra innings."

She examined his gym shorts and t-shirt in contrast to her jeans and floral tank top. "Guess we're staying in tonight."

He hesitated, looking back at her. "Did you plan to go out? You said come over. Want me to go back and change?"

Brila fought the urge to roll her eyes. "I said come over two hours ago. I figured we'd hang for a little while, then decide what to do for the night." She took a deep breath. It wasn't like she had planned for anything in particular. "It's not a big deal. We can stay in." She walked to her bedroom.

"Are you sure?" He followed behind. "We can go out. I'm good either way."

"No, it's probably for the best. We can order in and watch a movie or something."

"I like 'or something.'" He wrapped his arms around her as she pulled the tank top over her head.

"We'll see." She wiggled away from him to put on a t-shirt and then walked past him back to the living room.

D.T. grabbed the remote and sat at the far end of the couch. Brila sat at the other end. Her screen illuminated with new notifications. As D.T. scrolled through the list of shows, she unlocked her phone and read the messages.

"Who's that?"

"One of Shanna's friends. She wants me to do cupcakes for her sister's baby shower in a couple weeks. She was just sending me what she wanted."

He stared at her. Was he still hungover or did she not explain it right? She studied his face but couldn't read his mind. Instead of trying to figure it out, she returned to typing her response.

"So you're taking orders from strangers now?" he broke the silence a moment later.

She finished her message, reread it, hit the send button, and locked her phone. "She's not a stranger. I mean, I don't know her personally, but Shanna's introduced us before. She saw the post and asked."

"What post?"

He must have been out of it for the day if he hadn't been on his phone. She explained what had happened with the picture she'd sent Shanna and the resulting responses.

"This was a one-time thing. Just a hobby at best," he spit out her words from the night before. "Now you're taking orders and special requests from strangers. Exactly how many of these are you doing? And when's it going to stop?"

"It *was* a one-time thing." She sat up, crossing her arms. "I didn't ask Shanna to share that picture. I just sent it to her because ... well, I don't know why. But people kept asking questions and saying nice things. It felt good. And I like to do it, so why not do it for others and make a little money on the side? I'll do these and see what happens."

"Well, there go the weekends."

"That's a bit of an exaggeration." She thought for a moment. "I can do them after work on Thursdays or Fridays. I might have to be up early Saturday, but then I'm free the rest of the day. It's really not that bad."

D.T.'s eyes were focused on her as if he was trying to find more holes in her plan. "Sounds like your little hobby is turning into a business."

A laugh escaped her mouth. "I'm not qualified to run my own bakery."

"I don't think you know what you're getting yourself into."

"Thanks for your concern, but I'm not getting into anything." Another notification caught her attention. "Do you have any other issues with me that you'd like to point out, or can we enjoy our night?"

"I don't want to see you get hurt or stuck, that's all." He pulled her ankle, but she didn't budge. He repositioned himself next to her and pressed his lips into hers. "Now, what do you want to eat tonight?"

Brila let her gaze drop to the middle of the room. He couldn't make every fight end with a kiss. It didn't erase the fact that he doubted her ability, questioned her motives, and didn't support her in something that made her happy. Maybe he did just want to protect her. But why not let her take that risk if it was something she wanted to do?

"You decide." She leaned away from him. "I'm not that hungry, anyway." A grumble building in her stomach threatened to betray her. She alternated between sucking in and pushing out her abdomen to make it go away.

 D.T. studied her. Or maybe he was still hungover and she just happened to be where he was staring blankly. He blinked rapidly a few times and refocused on her. "Want Mexican since you left before we could eat last night?"

She rubbed her arm. "I ended up getting some after running to the store for a couple things I needed." She paused. "But I can eat it again if that's what you want."

He shook his head. "I just thought you'd want it. How about burgers?"

She did tell him to choose, and she said she wasn't hungry, so she didn't have much room to argue. "That's fine. Arrows?" They had a handful of restaurants they relied on for take-out. She pulled up the menu on her phone.

"Good with me."

She scanned the menu, settling on the same turkey burger sliders she always got. She then turned the phone to D.T.

He gently pushed her hand away. "Just get the usual. Are you going to call since you have the number right there?"

She nodded and selected the number to place the same order they placed each time. Their predictability teetered between comforting and unsettling. That alone sent a twinge of guilt into the pit of her stomach. Relationships weren't always easy, but a sense of familiarity should be as comforting as home.

Her phone lit up as soon as she set it down. As she reached for it, D.T. scooped it up, put it on the other side of him, slid closer, and wrapped an arm around her. "You can answer them tomorrow. Tonight, you're mine. And all you need to worry about is relaxing."

She opened her mouth to fight back but resisted. It was the low-key Saturday night she had hoped for. There was no need to ruin it just to have the final word.

EIGHTEEN

Brila jerked awake at the sound of her alarm the following Tuesday morning. She arched her back and twisted her head side to side, stretching her neck. A smile spread across her face as she reopened her eyes.

She pushed back the covers and shuffled to the bathroom. In just forty-five minutes, she would be leading her first yoga class. Excitement fluttered through her gut. She mentally ran through the sequence she had planned the week before. After reviewing it every chance she got over the past two days, even completing the full session three times in her living room, she could probably do it in her sleep.

As she pulled on a pair of navy leggings, she recalled her conversation with Callie a week earlier. She would lead the morning class on Tuesdays and Thursdays for the next two months. It was a small class, typically no more than ten people and a perfect way to start her career. Her career! The thought made her giddy. Could she be so lucky to only work at her favorite studio?

She laid out a pale blue blouse and black dress pants on her bed. She'd have a short window of time to get home from the class and get ready for work. It wasn't a huge time saver, but any little thing would help. Checking her bag one last time, she grabbed a banana from the kitchen counter and walked out the front door.

It was a short, ten-minute drive to the studio. The radio pumped out an upbeat pop song, but Brila barely noticed. Her thoughts had shifted from the sequence to the words she would speak. Greeting the class, offering words of encouragement, and answering questions would be easy, natural. The meditation made her nervous. What could she say to inspire others? What did she want to focus on? She had practiced a couple of different meditations and mantras, deciding that she would choose one during the session. The energy of the room would lead her to the right answer.

The studio sat dark, tucked between a law office and a design firm. She peered through the glass door before knocking on it. With no sign of Callie, she slid her phone out of the side pocket of her bag. She unlocked the screen and opened up her messages.

"I'm here," Callie called behind her. "Have you been waiting long?"

Brila shook her head. "Just got here. I was just checking the time."

She watched Callie unlock the door and followed her inside. The scent of lemon cleaning products filled the air. She flipped the light switches and helped Callie pull open the cream blinds for the windows on either side of the door, letting the glow spill out onto the sidewalk.

Taking a deep breath, Brila walked to the front of the room, slid her mat out of her bag, and unrolled it horizontally. She stood and stretched her hands above her head.

"Ready to go?" Callie smiled as she moved toward her small office in the back corner.

Brila nodded despite the knots twisting in her gut. "Ready as I'll ever be."

"You'll be great. The morning crew is a good one." Her infectious positive energy permeated everything she did.

"Thanks. I can't wait to meet them." Hinging at the waist, she folded forward and placed her hands on the ground.

Brila lifted her head at the creak of the door a few seconds later. She returned upright and smiled as a tall, gray-haired woman entered and walked to the right side of the room. "Good morning."

The woman smiled in return. She rolled out a purple mat, pausing as she looked at Brila's mat. "Do you want our mats to go side-to-side like yours?"

"Yep, horizontal mats today." She had been so focused on her own plans, she hadn't considered how the prior instructor had done things. She shrugged it off as the woman rotated her mat.

Two other women entered the studio and claimed their spots in the center of the room. After greeting them, Brila checked the small clock above the door. It was three minutes to six. Hopefully, the others would arrive soon. She didn't want to start without everyone, but she also didn't have much time to wait around. Based on the app Callie used for class sign-ups, there were four more to show up.

She continued to stretch her arms and back as the others trickled in. Watching the clock tick to six, her heartbeat quickened and sweat peppered her hands and back. She took a deep breath and began.

"Good morning." Her voice projected above the chatter, a sharp contrast to the overly soft-spoken instructor she'd witnessed in the first session in which she had assisted. "As you're probably aware, Liz is taking some time off, so I'll be leading this class for the next two months. I'm Brila. I look forward to getting to know you. This is actually my first session as an instructor, so I'm open to any feedback you have. We can work together to help y'all get the most out of these sessions."

Maybe she shouldn't have told them that. She rocked back and forth, moving her feet closer together. "All right, let's get y'all energized for the day." She lowered the volume of her voice back to its normal level. "We'll start out with mountain pose. This is an active standing pose. Stand with your feet hip-width apart, arms at your sides. Pull your belly button to your spine. Keep your shoulders back and lift your chest and the top of your head toward the ceiling."

She observed each individual in silence as they settled into the pose. While most had focused their eyes on a point straight ahead of them, the woman in the back right corner continued to look from the front wall to Brila. Did she want reassurance? Maybe she was new to yoga.

"Great start." She made eye contact with the woman before continuing. "Now let's move into chair pose. Raise your arms to the ceiling and sit your hips back as if there is an imaginary chair behind you."

She demonstrated, holding the pose for a few breaths, before walking around the room. Starting with the gray-haired woman in the front, she studied her position and gently pressed her arms to lift them a touch higher. She made her way to the back corner to the woman who still appeared to be looking for confirmation.

"Good," Brila whispered. "Just sit back a little further to increase the stretch." She put her hands on the woman's hips and pulled them back and down.

She smiled to herself as she continued around the others and returned to the front. "Stand straight and widen your stance as we move into warrior one."

Her nerves from the start of the session had melted away. Her preparation had paid off. Being so familiar with the sequence she had planned allowed her to hone in on each individual's needs. She made mental notes throughout the session of which poses were the most difficult for the class to execute and which poses they stayed in for an extra breath before moving to the next.

Her training and passion intertwined, filling her with pride as she led the class through the session. She glanced at the clock as she pressed her palms together and raised her arms straight above her head for their final pose. She was right on schedule with five minutes left for meditation.

"Okay, let's sit, cross your legs and rest your hands on your knees with your palms facing up. Close your eyes and clear your mind. Your day will be waiting for you after we're done. Right now, you only need to focus on your breathing. Take a deep breath in," she paused as she inhaled, "and slowly exhale."

She listened to the whisper of their collective breath, leading them through additional breathing exercises. She continued, speaking slowly, deliberately. "Bring your focus to your right hand. Notice each finger. Touch your thumb to your index finger. Thumb to your middle finger. To your ring finger. And to your pinkie. Relax your hand. Relax your fingers."

They repeated this mind-clearing practice with the left hand. "Now I want you to repeat these words to yourself: I am healthy. I am strong. I am capable." As she repeated the words out loud, she heard a couple of voices join hers. She wondered if the others were repeating the mantra silently or if they chose to not participate. It would remain a mystery as she kept her eyes closed.

"Take another deep breath in. Exhale. And with your next breath, slowly let your eyes open."

Brila smiled as her eyes readjusted to the studio light. She stretched her arms above her head and then stood. A low murmur echoed as the class began to move and roll their mats. "Thanks so much for coming this morning. I'd be happy to hear any feedback you have so I can make any adjustments for Thursday's class.

They looked at one another, and then the tall woman in front spoke up. "It's a minor thing, but could we do vertical mats next time?"

She'd never seen someone so concerned with their mat placement. "Sure. Not a problem."

"Maybe not so many one-legged poses. Not all of us have good balance." Another chimed in.

"Can we have more time for each pose?"

"No, I liked the faster pace."

Brila felt her cheeks warm. She had expected feedback more along the lines of "Great first session" or even "Can you talk quieter?". Maybe she shouldn't have asked.

The conversations had turned into more of a debate between the attendees of their personal preferences.

"Thanks for your feedback. I'll take it into consideration and look forward to seeing you all on Thursday. Have a wonderful day!" She smiled and watched them file out the front door.

"Great job." Callie stepped out of her office. "I like the flow you put together. Perfect for a morning session."

Brila stuffed her mat into its carrying bag. "Not according to the class."

"Oh, you can't worry about that. Everyone's going to have an opinion. Trust your instincts. After all, you're the one who's been through training."

"Thanks." A weight lifted off her chest. "I'll see you Thursday."

She stepped outside and headed toward her car. The time she'd have to get ready and make it to Halltown would be a little shorter than she had planned for, but she could still make it work.

She felt more awake than she had in a long time. Maybe she could get in the habit of waking up for morning sessions even when she didn't have class. A laugh escaped her mouth. It'd take a little more convincing for her to willingly get up earlier than necessary to exercise when she could easily do it after work.

A little pocket of pride warmed in her chest. There were some small changes she could make in the session, and she'd take the class's suggestions into consideration. Overall, though, it had been a success. At least Callie thought so.

Still, something seemed to be missing. Shouldn't there be some big "aha" moment, a sense of making it or a feeling that everything had fallen into place after finally realizing and beginning to live out your dreams? It had been rewarding to lead a great session, to feel the change in her own energy, and to be part of others' wellness journey. And yet she expected to feel something more. Where was all the happiness Angelle had wanted her to find?

Maybe that was unfair. She couldn't expect everything to change with just one session. She opened her car door, tossed her bag to the passenger seat, and started the ignition. She had plenty to be happy about. Things would get better as she continued to settle into a routine and into the yoga instructor she wanted to be. And when she did that, hopefully, the little nagging bit of doubt in the back of her mind would go away.

NINETEEN

Two Fridays later, the sugary smell of buttercream frosting filled
Brila's condo. She turned off the mixer and tilted back the head. As
she did, Shanna ran her finger along one side of the paddle.

She scrunched her eyebrows together as she licked the frosting.
"It's no good. Give me this batch and start again." She reached for
more, but Brila tapped her hand.

"You can't have all of it," Cameron chimed in, as he leaned over
the counter and snuck a taste of his own.

"Do I have to make you two sit in the living room with Tony?"
Brila pointed the rubber scraper at them.

"What about me?" Tony called from the couch, his eyes still
glued to the baseball game on TV.

"You might have some company soon if these two don't stop
eating all my frosting."

"You're eating frosting without me?" He appeared at the edge of
the counter. Waiting until Brila turned to get her piping bag, he
grabbed the little frosting that was left in the middle of the paddle.

Brila spun around to catch him. Her glare melted into a smile as
they all erupted with laughter. "I guess that means it's good."

Tony returned to the couch as the game came back from a
commercial break. "Best frosting in the city."

She scooped half into a piping bag, added purple food coloring to the other half remaining in the bowl, and turned the mixer on low. Once the frosting turned a muted shade of lavender, she placed it in a second piping bag.

"Time for the magic." Cameron grinned.

Brila rolled her eyes. "Roses are the easiest thing to do. Maybe I'll only take requests for bridal showers from now on."

"Yeah, right." Shanna reached over and grabbed the bowl. She held it between her and Cameron as they scraped out the frosting remnants. "I know how much you loved doing those monsters last week."

She thought back to the green and purple monster faces she had created for a five-year-old's birthday party and smiled. "Those did come out cute."

After she had piped the lavender frosting on a dozen chocolate cupcakes, she paused to pick up a container of silver pearl sprinkles. She extended it out toward her friends. "If you're going to be here, you might as well help."

Cameron grabbed the container and inspected it. "So do we just dump them on top?"

"No." Her eyes widened. "Here, pour them into this bowl, and use your fingers to set a few on each."

"How many do you mean by 'a few'?" If Shanna was going to help, it would be done to perfection.

Brila thought for a moment. "Six. And it's okay if it's one or two over or under. Just don't dump them." Her eyes narrowed on Cameron. She repositioned the piping bag but stopped before squeezing out the frosting. "Wait. Wash your hands first."

"I just came for moral support and free samples. I didn't sign up to work." Cameron tapped his fingers on the countertop.

Brila pressed her hand on top of his. "Could you stop?"

He pulled his hand free and went to the sink as Shanna turned off the faucet and reached for the dish towel. "At this point, I do it just to annoy you."

"Tell me again how D.T. got out of this?" Shanna teased.

"Got out of this?" Her hand and the piping bag collapsed to the counter as she turned. "You two wanted to come over here. No one forced you. And you really don't need to help if you don't want to. D.T. was going to the gym. He'll be here after he showers and gets ready."

"You know we're happy to be here." Shanna returned to her seat. She pulled a tray of lavender frosted cupcakes toward her and carefully arranged six pearls, one at a time, evenly around the top of the first one.

Cameron chuckled as he sat down and haphazardly dropped the pearls over a cupcake until seven stuck. "It doesn't have to be perfect."

He looked to Brila for confirmation, but she wasn't about to be caught in the middle of another one of their competitions. "However you get them on there is fine with me. It's one less thing I have to do before we leave."

Shanna smirked at Cameron as she moved onto the next one.

"At the rate she's going, we'll never eat." He continued sprinkling the cupcakes, finishing three in the time it took her to do one.

Brila finished piping the white cupcakes and watched her friends. She swallowed the lump in her throat and fought back the tears welling in her eyes.

Shanna looked up as she reached for more pearls. "Is everything okay?"

She nodded, unsure if she could speak without choking up. She forced a cough as if that would make it go away. "It just feels like it

did when Angelle and I baked together. I wish she could be here."
She pulled at the corners of her eyes.

Cameron walked around the counter. "I know it's not the same,
but we're always here for you." Standing at her side, he wrapped his
arms around her, pinning her arms to her sides.

She placed her hands on his forearm, closing her eyes as a tear
rolled down her cheek. Shanna joined them and Tony followed.

They were still in their group hug when D.T. walked in. "What's
going on?" he asked as they separated.

Brila dried her cheeks with the side of her hand. "Just another
Angelle episode." She looked down at the counter. "The good news
is, there's leftover frosting. Who wants some?"

D.T. joined them. "I'll get in on that." He hugged her and kissed
her cheek. Then he grabbed a handful of spoons from the drawer,
allowing each person to take one.

Brila squeezed frosting from the piping bags onto each spoon.
She tried a small taste of the lavender, using her index finger. Filling
the sink with water and dish soap, she set the mixing bowl, rubber
scraper, and piping bags inside it. "Let me go change quick, and we
can go."

When she returned five minutes later, she found Shanna and
Cameron washing the dishes. She swallowed hard, determined to not
release the tears that had returned. Being so emotional was
exhausting.

She looked at D.T. and Tony watching the game in the living
room to distract her before entering the kitchen. "You really don't
need to do that."

Shanna turned around as she handed the mixing bowl to
Cameron for him to rinse. "It's the least we can do. Are you ready?"

She covered the cupcakes and looked around until she spotted
her purse on the table. "I'm ready, but I don't know if the guys are."
When no response came from the couch, she repeated herself louder.

"The inning's almost over," D.T. answered. "Just a couple more minutes."

Brila watched the batter foul the next three pitches. "Are you sure?"

"They just need this last out. It'll be ..." His voice trailed off as the ball was hit deep into right field.

She looked at Shanna and Cameron then back at the TV. "What if we go grab a table, and you two can meet us when the game is done?"

Tony turned around to gauge Shanna's reaction.

She smiled. "It's okay. Stay and watch the game."

As the coach walked to the pitcher's mound, D.T. turned. "Are you sure?"

"We're ready to go. Might as well get a table so we don't all have to wait. Come after the game. It'll be fine."

"You don't want to stay?" Tony looked at Cameron.

He thought for a moment. "No, I'm good."

"So we're all good?" Brila surveyed the room. Without any opposition, she picked up her purse. "I can drive."

They sat at a six-person high-top table in the restaurant bar, where they were immediately greeted by their server. After ordering drinks, Brila texted D.T.

> The wait at Half Shell was too long.
> We're at Wings and Things.

He responded a minute later.

Well damn. There are ten different games there.
We're coming.

She shrugged and located the Astros game on the wall of TVs to get up to speed. As a new batter approached home, she looked at Cameron. "Please tell me you're watching."

He scanned the TVs to find what she was talking about. "The Astros? No, I want to hear about this new cupcake business you're starting."

"I'm not ..." She trailed off as the server returned with their drinks.

"Do you want to start with any appetizers?"

They looked at one another. Maybe they should have looked beyond the drink section of the menu. Shanna answered for the group. "Not right now. We have two more coming in a few minutes."

The young waitress smiled. "No problem. I'll check back later." Her voice was bubbly. She practically bounced as she walked away. Brila couldn't tell if it was her real personality or a persona she wore to make extra tips. Either way, she found it infectious.

Avoiding Cameron's question, Brila looked across the table to Shanna. "How's work going?"

"A little hectic right now. We're short-staffed with two out on maternity leave." She looked down at the menu.

A twinge of guilt rose in the pit of Brila's stomach. It had to be hard enough for Shanna to take care of new moms and their babies all day long. Watching her coworkers join the ranks of motherhood while she continued to struggle with fertility had to be a new kind of hell. And having your best friend ask about it like an insensitive jerk certainly didn't help things.

"I don't know how you do it. Any of it. I know you don't feel like it, but you have more strength than anyone I know." Brila gave a soft smile, wanting to rush over and hold her friend but not wanting to cause a scene or a breakdown.

The game broadcast and overlapping conversations from the surrounding tables still couldn't mask the heavy silence between them.

"So, are you still taking order requests?" Cameron wouldn't let her off the hook that easy.

"I haven't gotten any, but I guess I'd take them. The orders from Shanna's post will keep me busy for a while anyway." She eyed her friend, still feeling a mixture of gratitude and sheer shock that she'd been propelled into this new side gig.

"That's easily fixed. I'll post another picture when we get back to your place." Shanna's wide smile returned. "Or better yet, maybe you should start advertising your work on your own page."

"My work? It's just a hobby. And if you wouldn't have posted that picture, I wouldn't be doing this at all. It's okay if I don't have more people asking for them. That means I could actually have the weekend to do what I want."

"Like what?" Cameron challenged. "Watch TV? Sleep? You've hardly lost any time from your weekends. You're here now on a Friday night. What are you complaining about?"

Damn. She hated when he called her out on her exaggerations. "I could be at yoga or doing other activities. D.T. and I could kayak or go on a date. And what if I start getting requests for weeknights or Sundays?"

"Well, the nice thing about running your own business is you decide your own terms and availability. You don't have to say yes to everything. But that also doesn't mean you have to say no to everything." He smirked.

"You have a real gift," Shanna chimed in. "Why not share it?"

Brila would have been lying if she said she hadn't thought about it. As much as she complained about the extra time it took, she truly enjoyed it. That was her time alone to just do and create. Except for when the entire crew came over to watch. Even then, she didn't mind.

She also felt more connected to Angelle when she baked. It had been the one thing she had avoided after the accident, afraid it would intensify the loss. Instead, she'd denied herself the opportunity to remember those times they'd shared and to celebrate that part of her sister's life.

"I don't know anything about running a business. Or baking properly. What if it gets to be too much? What if I end up hating it because it starts to feel like work and not something I love?" She took a long drink to slow her pounding heartbeat.

"Well, it's not something you have to do right away. But it's definitely something worth thinking about, especially if you continue to have people interested in your work." Shanna smiled.

"Yeah, I guess I'll see what happens and figure it out as it comes." That didn't feel right either. She'd rather take the time now to decide one way or the other, rather than waiting around and feeling like the decision was made for her.

"What'd we miss?" D.T. pulled out the chair next to Brila as Tony kissed Shanna's cheek and sat next to her.

"Not much." She looked up at the TV and realized the score had changed.

"They scored another run since we left the house. You didn't see what happened?" D.T.'s eyes darted between her and the game.

"I must've missed it while we were talking. I'm sure you'll catch it in the highlights later." After all, it wasn't her responsibility to watch the game for him.

Tony jumped in. "Sounds like they started the party without us."

Shanna leaned toward him. "We're trying to convince her to start her own cupcake business. Don't you think she'd be great?"

"We all know she can bake, but she has to want to do it." Tony looked from his wife to Brila. "There's a lot that goes into starting and running your own business. I'm not saying it can't be done. There's just a lot to consider before jumping in."

Tony's parents had opened their own clothing store and expanded to five locations between Houston and Galveston. Tony managed the Houston stores and had begun learning the bookkeeping and other ownership responsibilities. She loved her friends and their enthusiasm, but she valued his honest input.

"I thought it was just a hobby." D.T.'s mocking tone made her stomach churn.

Brila folded her arms. "It is right now, but maybe it can be something more down the road. Who knows. At least I know I have people who support me regardless of what I decide." She looked at the wall of TVs, pretending to watch the game as she drank her beer.

"So, is anyone going to the fireworks next weekend?" Shanna wasn't one for conflict.

Cameron shook his head. "I'll probably stay at home and watch from the patio. There are few things sadder than a single man hanging around at the fireworks display."

"You're not alone if we all go together," Brila chimed in.

"We'll be in Galveston for the weekend," D.T. countered.

Brila tried to recall that conversation. A few weeks earlier, he had mentioned that some of his friends were going but never brought it up again. "We didn't book a hotel. Are you planning to drive back that night?"

"I'm sure we can find something."

"It's a holiday weekend."

"People cancel all the time. And if not, the guys have a rental."

If he was so adamant about going, why hadn't he said so when he'd first mentioned it, and why hadn't he already booked a room? Brila looked across the table to Shanna, whose wide eyes confirmed she was not being unreasonable. "Whatever. Guess we're out for fireworks. The three of you should still go. Maybe you can find a date for Cameron." She smirked.

"I don't want a random date, and I'd rather not be a third wheel. I have a perfect view from my patio. Don't worry about me."

The conversation continued for another minute then ended with no one going to the fireworks display. However, Brila only muttered a few words and occasionally nodded in agreement. Her mind was stuck on the idea of starting a cupcake business. Twenty different reasons for why she shouldn't do it filled her mind. Yet, she couldn't ignore the possibility. It fluttered in the pit of her stomach and twisted in her chest.

The other thing she couldn't shake was D.T.'s lack of support. Her friends were excited about the whole business idea. He should be her biggest cheerleader. Instead, he had more doubts than she did, if that was possible. Did he really think it was a bad idea? Did he not think she had what it took to run a business? Or was he just against anything that didn't fall in line with his idea of normal?

TWENTY

Brila had spent the Fourth of July watching D.T. drink his own twelve-pack of beer and take too many tequila shots to count, with his friends. As a result, it became her responsibility to get them back to Houston the next day.

While she appreciated that he'd wanted to include her, she wished he'd gone alone. His three friends with whom they stayed were all single. It wasn't that she had a problem with them under normal circumstances, but this 'frat boy' weekend wasn't her idea of fun. She'd felt like D.T. had been torn between dedicating his time to her and his friends. Not wanting to be in the way, she had assured him throughout the weekend not to worry about her, while secretly waiting for him to choose her anyway.

She could've spent the weekend with Shanna and Tony or Cameron. She could've slept in and binge-watched new shows. The only good thing to come from the weekend was all the time they'd spent at the beach between kayaking, jet skiing, and just lounging under an umbrella.

She glanced at D.T., who was sleeping in the reclined passenger seat of his Jeep. She'd already cleaned up the condo they'd stayed in, packed for all five of them, and now the stench of sweat and alcohol overpowered the saltwater breeze. Narrowing her eyes on the highway, she silently rehearsed the lecture she would unleash on him once they got home.

The time, 11:11 a.m., illuminated brighter than the rest of the display screen. She sighed heavily and gave a slight shake of her head. Her chest tightened as she refocused on the proposal she had to finish and present at work in the next two days, followed by the two cupcake orders she had for the next weekend.

Brila looked over at D.T. as she exited the Gulf Freeway. Clenching her jaw, she stomped on the brake at the traffic light.

D.T. jerked awake. "What the hell?"

"We're almost home." She scrunched her nose as the stench of the alcohol still on his breath wafted toward her. "Will you be able to drive from my place, or do I need to take you home?"

He returned the seat to its upright position. "I'm fine. Just tired."

She hesitated. "Well, then I guess it's good you brought me along."

"I could've driven if I needed to, but why not get a little rest if you're willing to drive?"

"Like I had much say in the matter. You threw me the keys and climbed into the passenger seat."

"Should've said something if you didn't want to."

"You also could've drunk less or gone to bed earlier. But why do that when you bring along your girlfriend to do everything for you and your friends?" She clenched the steering wheel.

"We're not doing this." He turned back to his other side and closed his eyes.

"Don't go to sleep. We're almost home."

"I'm not sleeping."

Continuing to argue would have been a wasted effort. She abandoned her rehearsed lecture and turned up the radio to fill the silence between them.

She parked the Jeep next to her car but left it running. Grabbing her weekender bag from the backseat, she muttered, "Hope you get some sleep," before slamming the door closed.

Her jaw remained clenched as she stomped up the stairs to her condo. She wanted nothing more than to call her sister and hear her soothing voice talk her off the ledge. A yawn escaped her mouth, her own exhaustion setting in. She kicked off her flip-flops inside the door then shuffled to her room and dropped the bag near her dresser before climbing into bed.

Did he really see nothing wrong with what had happened? She already knew the answer. As caring as he could be, as much fun as they had together, and as much as she believed he loved her, his own wants would always take priority over everything, including her. He was always right, and he found no fault in doing things the way he wanted.

She rolled on her side, trying to think of anything else so she could rest. The vibration of her phone against the dresser caused her to jump. One more reminder alert then she could get some sleep. Instead, three new messages came through one after the other. D.T. wasn't in any condition or mood to be texting. She knew only one other person who texted in rapid individual thoughts like that.

Sighing, she tossed back her covers and retrieved the phone to see what Shanna had to say.

How was your weekend?
Are you back in town yet?
What are you doing today?
Tony just made fresh salsa and is making fajitas
later.

She crawled back in bed, propping up her pillow so she could rest against the headboard. She hadn't planned on leaving her bed for most of the afternoon, much less her condo. Yet, maybe spending time with her friends would help shake her frustration.

We just got back. I'll be over in a little while.

She slid down, pulling the pillow flat onto the mattress. She could take a fifteen-minute nap and still get there before Shanna started checking on her. Her eyes closed, but her mind was wide awake. Pushing herself upright again, she resolved to go to bed early that night. The morning yoga class the following day was going to be torture.

She froze at this thought. She loved yoga. It had brought her happiness and purpose. Sure, she didn't enjoy getting up early, especially after a long weekend. Still, the excitement of leading a class and working toward the goal of teaching yoga full-time should have more than made up for that.

Truth be told, she never quite felt the fulfillment she'd hoped for in the morning class. She took pride in the progress some of the attendees had made. She enjoyed creating new sequences and the added benefit of starting her day off with a little boost of energy. Even with all those positives, something still seemed to be lacking. It didn't provide any spark. No greater sense of peace or belonging or anything else she'd expected to bring the purpose and happiness Angelle had advised her to find.

Sighing as her feet hit the floor, she knew she couldn't keep avoiding the doubts creeping in her mind about this new career she'd chosen. She'd been so certain of the signs all pointing to yoga. Now it felt like she had grasped at anything that gave her a new start.

Why couldn't she just bake for fun without worrying about the business side of things? That would solve all her problems. She could sleep in and bake when she wanted. She'd have peace and keep that bond with Angelle alive. She'd also have no money.

She made her way to the bathroom to fix her hair. Her eyes lifted to the ceiling. "You know, it'd be great if you could give me some guidance, some sort of sign to make this easier." Hoping for her sister's response but knowing she wouldn't get one, she pulled out her hair tie and reformed the messy bun on top of her head.

The smell of onions and jalapeños stung Brila's nostrils as she entered Shanna and Tony's house twenty minutes later. Her stomach grumbled, reminding her that she hadn't eaten since the night before. After greeting the couple and Tony's younger brother, Jorge, she placed a handful of tortilla chips on a plate and poured the salsa over the top before claiming the seat next to Shanna at the table.

Tony walked up and rubbed his hand along Shanna's back. "Where's D.T.? I was going to have him help with the grilling."

Brila's eyes scanned the room. "He's ... still recovering from last night."

"Have your brother help you," Shanna offered, smiling up at him.

"Yeah," he sighed. "I just thought D.T. was coming. He kissed her forehead and walked away.

Shanna leaned in and whispered, "What happened?"

With tears welling in her eyes, Brila breathed slowly, unable to speak.

Shanna grabbed her hand and pulled her onto the patio then toward the corner of the house where no one could see through the windows. "What's going on?"

"It was like some stupid frat party all weekend long. I mean, I'm all for having a few drinks and getting carried away once in a while, but we're not in college anymore. Who still wants to binge drink and get blackout drunk all weekend? I didn't have to be there. Why did he insist on bringing me? The whole thing was stupid. Then, of course, he was hungover, so I had to drive back while he slept the whole time. I'm just over it, but we can't talk about it like a normal couple because he doesn't think he did anything wrong, and I'm an idiot if I suggest otherwise." Brila folded her arms. Her tears retreated as her anger returned. Yet, it felt like a weight had lifted off her chest just by voicing her thoughts to someone who could rationally understand the situation.

"Sounds like an exciting weekend." Shanna raised her eyebrows. "I wish you would have stayed here. When Tony's family found out we didn't have plans for the Fourth, they invited us over. And now it's been something every day. Don't get me wrong, I love *la familia*, but they're better in small doses." She let out a quiet laugh. "I shouldn't complain. At least it wasn't a bro weekend."

Brila cracked a smile. "Go ahead. Rub it in." She looked toward the house, thinking she heard the door open. When no one appeared, she continued. "And you still can't pull that off."

"Now you're just being mean." Shanna jutted out her lower lip. It quickly pulled back in as her eyes lit up. "Maybe it's time for another girls' trip."

"That sounds like a great idea." Brila's shoulders relaxed. For the first time that day, she felt like herself again.

"Good news," Tony called from the patio door. "I texted D.T., and he said he's good. He'll be here soon."

Brila's eyes shifted between Tony and Shanna. "Oh, okay." It was all she could manage to sputter as her heart sank.

Shanna walked toward Tony. She whispered to him, and he looked at Brila.

"Do you want me to text him back and tell him never mind?" he called over to her.

That would have just caused a bigger fight. She couldn't keep him from being there. She was capable of not starting another argument. "You don't need to do that."

He looked back to Shanna, who shrugged, and retreated into the house.

Shanna returned to Brila. "Are you sure? We could come up with something."

Brila shook her head. "We're all adults. It'll be fine." She looked out to the yard. "Besides, he'll probably stroll in here like nothing's wrong. And I can pretend that's true."

As she predicted, D.T. arrived ten minutes later with a wide smile, shaking hands with the guys before hugging Shanna and pulling Brila in to kiss her cheek. "Why didn't you tell me we were invited over here?"

She stepped back. "I figured you needed your rest after last night and didn't want to bother you."

He dismissed this excuse with a wave of his hand. "You're not giving me enough credit. I feel great."

"Yeah, well, you still should've stayed home," she said under her breath.

His eyes bored into her as his jaw tightened.

"D.T., come help us with the grill," Tony called out before he could respond.

Brila watched him walk away with Tony and Jorge. He could've been on the verge of vomiting and still convinced everyone he felt great. He did look like his normal self. Maybe he'd rebounded. It didn't matter. She still didn't want him there. The sting of his actions throughout the weekend hadn't faded and, more importantly, a deeper issue had surfaced. Her stomach knotted at the thought of confronting him.

TWENTY-ONE

The following Saturday, Brila was baking vanilla cupcakes for a baby gender reveal party. The mother-to-be was Cameron's sister, Janae. Apparently, she had been keeping a secret at the wedding and had been rather convincing with her champagne flute of sparkling cider. While she had trusted Cameron to give Brila the envelope from the doctor, she had also given him strict instructions to not look. Of course, that didn't stop him from sticking around to watch Brila bake.

"Okay, you have to leave now." She smiled as she measured the powdered sugar for the frosting. "I need to make the filling and add the sprinkles for the reveal cupcake."

"Oh, come on. I can keep a secret for one day." He surveyed the counter and open pantry for clues. Unfortunately for him, she had set out both pink and blue food coloring and sprinkles.

"No, sir. What the mama says goes. And I'm not going to have your whole family mad at me for letting you find out first."

He folded his arms with a smirk. "Well, I can't argue with that. Why don't I go pick up some supper? I know you're not going to cook after baking all night."

She looked at the clock: 7:11 p.m. "I am getting hungry, and I guess that should give me enough time to finish before you get back."

"Great! What are you hungry for?"

She thought for a moment. "I don't know. Get me a salad or a chicken sandwich from somewhere on the other side of town."

"Yeah, okay." He walked out the door, then quickly pushed it back open in an attempt to catch her selection.

"Get out!" she laughed.

After the door closed, she looked back to the clock, just in time to see the minute tick up. It had been the seventh time she had seen the eleventh minute of the hour that day. "I see you." She looked from the clock to the ceiling. "I don't know what you're trying to tell me, but I'm listening." She soaked in the silence, hoping to hear something, feel something. Her eyes scanned the room. Nothing.

She inhaled deeply and scooped out a third of the frosting and set it aside. Using a paring knife, she carved a chunk out of the mini cake she had made for the reveal. She filled it with a variety of pink sprinkles. A smile spread across her face as she cut the chunk in half and placed the top half back on the cake to cover the surprise filling.

After returning both the pink and blue sprinkles to the pantry, she grabbed the bottle of pink food coloring. The spinning paddle blending the drops of color into the white frosting was mesmerizing. As it turned bubble gum pink, a strange ache grew in her stomach. It rose into her chest, and her throat began to tighten.

Then it hit her. It was July eleventh. Her due date. Or what would have been her due date. She managed to turn off the mixer before collapsing to the floor. Tears rolled down her cheeks and spilled into her hands, which were cupped around her face.

How different would her life have been as she prepared to welcome a little girl or boy of her own into the world? Would D.T. still be around? What would she have done after being let go from Southern? Who would have wanted to hire someone who was about to go on maternity leave?

Her arms wrapped around her stomach, which suddenly felt impossibly small and empty. A beautiful, tiny person should have been inside. Her chest rose and fell with each short breath. Her quiet condo, which had just been filled with laughter minutes earlier, now felt desolate.

Her mind went back to that dark day in November. She had still been coping with the reality of her pregnancy when a cramping pain in her abdomen started after lunch. D.T. had left the day before for a work trip, she wasn't ready to tell her family, and she didn't want to upset Shanna, so she had gone to the doctor on her own. While she was concerned, she had convinced herself that there'd be a reasonable explanation for the pain and bleeding, and it would be fine.

When the doctor told her that she had miscarried, she sat in stunned silence. A part of her was relieved. She wasn't ready to be a mom. But guilt for even thinking that pushed it away, and a deep sadness swept over her almost immediately. She had held life inside her and couldn't even do that right. Had she subconsciously caused the miscarriage because she hadn't been excited about being pregnant? Her thoughts shifted momentarily to Shanna, as she had a small glimpse into the suffering her friend had experienced for years. A roller coaster of emotions continued to bombard her that afternoon before she finally called Angelle to confess everything.

Angelle listened to every detail without interruption or judgment. She let her cry instead of trying to fill the void. And when it was her turn to contribute, she offered support with "these things happen without explanation" and "it's understandable to not know how you feel" and "one day you will heal from this." Finally, she told Brila that she had just finished baking and offered to come over to be with her. Brila insisted that she stay home, although she secretly longed to have someone with her so she wouldn't feel so alone.

Now, as the loss set in again, another thought weighed on her heart. The truth she couldn't shake no matter how hard she'd tried. If she hadn't miscarried, not only would she have a baby she'd also have her sister. There would have been no reason for Angelle to come visit, no reason for her to be on the road that night.

She could tell herself that God had called her sister to heaven, that it would have happened whether or not they had talked that night. These empty phrases of reassurance and the similar sentiments she received from her parents, friends, and therapist would never take away the what-ifs that loomed in the back of her mind. After all, she had still been the one texting her sister when she had gone off the road.

With her head resting on her knees and her arms still hugging her stomach, she sniffled and tried to gain control of her emotions. She could have her breakdown after she finished the cupcakes.

It was like she was watching a video of herself, just out of reach to do anything about it, so she remained helpless on the floor. Her thoughts continued to spiral around the baby she should be holding and its aunt—how they were both torn away from her in one wretched night.

"What's going on?" Cameron's voice and the touch of his hands on her shoulders startled her. His face was blurred through the tears as he knelt in front of her.

"I ... it's just ..." She couldn't tell him the real reason she was sobbing on the floor. She couldn't explain how this day would now be another on her list of difficult days or how decorating pink and blue cupcakes now seemed like an impossible task.

"Memories of Angelle?" Cameron offered.

She nodded. He was partially right. She dragged her index fingers under her eyes to pull away the tears that had slowed to a trickle. She looked to the floor, suddenly aware of how she must look with puffy eyes and a puddle of tears smeared across her face and hands. "Sorry. It just hit me out of nowhere."

"Hey," he waited for her to look up, "you never need to apologize for how you feel."

She locked eyes with him, finding gold specks and one dark freckle splattered in their sea of brown. Her breathing eased as she scrunched her eyebrows. "Tell me you didn't look at the counter."

He twisted his body and sat next to her. "It was a little hard to miss when I was trying to find you, but I promise I won't say anything."

"You better not. I'd never hear the end of it."

"I've already forgotten." He nudged her shoulder with his. "Do we need to finish them first, or can it wait until we eat?"

She gave it some thought as she attempted to dry her face again. "We can eat. I just need to cover the frosting first." Her stomach rumbled in agreement.

Cameron stood and grabbed her hands to help her up.

She hugged him tightly, breathing in the sweet scent of his cologne. "Thank you," she whispered before slowly pulling away. She would have stayed on the kitchen floor all night if he hadn't been there. She pressed plastic wrap over both bowls of frosting. "I'm going to fix myself up. Go ahead and start eating."

"You don't need to do that." He opened the cabinet to the right of her sink to grab a paper plate.

"I do. I'll be right back."

The drying tears that streaked along her cheeks and jaw were a reminder of what that day now meant, and for the moment, she wanted to forget so she could make it through the evening without another breakdown. She leaned over the bathroom sink, cupped water in her hands, and rubbed it over her face. The eyes reflecting in the mirror were red and puffy. Her skin was blotchy and void of the makeup she normally wore. She looked like she hadn't slept in two days. She pulled the hand towel from its hook and sighed as she dried her face.

Cameron stood by the table, reading his phone when she returned.

"I told you to eat without me." She forced a slight smile as he pulled out a chair for her before sitting down. "Seriously. I'm not broken. You don't need to take care of me."

"I'm not taking care of you." He read his phone for another moment then locked it and set it on the table. "You know this is ingrained in me."

It was true. Even in high school, he would pull out chairs, open doors, and help others as often as he could. His parents had run a tight ship and ensured he and Janae were raised to treat others with the utmost respect.

"Fine." She took the lid off her salad and poured the Italian dressing over it.

Cameron bit into his chicken sandwich. "I was looking online, and I think I get how you fill cupcakes. So I can help if you want. You know, to help you finish faster. I just can't decorate the tops. I don't want to ruin your reputation." He grinned.

"If I tell you no, will it stop you?" She asked between bites.

He pursed his lips as if he were giving it thought. "I don't think so. I mean, I did the research. I have to do it now."

As much as she wanted to push back and insist on doing it herself, the idea of working with someone else in the kitchen again was comforting.

After cleaning up from supper, Brila scooped half of the pink frosting into a piping bag and filled the center of a cupcake. She showed Cameron how to hold the bag, squeeze the frosting, and twist the top as it went down. She handed him the bag and held his hand to guide him and ensure he didn't break through the bottom of the cupcake or overfill it. She watched him do three others on his own and then used a spatula to add blue food coloring to the smaller bowl of frosting and mix it until it was the perfect shade of baby blue. She carefully filled a second piping bag by placing pink frosting on one side and blue on the other.

Once Cameron had the first dozen cupcakes filled, she took the tray and began piping large roses on top. While waiting for him to finish the second dozen, she covered the mini cake with the same roses then stood back and analyzed her work. The pink and blue twisted and blended together perfectly. She made a mental note to play with multicolor piping the next time she had extra frosting.

Finishing, Cameron laid the bag down and rubbed his wrist as he watched her finish. "I didn't even know you could do that. They look great."

"It's not that different from single color piping." Even as she said it, a warmth of pride swelled in her chest.

On a night that could have ended with numbing depression, being able to create something so beautiful for Janae and her husband to celebrate the new life they had created comforted her.

TWENTY-TWO

Two weeks later, Brila was at D.T.'s after work. These visits had become the norm at the start of the week since she had spent most of her Thursdays and Fridays baking and decorating. With his house being closer to Halltown, she also liked having the shorter commute to recoup before heading home later in the night.

"I don't know how much longer I can take this." Brila sunk into the couch. "These women are impossible." Her coworkers hadn't gotten any friendlier in her time with the company. To make matters worse, they were all focused solely on promoting their own work in hopes of advancement rather than working as a team. "I was working on a publication, and they actually gave me wrong information about the union. So when I turned it in, I looked like an ass." She sighed. "I didn't know we were still in high school."

D.T. laughed. "Should've checked your own facts."

Of course he had no sympathy for her. He was just like them, willing to throw his own team under the bus in order to get ahead.

She had noticed the cutthroat mentality was prevalent throughout the company. It made her stomach churn. "I don't get it. What is so difficult about being a decent human being? I'm not even a threat. I'm the newest one there, and I still don't know what I'm doing half the time. I'm not trying to get promoted. I just want to do my job until I can afford to do something else."

D.T. narrowed his eyes. "What's that supposed to mean?"

She held his gaze, deciding whether or not he was really that clueless. "It's not like this is my career. I'm grateful you helped me get this job when I needed it, but eventually, I'll find something I actually want to do."

"What's wrong with doing this?"

"Besides the high school B.S. I just mentioned? I don't enjoy the work I do or the people I work with. It's draining. I want it to mean something more than just getting by."

"You're influencing the public opinion of the company. That seems pretty meaningful to me."

"I don't understand why you care if I stay at Halltown or not. Don't you want me to do something that makes me happy?"

He walked into the kitchen and grabbed a beer from the fridge. "I do, but why can't you be happy where you are? It's like you're never satisfied with what you have."

She pulled her head back in confusion. "That's not true. But I'm also not going to settle, especially now."

"I get it. Losing your sister changed everything. Rearranged your priorities. But what if you're where you're supposed to be, and you're too worried about finding the next big thing to realize it? When's enough, enough?"

She took a deep breath. "Don't put this on Angelle or her accident. Yeah, everything changed after that night. But it doesn't change who I am at the core. I'm just trying to be true to who I am, even more so now. And I know doing this doesn't feel right. It's draining all my energy. I'm ready for something else."

"You can never be happy, can you?" He stood in front of her.

She felt her face warm. "I was perfectly happy at Southern until they took my job away."

"No you weren't. You were considering other jobs in your department before the budget cuts were announced."

"I wasn't looking because I was unhappy. I thought it'd be nice to branch out and learn more about other areas. You know, when I thought I'd be there for a while." She folded her arms.

How dare he question her, like she was incapable of holding a job? What was so wrong about wanting to find something more fitting? She never should have let herself get sucked into doing that interview. But what other choice did she have at the time? She needed a job and still did.

"I still don't know why you even care."

"I put my reputation on the line for you." He began to pace in front of the couch. "I told them you were perfect for the job and the company long-term. And now you want to walk away after a couple of months? It's going to look like I'm screwing them over."

"You're the one that pushed so hard for me to take this job when I wasn't sure. And you knew it wasn't my plan to stay long-term. If you made those promises to the company, that's on you. But I still don't get why you think my leaving will have any impact on the company or your reputation. If I find something better that fits what I want to do, who cares? They'll probably have a replacement for me before I walk out the door."

D.T. took another drink and sighed. "It's going to look like I did it just to get the referral bonus."

Brila squinted, unsure she heard him correctly. "You got a bonus for referring me?" His silence was all the confirmation she needed. "And you weren't going to tell me about it? What the hell is that about?"

"I used the money on our Galveston trip. What does it matter?"

"Oh, you mean the trip where you spent all weekend with your boys?" She stood and brushed past him. "I might as well have not been there. So great. Thanks." She slid her feet into her shoes and grabbed her purse. "So sorry you think your stupid bonus and reputation are on the line. Excuse me for wanting to be happy for once in my damn life. Especially after everything I've been through. But I guess it's too much to ask you to give a shit."

"Don't you think you're overreacting?"

"No." She yanked the front door open and slammed it behind her.

She huffed as she stomped to her car. As she started the ignition, 6:11 p.m. illuminated on the dash. "Dammit. I know you're not showing up right now to take his side. I'm not the one who's wrong here."

Turning left out of D.T.'s neighborhood, she rolled her eyes. Now she was arguing with a number on a display screen. The same number, that stupid eleven, popped up multiple times a day and stopped her in her tracks each time. She had convinced herself it was Angelle, certain that her acknowledgment would make it stop or somehow all make sense, but that never happened.

Maybe it was God or a guardian angel or some sort of karma-driven sign from the universe. The more she tried to figure it out, the more confused she became. Whatever it was, it had her attention. If only it would be a little clearer on why it insisted on pestering her. Maybe it was nothing but a coincidence. But if that's all it was, why did it feel like something more? Why did it surge through her veins and shake her to the core?

Music reverberated inside her car. She told herself she wanted to forget what he'd said. She tried to sing along with the music as she turned it up another notch.

Who did he think he was? He didn't have any right to tell her what she should do. Why should she stick with a job just because he wanted her to? Everyone else had been supportive. Why couldn't he? He's the one who should be there by her side no matter what. Maybe he wasn't the person she thought he was.

She snorted. He hadn't changed. He was exactly the same as the day she had met him. She had changed. It wasn't just the miscarriage or losing Angelle. She had been in the process of finding herself when they'd started dating. She had grown as a person. Her goals and desires were in flux. His were firmly set on advancing his career and finding the next adventure. As much as Brila hoped he'd want to get married and start a family, it didn't seem to be anywhere on his radar.

As the next song started, she tried again to clear her mind. She practically shouted the love ballad lyrics. Turning onto her street, tears began to fill her eyes, threatening to spill over. She inhaled deeply, pushed them away, and mentally scanned the inside of her fridge. There was nothing appealing but enough lettuce and leftover chicken to avoid a drive-thru.

After putting the car in park, she debated calling Shanna. She scrolled through her recent call list while walking to her condo. Unlocking the door, she closed her phone. She didn't need to bother her with this. To be honest, Brila didn't want to be bothered with it herself. This was something bigger than an argument, and she didn't have the energy to deal with it.

It took D.T. two days to contact her. And he had the audacity to do it through instant messenger at work.

Is the group still going out Friday night?

No apology. No sense of regret. Of course not.

He could've asked Tony. Instead, he chose to ask her. As if nothing was wrong. Like she hadn't stormed out of his house. Like their entire relationship wasn't hanging by a thread. She rested her chin in the palm of her hand. It wasn't worth dignifying with a response.

She had spent the past two days agonizing over their last conversation and scrutinizing every detail of their relationship. Time spent crying and screaming into pillows. Wishing to be in his arms and wanting to pound his chest in anger, back and forth and back again.

They needed to sit down and talk about where they stood and where things were going. She needed to know he supported her dreams and could commit to a long-term future with her. Still, she expected him to have some sort of empathy toward what she had felt that Monday. Given his message, there didn't seem to be much hope for that.

She texted Shanna instead.

> Do you know if Tony's heard from D.T. lately?

She minimized his message and continued proofreading her latest statement.

> Not that I know of
> > He just messaged me asking about Friday.
> > Who does that?

Her shoulders pulled toward her ears.

> You can lie and tell him no. How many orders do you have this week?
> > None. Surprisingly. I don't know why he has to ask me.

She folded her arms and sat back in her chair.

Because you're his girlfriend. Maybe that's his
way of apologizing

Well it's bullshit.

True but you still have to talk to him

Brila sighed. Shanna's honesty was admirable, but couldn't she
occasionally let her make poor and irrational decisions? Couldn't
she allow her to stew in her anger without suggesting reasonable
alternatives? She reopened the conversation with D.T. and
responded.

Is it okay if I stop by after work?

She rested her elbows on the edge of her desk while waiting for
a response. His status showed he was available. Maybe he was
talking with a coworker, hopefully not about her. She scanned
through her emails but didn't actually read any of them. Instead, her
mind conjured up potential responses from D.T.

Ten minutes later, the message flickered on her screen.

Sure. You know you can always come over.

Was he oblivious to how upset she had been, or did he just want
to move past it? Maybe Shanna was right, and this was the best
apology he could muster. Maybe they'd be able to hash it out and
move forward.

TWENTY-THREE

Brila pulled up to D.T.'s house shortly after five o'clock. She put the car in park but didn't turn off the ignition. Gripping the steering wheel with both hands, she inhaled deeply. Two young girls were running through a sprinkler three houses down. A smile crept up as she watched them. She and Angelle had spent many summer afternoons in sprinklers, small inflatable pools, and even a makeshift slip 'n' slide their dad had rigged together. If it involved water, they had been all about it.

She took another deep breath and turned off the car and opened her door. The sidewalk to his front stoop felt like it was a mile long, yet when she arrived, she wished it had been longer. She raised her hand to knock, but the door opened before she could make contact.

D.T. leaned in to kiss her as she stepped inside. She turned her head to the left for him to kiss her cheek instead of her lips. Whether it was an apology or ignorance of the situation, she wasn't ready to receive or return his affection.

Her heart pounded as she slipped off her shoes, dropped her purse, and made her way to the couch.

"Want a drink?" D.T. held the refrigerator door open.

"I'm good," she answered reluctantly. A drink or two would have helped calm her nerves, but it also could've led her to say words she didn't mean or cause her mind to wander from the matter at hand. She needed to stay focused.

He joined her on the couch a moment later, beer in hand. "So, what did you want to do tonight?"

Brila furrowed her brow. "I came over so we could talk."

"About what?" His head cocked to the side, like a puppy trying to comprehend its owner's words.

" 'About what?' Are you serious?" She threw her hands in the air and rested them on top of her head. "Was I the only one in this room two nights ago? Maybe I was just the only one in the conversation." So much for staying calm.

"Wait. You're still upset about that?"

An exasperated laugh escaped her mouth. "Of course I'm still mad. And I have every right to be."

"Is it about the bonus? I'll give you the money if it means that much to you."

She stood and paced in front of him. She clenched her jaw, fighting the urge to scream at him. "This isn't about the damn money. It's about you caring more about your reputation and your idea of success than my happiness." Her arms folded as she gave him a chance to respond.

"That's not true." He took a drink, still relaxed on the couch. "Why would you think that?"

"Because that's all you talk about whenever I mention finding another job or starting my own business."

"I never said I don't support you. But have you really thought those things through?"

"Did it ever occur to you that I have thought about it? A lot. That when I say I'm not happy and don't want to stay in this job, I mean it. I'm not just whining or being difficult. Just because this company and the fistfight to the top of the ladder is your idea of fun, doesn't mean it's what I want."

"Fine. But do you really think you're going to be happy baking for the rest of your life? And will it be enough to support yourself?" He took another drink and then held his beer bottle on the armrest.

"You know what? I'll figure it out if it comes to it. I can still bake part-time until I can build up the business and, if I ever decide it's no longer what I want, I'll find something else. It's just something that I feel in my gut I have to do. For myself. For Angelle. I've tried to ignore it, but it keeps coming back." She sat back on the couch; her arms remained crossed in front of her chest.

She hadn't admitted to anyone that she had started contemplating how to go about turning her baking into a side business. She'd hoped to have the details ironed out before telling anyone, but she couldn't take it back now. It was probably for the best. If they were going to have this conversation, everything needed to be out in the open.

"If you say so." He chuckled a bit. "But the connection to Angelle doesn't mean you should give up a good job for it. You can bake and reminisce about your sister anytime you want without turning it into a business."

"It's not just the connection. It was her dream, and now it's mine. Why can't you see that I want to do this, and all I'm asking is for you to stop criticizing me."

"I'm just having a hard time seeing how this will work for you."

"You really can't say anything positive?"

"Your cupcakes are good, but there are a hundred bakeries in the city. It's not like you do anything they don't do."

"Great. Thanks." She sighed.

He stood and walked to the kitchen. "So are you staying for supper?"

She stared at the floor; the tightness from her jaw moved to her ears and a lump lodged in her throat. "This isn't going to work." Her words were barely audible.

D.T. peered around the pantry door. "What do you mean?"

She stood and turned toward the kitchen. "This. Us. You not supporting me and thinking you're never wrong."

"Whoa. Calm down. You're going to throw away our whole relationship over one disagreement?"

"Having you in my corner is a big deal. Even if you don't think so. Even if you don't understand it. Just be encouraging instead of telling me all the ways I could fail. And it's not just this. Every time we have a disagreement or difference in opinion, you can't even consider my side. If I dare question you, I'm just an idiot. I'm so tired of you doing what you want, when you want, then questioning my thoughts and actions. I'm tired of being the only one who puts effort into this relationship. What are we even doing?"

"I thought we were having a good time together. I thought we had something special. But now you want to walk away like it's meant nothing."

"This isn't easy for me!" her voice cracked. Her heart twisted in her chest. How had it come to this? "Do you know how much I've agonized over this? How many times I've tried to talk to you about it, and you just dismiss me for overreacting? It's exhausting. It's clear you're not going to change, so why keep this up? I can't do it anymore."

"So that's it? It's coming down to this?" He slammed his beer on the counter. "Fine. Go. You'll realize you've made a mistake before you get home."

She walked toward the door, tears welling in her eyes. "All I asked was for you to put aside your idea of what's important and try to care about what I want. And you can't even do that."

D.T. opened the door and leaned against it. "Yeah, I'm the jerk here. Whatever you want to tell yourself. Sounds like you were just looking for any excuse to walk away, and this is it."

She gasped. "I can't believe you just said that. That's really how you want to leave things?"

"You're not denying it."

"I have let these things go for so long. I'm finally standing up for myself, and you still don't want to hear me."

"Whatever you want to tell yourself. Good luck with the cupcake thing. I'm sure it won't be a complete failure."

She stepped outside and turned back. "Thanks for the—" the door slammed in her face, "vote of confidence." Tears rolled onto her cheeks as she walked to her car. How could someone who claimed to love her be so against her following her heart?

Staring at the now empty yards down the street, she already knew the answer. She had held on longer than she should have. Because she'd held out hope for who she wanted him to be. Because she thought conceiving a child with him meant they had a deeper connection worth holding on to. Because after losing their unborn child and her sister, the thought of losing him too had been unbearable.

Those reasons were no longer enough. She deserved more. She had enough self-doubt. She didn't need someone who supposedly loved her also questioning her every move. If only Angelle were around to give her the boost of confidence she needed.

She started the ignition. One hundred eleven miles to E illuminated on the dashboard. A smile pushed up her cheeks as she dried her tears and shifted into drive.

TWENTY-FOUR

Once she was home, Brila texted Shanna.

> It's over. Mr. Can't Do Wrong had no clue what the problem was. He actually thought he was helping. He couldn't even say one supportive thing without being an ass. Why did you let me stay with someone like that for so long?

She changed out of her work clothes. As she pulled a tank top over her head, her phone chimed. Before she could pick it up, it started ringing.

"I know you're not blaming me," Shanna started before Brila could say anything. "You're a grown woman capable of making her own relationship decisions. No matter how many times I questioned his commitment to you."

Brila huffed, unable to disagree. "You could've told me how stupid I was a few more times. Maybe eventually I would've listened."

"We both know that's not true. Besides, you were happy most of the time." There was a short pause. "But you shine like the sun. You deserve someone who's willing to get burned standing in your light, not someone who will try to eclipse it."

A warmth filled her chest. She needed that kind of love. Everyone deserved that kind of support. She was so blessed to have Shanna in her life.

"That's by far the sweetest thing anyone's ever said to me. Do you think Tony would mind sharing you? I get all the talk and cuddles. He can keep all the sex."

"I thought that was our arrangement. I'm pretty sure it's in our vows somewhere."

Brila laughed as she searched her kitchen for something to eat. "Good. So I didn't just make a huge mistake?"

She grabbed salmon and green beans from the fridge and then wrestled a baking sheet from the cabinet next to the stove.

Shanna waited for the clatter to stop. "The only mistake was giving him so many chances. You know you deserve better, and when the right one comes along, you'll notice the difference immediately."

Brila smiled as she tore two sheets of aluminum foil. "I hope you're right, but I can't even start thinking about dating again. I have plenty of other things to worry about right now."

"Yeah, take some time for yourself. It'll come together when you're ready. So what's for supper?"

"Salmon and green beans." She laid the green beans on each sheet of foil, placed a salmon fillet on top of each pile, then turned to the fridge to find the garlic butter.

"Sounds great. I have a meatloaf in the oven. Actually, it's probably about done."

"I'll let you go. I'd hate to ruin your meal and have Tony mad at me," she chuckled.

"Oh, he'll be just fine."

"Well, thanks for the talk and helping me feel a little better." She wrapped the foil into little packets around the green beans and salmon, placed them on the baking sheet, and put it in the oven. At least she wouldn't have to worry about what to make for supper the next night. She really should consider doing more meal prep to save time throughout the week.

"I'm always here for you. And good luck with seeing D.T. at work. Hopefully, that isn't a complete disaster. Let's do lunch later in the week."

Shanna's words stuck with her after she ended the call. Sharing the same employer wasn't ideal for a breakup. Luckily, they sat on different floors and in different parts of the building. Running into him in the halls would likely happen even less, now that she'd be trying to avoid him. It gave her additional motivation to get out of there as soon as possible. Seeing him would be uncomfortable but not unbearable. The company gossip would be much worse.

After changing her clothes, she slumped onto the couch. Her phone illuminated as she lifted it to check the time. The picture of her and D.T. from their first kayak trip together stared back at her. She had made it her lock screen picture after their Fourth of July argument, her one-sided argument, to remind her of the joy and simplicity of the early days in their relationship.

Had it really come down to this? After all the ups and downs, after all the disagreements and insecurities she faced in their relationship, she never expected to walk away. And for D.T. to accuse her of looking for any excuse to leave, to let her go without a fight. Didn't he think they were worth fighting for? Was she not worth fighting for?

She opened her text messages to read their recent exchange. Maybe he never really loved her but, rather, loved the idea of having someone to spend time with. What would have happened if she'd pressed the issue of marriage? What if she had told him about her pregnancy and miscarriage? Would he have stayed and committed to her or would he have been the one to walk away? Both options made her uneasy. Not that it mattered anymore.

When her meal finished cooking, she unwrapped the packets, transferring one to a plate and leaving the other one to cool.

She ate in silence. No TV, no music, just her thoughts. She had chosen to end the relationship. She had decided she needed something more, someone who could support her, lift her up, and have respectful conversations and disagreements. So why did it feel like he had broken up with her?

She sighed as she jabbed her fork into a green bean. After all they had been through, she had still held out hope that he could put aside his narrow-minded vision of what a career path should be and care about what she wanted.

As she finished supper, she craved something more, although she had eaten plenty. She placed her plate and fork in the dishwasher, transferred the second packet of food to a container, then grabbed the leftover frosting sitting in the corner and a spoon.

This was a cupcake moment, but she had no desire to make them. She needed her sister to lean on as she ate two too many cupcakes and let all the irrational thoughts in her mind spill out of her mouth. Would she ever stop craving those things? Could she learn to rely on herself? Even more unfathomable, could she find someone else who would be there like Angelle had always been? As much as she loved her parents and Shanna, as much as they supported her unconditionally, going to them would never be the same. No, there was no replacing Angelle's place in her heart, but perhaps she had enough love in her life to make the void a little more manageable.

TWENTY-FIVE

The following Sunday, Brila went to her parents' house for brunch. When she'd started college, their family made a point to get together for a big meal once a month. After Angelle's accident, though, their tradition of eating, visiting, and playful ribbing had been clouded with an incessant reminder that they were no longer whole.

In the past four months, Brila had made excuse after excuse to miss brunch. It was no longer the same. However, with the breakup still a fresh wound in her heart, she welcomed the comfort of home and her parents.

Her dad greeted her at the front door, wrapping his arm around her shoulders. He kissed the top of her head. "He was a bum, anyway." He closed the door behind her. "He never deserved you in the first place."

"You said he was like the son you never had. And you don't even know what happened. I could've been cheating on him. I could've broken up with him for no reason."

"Oh, I just said that to make him feel like part of the family. And it doesn't matter what happened. If he didn't make you happy, he wasn't worth keeping around."

She smiled and hugged him. "Thanks, Dad."

They followed the scent of cinnamon to join Lyla in the kitchen.

She wiped her hands on a navy blue towel on the counter and hugged her daughter. "Your dad's right. He didn't deserve you."

Brila's cheeks warmed. Deep in her heart, she knew they were right. After all, she had broken up with D.T. because she believed she deserved someone more supportive and more understanding of her feelings. However, so much had felt right with him. She had been sure they would get married one day, even if he never wanted to talk about it.

If she'd been wrong about D.T., how would she know when she did find the right one? Maybe it wasn't a matter of finding the right one, but being content with right enough.

Her mom pulled the cinnamon rolls from the oven, flipped the hash browns in their pan on the stovetop, and then returned to the island to slice the strawberries. "So, tell me what happened."

She sighed, afraid the reason for ending their relationship would sound trivial. She could lie, say that he cheated or talked down to her, but only the truth found its way to her lips. "I just realized that he was never going to care about me, my feelings, or my dreams the way I need him to." She looked up from the counter to her parents who were studying her face. "I know. It probably sounds stupid. I guess I just stopped being able to see a future with him in it."

Her parents looked at one another and then back to her. Lyla spoke first. "You need someone who will be there for you no matter what. If he can't do that, you were right to let him go."

"Yeah, good riddance to him," Brian chimed in.

Brila forced a smile. "I guess. I just feel a little lost. After two years, I thought I knew him better. I thought we were in a different place. It's like I don't know who I am or what to do with myself now."

Lyla scooped the strawberry tops into the garbage can and turned back to her. "Maybe you've changed and he hasn't. And there's nothing wrong with that. I've seen you become more confident and happier than I've seen you in a long time. If he's not willing to embrace that and support you, you're right in thinking he's not meant to be in this next chapter of your life."

Her stomach fluttered. Had she really changed enough for her mom to notice? She didn't feel much different. Perhaps there was some validity in what she believed had been missing from her relationship with D.T., after all.

Brila moved around the island to the stovetop, where she used a spatula to push the hash browns around. Grabbing a butter knife out of the drawer, she spread icing over the tops of the cinnamon rolls. When she was done, she made a mental note of which one had the most icing as she licked what was left on the knife.

"That's a good way to cut your tongue." Her mom's narrowed eyes pleaded for her to stop.

Brila glanced at her dad, who turned to hide his smirk. "I've been doing this since I was five. When we were little, Dad would use two knives just so Angelle and I could both have one."

Lyla's glare refocused on her husband, but she was losing the battle with the smile she tried to hide. "Just because your dad allowed it, doesn't make it any safer."

"It's not like I gave them steak knives to play with," Brian defended himself. "That came when they were teenagers and wouldn't stop bickering."

Laughter swirled around the kitchen but faded as the absence of Angelle's belly laugh sucked the air out of the room.

An ache wiggled through Brila's chest as she attempted to revive the moment. "Okay, I'm picking up the very dangerous butter knife." She dropped it in the sink as she eyed the cinnamon rolls. "Is it time to eat yet?"

Her dad handed her a plate. "Everything looks ready to me."

Lyla shot another look at her husband. "Excuse me. I did the cooking. I'll say when it's time to eat." She snatched the plate from his hands and set it on the far side of the counter, grinning as she placed the roll with the second-most icing on her own plate.

Brila reached over her mom's shoulder and grabbed the one she had dedicated to herself moments earlier.

Brian filled three champagne flutes with mimosas and set them on the table before reclaiming his plate. Having a table for six may have been odd for a couple with no children living at home and who rarely hosted company, but it was more comforting than a table that seated four. Three empty seats for others who hadn't shown up for the party were better than one empty seat for a family member who would never join them for another meal. They ate and made small talk because it was all they could do to suppress the pain in their hearts.

"So tell us about this dream you're chasing after." Lyla smiled at her daughter as she broke apart her gravy-covered biscuit with the side of her fork. "Do you really want to bake for a living?"

It had never been her dream. Angelle had tried convincing her it would be their retirement plan, but Brila had never seriously considered it—before or after the accident. Yet, the more she baked cupcakes for others, the more she enjoyed it and the more this dream burrowed into her heart.

She shrugged her shoulders. "I know it sounds crazy. It's not like I have any sort of training or experience. And I can't say with any certainty that it's what I want to do for the rest of my life. But it feels right, right now."

"What's your business plan?" Brian asked through a mouthful of food.

She stared back at him. "Like what?"

He and Lyla exchanged a look. "If you're going to start your own business, you need to have a business plan, especially if you're going to take out a loan."

"What do I need? Just what I plan to sell, the name, and all? I know I only want to do cupcakes. And I've started working on costs and pricing."

Brian nodded. "That's a start. You'll also need to figure out where you'll operate your business, which permits and licenses you'll need, how you're going to differentiate yourself, what kind of clientele you plan to target, what kind of competition is already out there, how you're going to market your business beyond your family and friends ..."

Brila's pounding heartbeat drowned out his never-ending list. She didn't have any of those things figured out. She'd planned to work out some of those details before she started, but this seemed like a lot more work. And did she need a loan? Maybe she should invest in more pans and tools to go all in. Not to mention the packaging and all the extra ingredients she'd need.

"And you'll want to set it up as an LLC," her dad continued, "so you're not personally liable for anything related to the business. You'll probably want to consult a lawyer for that."

"Well, it sounds like I have a lot to figure out." The ache that had fluttered in her chest earlier sank like a stone into her stomach. She leaned back against her chair. The remaining food on her plate no longer looked appetizing.

She didn't have any steady clients. After all, birthdays came but once a year. And how often does anyone want to splurge on cupcakes for no reason? And if they did, it was likely an impulse buy while passing through the bakery of the grocery store. How many of the people she knew would actually support her, repeatedly, if she did start this business?

She had been focused on the baking details, like learning new piping techniques and trying different flavor combinations. She hadn't given much thought to the business. She had so many decisions left to make, and her dad's questions were likely just scratching the surface. Was it really worth all that work? How much did this spark of a dream desire to be a flame? Maybe baking on the side for a few friends here and there would be good enough.

"Is everything okay?" Her mom asked. "You can't be full already."

Swallowing hard in an attempt to bury all those questions, she shimmied back up and lifted a forkful of hash browns to her mouth. "It's just a lot I hadn't considered." She continued chewing, washing it down with a long swig of the tart mimosa.

"Well, sweetie," her dad chimed in, "these are all things you need to figure out. Starting a business is no cakewalk." He chuckled at his wordplay. "It's hard work—not something you just do on a whim because you feel like it could be fun."

It was far from a whim. In fact, she had fought the notion of her own cupcake business from the moment it was first mentioned. She had meant it when she'd told D.T. and her friends that she would just do those first orders and be done. Somewhere along the way, though, something started to change within her.

In those moments of watching the batter come together in the mixer, adding food coloring one drop at a time to find the perfect shade of ocean blue frosting, or working on her piping to shape just the right flowers for a bridal shower, she found peace. The outside world drifted away to leave her alone with her thoughts, like a new source of meditation. And in many of those moments, it was almost as if Angelle had been there, whispering the directions, guiding her hands, and showing her what to do next.

How could she articulate that to anyone without sounding like she had lost her mind? Instead, she simply nodded and muttered "I understand" between bites. She continued to shovel in her food now. The sooner she could end this conversation, the better.

"It's not a bad idea." Her dad pressed on. "You have potential, but you need to have a plan if you want to succeed."

Brila tipped her head back and her glass upside down to get the last drops of the mimosa. "Got it. I'll work on it."

Her mom reached out a hand, touching her forearm. "We just want to make sure you've considered everything. We'd hate for you to get in over your head and not have a fair chance at this."

Sure, she'd rather hear this from her parents than be turned down at a bank or shut down by some governing agency she didn't know existed. But as her visions of this cupcake business were crumbling around her, their words stung more than they healed. "I know. I actually have a lot to get done today. And now it sounds like I have a lot more to figure out, so I should probably get going."

She carried her dishes to the sink, where she rinsed them off before placing them in the dishwasher. A few moments later, she kissed her parents goodbye, scooped up her purse and keys, and walked out the front door. As it closed behind her, a twinge of guilt twisted in her gut for not staying longer, for not helping clean up the remaining food and dishes—but not enough to make her turn around. Instead, she quickened her pace until she reached her car in the driveway, which was parked under the pergola connecting the house and one of their sheds.

In the safety of her car, she gripped the steering wheel and screamed at the windshield. Tears began to well in her eyes. She clenched her jaw, refusing to let the tears fall. Afraid her parents might see her car still idle, she backed into the street and navigated her way home.

For twenty-two minutes, she swallowed the lump in her throat and inched the radio volume and her singing voice louder. Refusing to make eye contact with other drivers, she weaved through traffic, afraid to let them see her heart break and give a sympathetic nod of approval to release the emotions she struggled to bury.

The moment she crossed the threshold of her front door, the floodgates broke open. Tears streamed down her face before she could slide out of her sandals. She dropped her keys and purse, leaving only her phone in her hand as she staggered toward her room.

She collapsed on her bed and cried out, "I need you here!" Her body shook with each sob.

Angelle would know what to do. She'd be the one with a checklist, research, and statistics. Everything they would possibly need to know would have been detailed, planned, and calculated. And Brila would be baking alongside her sister.

That was the hardest part. It had been Angelle's dream. Brila had just agreed to make her happy. She had been there for moral support. And it had all been hypothetical. At no point had they made any real plans to start a business. How had this transformed into her own dream? Was it really her dream now or was she simply carrying it on for her sister?

She let that churn in her mind. Would it be such a bad thing to do it for Angelle? Honoring her sister and living out her dream would be the greatest accomplishment she could imagine. Angelle had such a beautiful spirit and so many goals and dreams she'd never get to realize herself. Brila certainly wasn't going to step into a middle school classroom to impact the lives of students the way her sister had. But baking cupcakes ... that was something she could do. As her tears dried, she checked her phone: 1:11 p.m. And just like that, the tears flowed again. "What do you want me to do?" She dropped her phone on the mattress, staring at it until the screen went black. "It wasn't supposed to be this way. I can't do this on my own." She turned her head and screamed into her pillow.

What other option did she have? She couldn't keep working in the hell of Halltown PR, not with her bloodthirsty coworkers and D.T. there. Working in marketing or social media was still an option, but where?

She sighed at the thought of starting another job search. Sure, she had created her résumé and interviewed for her current job, but D.T. had guided her through the whole process. Even if she did go through with this cupcake business, she'd still need a second job until she built up a decent customer base and a regular income. But how would she be able to build her business if she was busy working?

She rolled onto her back, pushing her hair from her face as she stared at the ceiling. "I don't think I can do it," she whispered, her voice breaking. A knot twisted in her gut.

Brila thought back to the prior August when she had promised Angelle that they could take a day trip to Galveston. It had been the last weekend before her sister would report back to school to prepare for the new year. The Thursday night before they were supposed to leave, D.T. had told her that his parents' anniversary party was also that weekend. He'd begged her to go with him. "You know my mom loves you. If you don't come, I'll never hear the end of it. And you're the only one who can tolerate Dad's jokes."

After much debate, she'd reluctantly called Angelle and backed out on their plans. Although her sister had said she understood, Brila knew she'd been disappointed. She'd promised they'd take a small getaway trip to Dallas or New Orleans over the holiday break to make it up to her, but she never got to fulfill that promise.

She had never promised Angelle that they'd start this business together. Yet, by not following through now, it felt like she was letting her down again. While logic insisted it wouldn't be possible, her heart argued that she still had to try. But if she did it simply to realize Angelle's dream and not out of her own desire, how long would it be before she resented the decision and fell into a hole deeper and darker than she had ever experienced?

TWENTY-SIX

Over the next few weeks, things didn't get much easier. Brila had applied for four different jobs outside of Halltown, only interviewed for one, and did not get the job offer. Work continued to be insufferable as her coworkers often ignored her, except to ask what had happened between her and D.T. One had even gone on a date with him two weeks after the breakup and loudly bragged the following Monday about how sweet he'd been.

Thankfully, she rarely saw him at work. Although, it proved to be more difficult for him to stop showing up at the same bars and restaurants she and her friends frequented. She hadn't decided if it was out of habit or out of spite, or if it was a half-hearted attempt to get her back.

It became easier to cancel plans with Shanna and Tony than to figure out where he might show up. She insisted that they needed time—just the two of them—anyway. Although she never felt like a third wheel, it also wasn't fair for them to spend all their time making sure she was okay. Besides, the added stress of their fertility struggles had put a strain on their relationship. It was good for them to focus on each other again.

Her baking had become another source of frustration. She'd started researching business plans and bakery requirements in Houston. There was so much to learn and so much to decide and do.

Did she want to do gourmet cupcakes or mini cupcakes? Simple flavors or crazy new combinations? Would she keep working out of her condo or try to open a storefront? Which licenses and permits applied to her, and did she need to complete any classes to get them?

She'd become overwhelmed. Her excitement about pursuing a cupcake business deflated. She stopped talking about it, stopped sharing pictures, and as a result, stopped receiving orders. Her dream—her sister's dream—seemed to be slipping out of her grasp. She couldn't let it fall apart now, but she didn't know how to get back on track.

She tried to pour her energy back into yoga, but the spark she had felt when she had initially gone through training seemed so distant now. She still enjoyed the exercise, both through leading the morning sessions and attending classes in the evenings. However, she would be happy once the morning classes came to an end. As much as she'd tried to convince herself that she'd get used to the new schedule, she continued to struggle to get out of bed each day she had class.

One positive thing to come out of her regular practice was a newfound sense of peace in the meditation. She made it a standard part of her routine each evening, either in class or at home.

At first, she had focused on finding strength in herself to move on from her relationship. She didn't need a man in her life to be happy. D.T. had just been such a large part of her life for the past two years, it had been an adjustment to be without him—for him to no longer be the one she called first to celebrate successes or gripe about problems, the one she spent her weekends with, the one she imagined in her future. She hadn't lost herself in him, but she had grown accustomed to factoring him into so much of what she did.

In the past week, however, her focus and mantra had shifted. After returning home from work Friday evening, Brila changed into leggings and a tank top then rolled out her yoga mat in the middle of her living room. She transitioned through a handful of poses to stretch her back and shake off the stress of the day. She sat cross-legged on the mat with her hands resting on her knees so that her palms faced the ceiling; she closed her eyes and inhaled slowly. "I am enough. I will fulfill the purpose placed in my heart," she whispered. She repeated this with each of her next four breaths and quieted her mind.

She focused on the sound of her breathing, the rise and fall of her chest, the darkness behind her eyelids. She relaxed into the quiet. A minute or two later, the darkness turned to light, and she was transported to her parents' kitchen. She watched herself and Angelle as she measured ingredients and mixed them together to create cupcake batter. Her chest tightened as they laughed and argued about which of them would get the leftover frosting.

She squeezed her eyes tighter to push the image away, committed to clearing her mind in meditation. "I am enough. I will fulfill the purpose placed in my heart," she repeated.

The vision returned moments later.

Sighing in frustration, she opened her eyes. Once she adjusted to the evening light that flooded her living room, she stretched her legs in front of her and then stood to roll up her mat. Part of her wanted to close her eyes and summon the vision back into her mind just to see Angelle again, but she remained frustrated that she couldn't stay focused for even ten minutes.

Those times of peace and refocusing on herself had helped her start to move forward after the breakup. She had hoped that it could also help her figure out what she should do next. It would be impossible to tune into what her heart was guiding her to do when she was continually interrupted by other thoughts, especially memories of Angelle.

She picked up her phone: 6:11 p.m. She'd decided to use these moments of eleven to check in with Angelle. "I miss you, too," she whispered. Not that she needed a number to be reminded of her sister. The gaping hole in her heart would always be there. Still, these moments occurred frequently enough that they'd become an additional connection for her. Whether they were intended to communicate something else, like she had read about with angel numbers or had just created a heightened awareness of the number, it didn't matter anymore. Each eleven sent a wave of calm through her body and a warmth in her chest. Everything around her faded for a few seconds, providing space for her and Angelle alone.

As the time changed, she unlocked the screen and began scrolling through Facebook. A minute later, a text message from Shanna popped up.

> You need to eat
> I know you have nothing at home
> Come to Vinny's with us
> Cam's meeting us too

She hated how well her friend knew her. Actually, she hated being faced with truths she didn't want to admit herself. Like it or not, she could always rely on Shanna for that.

Nothing in her pantry or fridge looked appetizing. She double-checked, trying to convince herself chicken and rice would be fine. Besides, if she went out tonight, she'd be off the hook for the rest of the weekend and probably the next few weeks.

> Fine. I'll be there at 7.

She slid her yoga mat into its carrying bag and propped it next to the front door. Rubbing her thighs, she entertained the idea of staying in the clothes she had on. Leggings were acceptable pants these days, and who cared if she showed up in workout clothes? She didn't need to impress anyone.

She forced herself to keep walking past the couch and to her room. If she sat down now, there'd be no getting up for the rest of the night. A rumble in her stomach insisted that her need for food was greater than her desire to stay in the comfort of her living room.

Standing in her closet, she changed back into the jeans she had worn to work. Removing her tank top and replacing her sports bra with an equally soft bralette, she flipped through her shirts. She couldn't find anything she wanted to wear, yet she didn't want to get rid of anything either. Finally, deciding on a simple purple t-shirt, she moved on to the bathroom where she reapplied eyeshadow and lipstick. Pulling out the hair tie that secured the messy bun at the top of her hair, she quickly braided her hair so that it lay on her right shoulder. Approving her reflection's appearance, she headed toward the front door.

At Vinny's, she found Cameron standing at the end of the bar. "Hey, stranger," she said as she walked up behind him.

He turned and smiled. "Look who decided to come out of her holding cell. No cupcakes tonight?"

She shook her head. "I think those days are over."

He twisted his face. "What do you mean? I thought you were going to make it a legit business."

She shrugged her shoulders. "It's too much. I'm not cut out for the entrepreneur life. I guess it'll just be a side thing for friends or something. No new orders lately, so I may actually have some free weekends coming up."

"Well, funny you should mention that. I need you to make cupcakes for my parents' anniversary party in a couple of weeks. They loved the ones you did for Janae's reveal party. Whatever you want to do. You're the expert."

She shifted her weight. A twinge of joy flowed through her, but it intertwined with the disappointment of this not being her full-time work. How great would life be if she could figure out the business side and actually get to bake for a living?

"They're your parents. Just tell me what they like."

Cameron chuckled. "Don't act like you've never met them. I'm sure whatever you do will be perfect." He ordered a beer for Brila and scanned the restaurant. "Where's the happy couple? Shouldn't they be here?"

Brila peaked at his watch as he checked the time: 7:12 p.m. Damn. Just missed it. "I guess we can grab a table. I'm sure they'll show up soon. You know how much Shanna hates being late." She reached past him to pick up the pint glass and tapped it against his glass. "Thanks for the drink. Next round's on me."

Once they were seated and looking over their menus, Shanna and Tony arrived. Brila joined Cameron on the other side of the booth so the couple could sit together.

"So sorry we're late. Time got away from us." Shanna sighed as she slid along the bench.

"What took y'all so long?" Cameron asked. "We were starting to think you ditched us."

Brila examined Shanna's flushed face and a single misplaced curl in her hair. "Really? You couldn't wait until you got back home?"

Shanna's eyes grew wide.

Tony laughed. "I can't help it. It's too hard to keep my hands off her."

"Stop!" She playfully pushed her husband away but immediately leaned back into him. "We just got caught up in the moment. We didn't mean to keep y'all waiting." She interlaced her fingers in his as they shared a menu.

Brila couldn't help but smile. Usually, public displays of affection caused her to have one of two reactions—cringe in disgust or an eye roll in annoyance. She had no interest in starting a new relationship, but seeing Shanna and Tony's connection had given her hope for something better in the future. That kind of love was worth waiting for, worth hoping for.

"What do you think?" Cameron motioned to her menu. "Chicken wings, mozzarella sticks, or jalapeño poppers?"

"Of course you had to pick out my three favorites. Make those two decide." Brila spoke a little louder to get their attention.

"Why not get all three?" Shanna chimed in.

Brila stared at her. "And who's going to eat all that? Are we not getting pizza?"

"Cut her some slack." Cameron grinned. "They just worked up an appetite."

They all laughed as the waitress arrived at the table.

"Fine, but I'm not taking home any leftovers," Brila whispered.

Tony ordered drinks for himself and Shanna, the appetizer sampler, and the usual large deluxe pizza.

Brila's pregnancy theory was squashed with the margarita order. Still, Shanna was hiding something from her. Something more than their impromptu romp-in-the-sack had to be going on. What was it? Could she call her out in front of Cameron? Possibilities ran through her mind, ranging from a new house to a new job to positive medical news.

She turned her attention to Tony as he talked about their weekend plans. She could get a better read on her friend, but maybe he would have his guard down and give away some clue for her to piece it together.

"And Labor Day weekend we have a back-to-school party for all my nieces and nephews." Tony's family turned everything into a large event. "Which I wanted to ask you," he looked at Brila, "if you could whip up some cupcakes for us to bring."

"You have to say yes." Shanna beamed. "Something cute like apples. Or you could just do navy and silver for their school colors. I'm sure whatever you do will be great."

So all the excitement was just about a cupcake request. Brila smiled, trying to hide her disappointment. "I can do that. Not like I have anything else going on."

"Well, that won't be the case after next weekend." Shanna smiled.

Brila scrunched her eyebrows. "Why's that?"

"Between all those kids' birthdays and every family gathering, you'll have plenty of orders to keep you busy. And after I post pictures, everyone will be hitting you up with requests again." She grabbed the margarita from the waitress who had returned. Before setting it down, she swung the straw around and took a sip.

"Why would you share pictures?"

"The question is, why don't *you*? You're the social media guru. If you really wanted to make this a business, you should be all over that. Creating accounts and pages and sharing the hell out of everything you make."

Shanna's eyes cut like daggers ripping into Brila's gut. She hadn't even decided on a name for her business. Sharing pictures with nothing to back them up would do her no good. Still, her friend had a point. She had the ability to market herself and gather customers if she wanted. If only she could figure out the whole creating-a-business part of it.

Three sets of eyes were now intently focused on her. She uncrossed and recrossed her legs. An extra gulp of her beer bought her another second or two. "Maybe I don't really want to make it a business after all." She kept her eyes on the table, picked up her glass again, and looked around the restaurant.

"That's bullshit, and you know it." Shanna quipped.

Cameron's ringing phone silenced their conversation. "I need to get this," he said, motioning for Brila to move.

"I don't know why you can't just answer it here." She scooted to the edge of the bench and stood. "Are you hiding a new friend from us?"

He looked from the phone to her then back at the phone. "Just a call I've been expecting, and it's too loud in here." He answered the call as he walked away.

"Who would call back on a Friday night?" Brila returned to her seat. "If it was so important, wouldn't they call during normal business hours?"

"Booty calls don't follow business hours." Tony chuckled.

Shanna and Brila laughed too. Then Shanna looked to her husband and raised her eyebrows, to which he nodded.

"What?" Brila folded her arms. "Stop having secret telepathic conversations."

"I'm actually glad he stepped out." Shanna smiled. "There's something I wanted to tell you."

"I knew it. You're even more cheery than normal, and I know the sex wasn't that good." Her eyes darted around the room as she realized her comment was louder than it should have been. Luckily, no one around them seemed to notice.

"Hey!" Tony threw his hands in the air. "I'm right here."

"I don't know how long Cam is going to be out there, so can I just tell her the news? I'll be sure to tell her how great you were later." Shanna winked at Brila.

"I saw that!" Tony narrowed his eyes but still smiled.

"Anyway, I wanted to tell you we've decided to adopt."

Brila's mind went blank. "Are you sure that's what you want?"

"We've talked a lot about it since the last miscarriage and even some before that." Shanna grabbed Tony's hand. "Of course we want to have our own kids, and maybe one day we will. But right now, the chances of that seem pretty small. And how great is it that we can give a child the loving home they deserve?"

Brila smiled. Her friend's resilience never ceased to amaze her. "Yeah, that's great. I'm so excited for y'all! I just wanted to make sure you were really okay with this, but it sounds like you've thought it all through. So what happens now?"

"We filled out the application. I hope you don't mind, but we listed you as a reference."

"Of course I don't mind. Anything I can do to help; I'm all for it."

"We have to go through background checks and home checks and who knows how many other steps. Then we wait for someone to pick us."

"We're trying to not get excited too early," Tony chimed in, "but it's also like a weight has been lifted."

"Y'all are incredible and are going to be the best parents. Anyone would be crazy not to pick you." Brila reached out and squeezed their clasped hands.

Tony looked toward the door before continuing. "And we don't plan to tell anyone until we've been matched."

"We just don't want everyone voicing their opinions or asking for updates every time we see them," Shanna added.

"I completely understand. I won't say a word." Brila pretended to lock her lips and throw away the key. She raised her glass and the couple followed suit. "Here's to the next chapter. May it bring you everything you've hoped for."

As their glasses clinked, Cameron returned. "What'd I miss? Why are you toasting?"

Brila looked across the table before sliding out of the booth to let him in. She wasn't prepared to come up with a cover story so soon.

"Brila's new business," Shanna offered without hesitation. "She's going to start baking again. Not just for us. It's time to go all in."

"I don't know about 'all in'." Brila narrowed her eyes on her friend as she sat back down. "There's still a lot to figure out, and I can't just stop working and live off hopes and dreams." She refused to let Shanna use this as an opportunity to force her into starting a business.

"That's great!" Cameron lifted his glass to her. "Congrats! If anyone can make it work, it's you."

She reluctantly tapped her glass against his. "So, what's so important it couldn't wait until Monday?"

"I told you; booty calls don't wait." Tony grinned.

Cameron shook his head. "Just a friend that's helping me with something for my parents' anniversary. Why do y'all always make me out to be some kind of man-slut? So I go on dates. That doesn't mean I'm sleeping around with everyone I see." He looked at Brila as he took another drink.

"Don't look at me! I didn't say it. I don't see anything wrong with your dates." She wished he'd find someone he could settle down with, but who was she to judge? She no longer had anyone either.

"I see your judging eyes. You're back in the dating world too. You'll see how hard it is."

She sighed. The thought alone was exhausting. "I'm just going to wait for you to find me someone again, so I don't have to go through all that work."

He pulled his lips to the side and squinted in thought. "I actually have someone in mind, but I'm not sure he's your type."

Her heart began to race, and jumping beans danced in the pit of her stomach. "I'm not sure I'm ready to date just yet."

"That's fine. We can talk about it when you get there."

TWENTY-SEVEN

Shanna's fake toast weighed on Brila's mind for the next week, and that alone annoyed her. It had been a simple cover story, an easy one since they had been talking about her baking before Cameron had stepped away. Still, her friends had been so confident that starting her own business was a logical step—as if it were her only option.

What would they say if she didn't follow through? What if she found another desk job? She did enjoy creating social media posts and interacting with people online. She could even see herself working in web design. Who said your purpose had to be some big, dramatic thing? The world needed corporate employees after all. Plenty of people baked for fun, and surely their friends all encouraged them to bake for others. That didn't mean it was supposed to be their career. That didn't make it their life's purpose.

Yet, no matter how many excuses she had, no matter how sure she was it'd be a failure, a persistent tug in her heart would not let the thought of starting her own cupcake business die. In fact, the more she tried to push it out of her mind, the more it pushed back. It also didn't help that her excuses and rationale for not doing it started to sound a lot like D.T., and that was something she couldn't allow.

Visions of her and Angelle baking together continued to flood her meditations. She found herself searching for information on business plans and loans when she was bored at work. In quiet moments at home, she spent her time watching videos of different piping techniques, looking at new flavor combinations and recipes, and screen shopping for new equipment. On her phone, she started a list that included ingredient costs, pricing from local bakeries, her favorite flavors, and even potential bakery names.

As she opened the list that Friday evening to add a commercial-grade mixer she had her eye on, she stared at the phone then shook her head and let out a small laugh. This was not the behavior of someone who had given up on the notion of starting her own bakery.

She cradled her forehead in her hands. Was she really going to do this? How? Could she still work full-time and run a business? She would have to. The amount in her bank account would only go so far, and she couldn't guarantee steady work for any period of time. What if she tried a little harder to get clients and did it on the weekends like she had before? Maybe if that went well, she could look into the business aspect. That way, if she fell on her face, she could say she tried and move on once and for all.

She nodded, content with her decision as she looked at the clock: 6:11 p.m. That eleven again. Was it approval of her decision? Confirmation that she should go all in? She didn't have time to dwell on it. She needed to finish the cupcakes she had made for Cameron before he arrived to pick them up.

Not that she could make sense of it. The number eleven constantly appeared around her. It didn't matter what she was doing. Positive thoughts. Negative thoughts. Working on ideas for the bakery. Convincing herself the bakery was a terrible idea. Watching TV or eating or desperately trying to fall asleep. The elevens were always there. She decided it was Angelle's way of making her presence known, but she still longed to hear her sister voice her opinion.

Each appearance of an eleven shot a warmth surging through every inch of her body and often pushed a smile to the corners of her lips. Yet, in moments like this, where she hoped only for her sister's guidance, the elevens seemed to offer little help. Even when she sensed a deeper meaning existed in the appearance, she just as easily convinced herself any interpretation aligned with what she wanted, not how her sister would respond.

As she often did, she talked back to Angelle, as she longed for an answer. "Can't you just tell me what to do? I'm lost. I don't know what I'm doing. Do you want me to start this bakery in your memory, or do you want to keep your dream with you?" She looked around her condo, waiting for something to move or to hear her sister's voice but secretly terrified to experience something so supernatural.

After thirty seconds of nothing, she gave up and debated how she wanted to finish the angel food cupcakes she had made. She had ingredients for three different ideas, but she finally settled on a strawberry filling. She took the diced strawberries out of the refrigerator then gathered sugar, cornstarch, and lemon juice in her arms before dropping them all on the counter next to the stove.

As she stirred together the filling ingredients, another check of the clock confirmed her fear.

Brila picked up her phone and texted Cameron.

> This is taking longer than I thought. Do you want me to bring them to you tomorrow morning?

She turned off the stove and slid the pan to the back burner to let it cool. She shook her head, realizing she should have decided on the filling and finished it with the cupcakes the day before so she'd only have to assemble and frost them. At least they were for Cameron and not a stranger. He wouldn't mind the delay.

Her phone buzzed with his response.

Are you not finishing them until tomorrow?
I'll be done tonight but don't want you to
wait around. I can bring them by in the
morning.
Or I can come hang out and watch the magic
happen. As long as you don't mind the company.

Brila smiled. Having someone around to fill the silence and keep her distracted from the tug-of-war taking place in her mind would be nice.

Come on over. I accept food as payment.

She pulled the mixer out from the corner and plugged it in before gathering the ingredients to make a whipped cream frosting. She froze, realizing the cupcakes would need to be kept cool. Pulling open the refrigerator doors, she inspected the space. After rearranging her leftovers and random ingredients that couldn't piece together a single meal, she had an empty shelf now dedicated to the cupcakes. She logged a mental note that keeping open fridge space would be necessary if this business thing were to take off.

Returning to her makeshift frosting station, she used the knuckle of her index finger to scroll through the recipe on her phone and then measured the ingredients into the mixing bowl. She turned on the mixer and washed her hands. Once the frosting formed, she placed the bowl in the fridge and returned to the stove to check on the strawberry filling. It still needed time to cool off. Looking around the kitchen, nothing else could be done at the moment. She scooped up her phone, sank into the couch, and scrolled through a list of shows on the TV.

Twenty minutes later, a knock jolted her out of a trance. She opened the front door to find Cameron holding up a bag of food. "I brought tacos."

"The second best form of payment," Brila smiled and grabbed the bag, "after alcohol, of course."

"I thought you might say that." He pulled a six-pack of hard root beer from behind his back and stepped inside.

"Have I become predictable?" She pulled the Styrofoam boxes out of the bag and opened the first one. Shredded chicken tacos, rice, and beans. It was what she ordered nearly every time she ate at a Mexican restaurant. She opened the second box and found the same thing. She handed it to Cameron, who traded an opened bottle of beer for the tacos.

"So what's baking?" He peered over to the far counter as they pulled out stools on the other side of the island. "You never told me what you decided to make."

"That's because I wasn't sure it would work. They're angel food cupcakes with strawberry filling and whipped cream frosting."

"Sounds delicious. They'll love them."

"Yeah, well, I didn't quite think things through. I should've made the filling last night so it could cool. And I overlooked the fact that they'll need to be refrigerated."

Cameron stared ahead for a moment, squinting slightly. "I think I have room in my fridge."

"Good. If not, you just came over for nothing."

"Not nothing. I had to bring your payment." He grinned as he held up his half-eaten taco. "Besides, when's the last time we hung out just the two of us?"

She ran through a mental list of the times she had seen him recently. "Other than work?"

"Other than work and lunch."

"Well, we had breakfast together a while back"

He smiled. "True, but that wasn't planned."

She thought some more. "No, wait. You came over when I did the gender reveal cupcakes." An image of her collapsed on the floor flashed in her mind. "Of course, that wasn't the best of days for me."

"I'm glad I got back when I did. You shouldn't have been alone." The look of concern he had that night returned to his eyes as he paused. "But before then, it's not like we've spent much time together lately."

"Well, I guess we're always making plans as a group. And when I was with D.T., I spent most of my free time with him."

"Then I guess we get a rare night just us two. Unless you finish these cupcakes and send me on my way."

A laugh escaped her mouth. "Of course not. You can hang out until you're tired of me. But I'll warn you, I'm not very exciting."

"That's okay. You never were." He grinned.

She gasped dramatically. "You're not supposed to agree with me."

"I'd take boring over dramatic any day."

"Fair enough. I guess I would too."

After they finished eating and cleaning up, Brila dipped a spoon in the strawberry filling. Tasting it, she confirmed that it had cooled. She removed the frosting from the fridge, moved the cupcakes to the island, and used a small scoop to hollow out their centers. Using a piping bag, she began to squeeze the strawberry filling into each one.

"Anything I can do to help?" He leaned forward on his stool. "I'm basically a professional cupcake filler now."

Brila barely glanced at him but smiled as she answered, "That might be true, but I'll be done in a few minutes."

"You make it look easy. I can't wait to see what you do with your business."

She turned the bag up so it wouldn't drip and scrunched her eyebrows as she straightened her back. "And what if I don't start my own business? Or what if I do it and end up failing?"

"If you don't do it, you'll be depriving people of your incredible work. And if you fail, which I doubt you will, at least you tried and can walk away knowing you gave it your all and it's time to do something else." He smiled as she returned to filling the cupcakes. "But what if you don't fail? What if you become the best-selling cupcake baker in the city?"

She laughed. "Don't get carried away."

"You'll never know until you try. But you have to be all in. You can't do it because we think you should or just because you like to do it and don't know what else to do. You can't even do it just for Angelle. If you're not fully committed to making it work, you'll never stand a chance."

"What if I'm fully committed to making it work because it was her dream?" She met his eyes as she set down the filling bag.

"I'm not saying there's anything wrong with wanting to do this for her, but if you don't enjoy doing it or if that's the only reason, you'll eventually burn out. But I see the passion in your eyes when you're baking and decorating. You have the desire. You have what it takes."

She groaned as the time on the stove caught her eye: 7:11 p.m.

Cameron followed her glance. "What's that about? Are you missing out on something right now? Because you didn't have to do these."

"It's not that. It's just ..." She hesitated. "Do you ever get the feeling you're seeing a sign or symbol or something?"

"Sure. Like when I see a cardinal, I always feel like that's my grandpa watching over me."

"Yeah, like that. Well, for the past few months, I've been seeing elevens. Mostly it's the time, but I see it in totals on receipts, on license plates, the distance to empty in the car, TV, everywhere."

"And you think it has something to do with Angelle?"

"I think so. It's almost like I'm supposed to be getting some kind of message, but I have no idea what it is. I mean, they show up all the time. There's no connection, no consistency. At first, I thought it meant I was supposed to do the whole yoga teaching thing. Then I thought it meant I was supposed to be baking for her. Then I turn around and see elevens when I'm thinking about not doing it. It's driving me crazy, but at the same time, I love feeling that connection." She exhaled and her shoulders fell, seeing that the minute had ticked up to twelve. "That probably sounds crazy."

He smiled gently, tilting his head slightly. "It's not crazy. It's like our loved ones are letting us know they're still with us. Like we get to stay connected even after they're gone. Isn't that what we hope for? It's great that you get to have that connection with your sister. Hold onto it. Treasure it. Why stress about trying to come up with some sort of deeper meaning? Why not just enjoy those special moments?"

Brila clenched her jaw and swallowed hard, fighting back the tears that began to well in her eyes. "Thanks. I'll have to remember that."

Maybe she'd been putting too much pressure on herself. Maybe there was no message. She longed for her sister's guidance. Angelle had always been there to give her advice, even if she hadn't always taken it. What she needed more than guidance, though, was her sister's presence. At least Brila could feel like she was there in spirit, even if it was for brief moments.

She stirred the frosting before scooping it into a piping bag. "You're so helpful. You should've been a psychologist or life coach or something." She grinned, remembering Cameron's high school declaration that he would become a guidance counselor.

He smiled back. "Funny you should say that. I've been thinking about going back to get my master's in psychology. Your pursuit in finding your purpose has made me curious about finding my own. I always liked helping others. Maybe there could be something there."

"That's awesome. You'll be great, no matter what you do. And you could always counsel at Halltown. Lord knows those nut jobs need all the help they can get." She chuckled.

"Hey, now! I'm still one of those nut jobs. And last time I checked, so are you."

She sighed. "Don't remind me. I'm trying to fix that, too. But how the heck am I supposed to find a new job and kickstart a business? That seems a bit ambitious."

"There's actually a lot of opportunities in digital marketing to do contract work and work remotely. My cousin does marketing work from his home in Austin for a company somewhere in Colorado. Why not do something like that? Make your own schedule and work while you bake."

How hadn't she thought of that on her own? "Well, you just have all the answers, don't you? Now I just need to figure out this whole business plan thing. Want to do that for me, too?"

"I don't have all the answers. Just trying to help however I can. And for the business plan, you can probably find examples and templates all over the internet."

Brila grinned. "Yeah, I found some. Guess I just need to sit down and finish doing the work."

She looked up to find him smiling at her and felt her cheeks flush. His eyes locked with hers. His confidence in her permeated the space between them and soaked into her bloodstream. She didn't know what it was about him, but just being around him made her want to do better.

"I really don't know what I'd do without you." She piped a large puff of whipped cream frosting on the last cupcake and inspected the small amount left in the bag. "Want the rest?"

"Do you need to ask?" He grabbed the piping bag and squeezed the remaining frosting into his mouth. He rolled his eyes back. "You could fill a kiddie pool with this, and I'd eat it all."

She laughed as she carefully transferred the finished cupcakes into boxes, which she then placed in the fridge. "Don't forget these when you leave."

Cameron carried the piping bag to the sink and turned on the water. Before Brila could do it herself, he grabbed the saucepan from the stovetop and the mixing bowl from the counter.

"I don't think I've ever seen you do dishes without being forced to. You really don't need to start doing them here."

"I do dishes all the time. And it's the least I can do."

"Well, then you wash and I'll dry." She walked up next to him as he handed over the rubber scraper. "Look at us. We're like an old married couple."

They laughed together. "So this is what old couples do?" Cameron looked at her. "I could handle that."

A flutter passed through Brila's stomach. She felt his eyes still on her as she dried the mixing bowl.

Once the dishes had been washed, she made her way to the living room. "What do you want to watch? Superheroes or rom-com?"

"What kind of choice is that? Superheroes always win." He grabbed the remote and selected the first movie on the list before falling onto the couch.

Brila grabbed two blankets from her storage ottoman, offering one to Cameron before sitting on the opposite end of the couch. It was strange seeing him in the space D.T. used to occupy. Plenty of other people had sat in that spot. In fact, it had been her seat of choice until D.T. beat her to it once. It was just a seat, but seeing Cameron there now reminded her that chapter of her life was over. She continued to be surprised when something so seemingly insignificant triggered an emotional connection to D.T.

"Are you sure you're okay with me staying? You just gave me a weird look." Cameron held the blanket as if he expected her to take it back.

"I didn't mean to if I did. I was just trying to remember the last time I had watched a movie here with anyone else."

He looked from her to the TV then back again. "Do you miss him?"

"It's not that I miss him but adjusting to not having him around and not having to consider him in my decisions is taking longer than I expected." It felt surprisingly good to admit that out loud.

"That's understandable. I guess I'm too selfish to consider someone else in anything I do. Probably explains why I'm single." He chuckled.

"That's not true. You're always thinking of and helping others. We make time for what's important to us. Maybe you just haven't found anyone worth considering yet." She studied his face as it twisted into a half-smile. "Is that what you want, or would you rather not be tied down?"

"I enjoy getting to know new people, and if I'm being honest, I'm not the easiest person to be with, but I think I'm finally ready to be with someone special and have a meaningful relationship."

She opened her mouth, hesitated as she considered her words, and started again. "Here's the problem. You're too picky. You're never going to find the perfect person. You have to learn to love someone in spite of their messes."

"I'm just looking for someone with a dream that doesn't involve the number of beers they can drink and the ambition to go after that dream, even if they're not sure what they're doing. Someone I can laugh with and be myself with. Someone who's comfortable going out and staying in. I don't think that's too much to ask." His eyes stayed locked on hers.

Brila's heart beat faster. Was he trying to describe her to see if she was paying attention? Of course not. That description probably fit a lot of people. Hell, she could say those same things about Shanna. "That doesn't sound like too much. In fact, I'm sure there are plenty of people like that. Have you really not found anyone that fits what you're looking for?"

He looked at the TV. "I might have found someone who's all that and more, but there are other complications."

"Too much baggage?"

He hesitated. "Maybe just bad timing."

She thought back through his relationships, trying to pinpoint who it might be. "Well, then maybe it's worth trying again when the timing is right."

"Maybe. Even if the timing is right, though, I'm not sure she'd want to go down that road."

"So it's a she." Brila's eyes grew wide, as she narrowed the list to his prior girlfriends. "Do I know her?"

"I'm not answering that." He pushed the blanket to the side and stood up. "Do you want anything to drink?"

"Oh, you know what we can do? Let's make floats with the beer you brought. I'm pretty sure I have ice cream." She jumped up from the couch. "I'll get it. Stay here and watch the movie."

"I'm already up." He smiled as he continued to the kitchen cabinet and pulled down two mugs. "I don't know the last time I had a root beer float." He set the mugs down and grabbed the beer bottles as Brila scooped the ice cream. "It had to be when you made us do it for our last college movie night."

She smiled at the memory. By their senior year of college, they each had various friend groups and plenty of activities that kept them busy, in addition to their course loads and preparations for the real world. What had once been a regular occurrence had become a rarity.

When they found themselves with a free Sunday two weeks before their last finals week, she'd proposed a movie marathon. They had watched all their favorites from the prior four years, argued which characters deserved what they got, and ate nothing but junk from popcorn and candy to pizza and root beer floats. The day remained one of her favorite college memories.

"I promise not to fall asleep this time." She grabbed her mug and returned to the couch.

Cameron chuckled. "You always fall asleep. It's a movie night tradition at this point."

"Hey," she narrowed her eyes, "I can stay awake." She drank her float and pulled the cozy blanket over her legs. Just the feel of the fleece made her eyes grow heavy. She refocused on the plot of the movie, hoping the action would hold her attention. "What?" She felt his eyes still on her. "I'm watching the movie. Shouldn't you be doing the same? You're the one who picked this."

"It's just funny to watch you try so hard."

Now she had the motivation to prove him wrong. She intently watched the rest of the movie, even though she had to shift in her seat every five minutes and get up three times to keep awake.

Once it was over, she retrieved the cupcakes from the fridge. "Sorry again that they weren't ready sooner, but I'm glad you still came over to hang out. We really should have movie night more often. You know, on the rare occasion you don't have a hot date."

He pulled on his shoes. "I think I'm taking a break from dating for a while. At least until I can figure some things out."

"Still waiting on that timing?"

"I think I just need to figure out what I really want first. Besides, I'm not sure I have much to offer."

"Why would you think that? You're one of the nicest people I know. You have a great sense of humor, you're laid-back, and you always put one hundred percent into everything you do."

He let out a lighthearted laugh. "Thanks. I guess we'll see."

"If anyone should be worried, it's me. I'm quite the mess these days."

"Not even close to it. Life gets messy sometimes, but you always find a way to come out better on the other end. You deserve to be with someone who appreciates all that you are."

"See. Nicest person I know." She hugged him, her head leaning against his chest. His heartbeat thumped against her temple. She smiled as she pulled back to look up at him. Her own heart pounded, and her stomach flipped. With his eyes still locked on hers, she fought the urge to lean back into him.

Instead, she released her hands from his back, slid the cupcakes off the counter, and pushed them toward Cameron. "So, just remember to put them on the floor, drive carefully, and keep them in the fridge when you get home." She held on to the boxes between them for another moment before letting go. "I hope your parents like them."

He gave her a crooked smile. "They're going to love them. They're perfect. You really have something here. I hope you don't let it go." He walked to the front door, and she followed behind him.

"Do you need me to help open your car door or anything?"

He thought for a moment. "I should be able to get it. Thanks again. Next movie night is at my place, and you can bring the food."

"Deal." She swallowed hard and opened the door. She watched him walk halfway down the stairs before closing it.

Her right hand clasped her forehead as her back fell against the door. "What the hell just happened?" Her wide eyes searched the living room for answers. All she found were blankets, mugs, and empty bottles. She busied herself with picking up, but no matter how hard she tried, she couldn't shake a longing to be in Cameron's arms again.

TWENTY-EIGHT

Over the next week, Brila reorganized the list on her phone. Cameron's encouragement stuck in her mind. She researched business plans and started pulling one together for herself, surprised at how much information she had already gathered in her list. It would be a lot of work, quite possibly more than she could imagine, but she set her mind on doing whatever it took.

She returned to baking over Labor Day weekend, this time for Tony's family gathering. Keeping it simple, she'd made vanilla cupcakes with red frosting to resemble apples. However, as she checked them that Saturday morning, they were less than stellar. They were plain, boring, and not apples at all.

As she whipped together some scrambled eggs for breakfast, she contemplated ways to fix them. Did she have time to scrape off the frosting and redecorate with the school colors Shanna had mentioned? First, she would have to remember what those were. The cupcakes had probably been stained with the red food coloring. Trying to redecorate would make them worse than they already were. She agonized over her failure as she ate her eggs.

After cleaning her dishes, she placed her hands on the edge of the counter where the cupcakes sat, mocking her. She couldn't give these to Shanna and Tony. She turned to the pantry. As she pushed around her baking ingredients, something caught her eye. A bag of pretzels. She pulled it out and broke one of the skinny sticks in half. She inserted a piece into the side of a cupcake to resemble a stem.

She leaned back to inspect the addition. It was certainly an improvement, but it still didn't look quite right. She pressed the pretzel stick halves into the remaining cupcakes. Then she scurried around the kitchen to gather the standing mixer and her buttercream frosting ingredients.

Mixing up a small batch of frosting, she colored it bright green then retrieved a piping bag and a piece of parchment paper. She made a row of leaves of different sizes before settling on the right one. Scooping her practice results back into the bag, she piped little leaves next to each pretzel stem. When she finished, she stepped back with a smile on her face. They were perfect. Why hadn't she thought of that the night before?

As she closed the lids on the cupcake boxes, her phone chimed with a new text message. She returned the ingredients to the pantry and moved the dishes to the sink before she checked her phone.

A message from Callie waited for her.

Can you cover the 11:30 class today?

Brila checked the clock. Why were instructors always waiting until the last minute to cancel? She hadn't planned to leave her condo, but she needed the exercise. Why not get paid to do it?

Sure. I'll be there soon.

Thankful to be in leggings and a tank top already, she retreated to the bathroom, fixed her ponytail, and brushed her teeth. Once she located her mat and tennis shoes, she headed out the door.

When Brila showed up at the studio, she hadn't expected to be greeted by Callie.

"Don't mind me. I have a little work to catch up on," she offered as they walked to the front of the room.

Brila rolled out her mat and reviewed notes of the position sequence she planned to execute. As the class filled with fifteen people, the pounding in her chest grew. She checked the clock hanging in the back of the room, watching it tick to 11:30. Taking a deep breath, she smiled and began the session.

Her shoulders relaxed as they started with prayer pose. Moving into warrior one, she spotted Callie watching from the office doorway. Brila refocused on the session, enjoying the stretch in her body and the peaceful focus of the others in attendance.

As they neared the end of the session, she instructed the class to lie on their backs and led them through a short meditation, allowing them to relax and clear their minds. Although she wanted to melt into her own meditation, she stayed focused on leading the class. She would have her regular meditation session at home later that evening.

Once the class ended and the studio cleared, Callie stepped out from the back hallway. "Great session today. You really know how to connect with the class and keep them in the moment."

Brila smiled. "Thanks. I just try to piece together what I enjoy most from yoga sessions." She slid her mat in its carrying bag.

"Well, it works." Callie paused for a moment. "How are things going with the morning session?"

"It's okay." Brila rubbed her arm. "Although, I'm not much of a morning person. Do you think one of your other instructors would want to pick up the class?"

"Oh." Callie folded her arms. "Sure, I can ask around. Are you still interested in teaching at other times? The instructor for this class actually quit this morning. She had this session and a couple of others during the week. Would you have any interest in picking up some or all of them instead of the morning class?"

Brila picked at her fingernails as she considered the offer. She'd hoped for an opportunity like this just a couple of months ago. She could probably swing a class or two on top of work and baking, and the extra income would help fund a new business.

As she prepared to ask for time to think about it, her heart gave her mouth a different response. "I appreciate the offer, but I have a lot going on right now. As much as I'd love to, I'm not sure I can commit to any classes at this time."

Callie's smile faded. "So you're not looking to make it a career anymore?"

She had been so sure she wanted that just a few months earlier, certain it'd be the start of the next chapter in her life. That felt like ages ago. She still loved yoga and enjoyed leading sessions, but so much had changed since then.

She'd rediscovered her love for baking and felt more connected to Angelle than she had since her death the prior November. She'd stood up for herself and lost D.T. in the process. What she'd thought would bring her purpose and happiness back in April no longer made sense. A new dream had gripped her heart, and no matter how much she had tried to fight it, this one wasn't going away.

"No, I think I've found something else that's a better fit for me." Brila shifted her weight as Callie's deflated energy seeped out of her downcast eyes. "But I can help fill in until you find a new instructor if it'll help you out."

"That would be great." Callie's head snapped up. "I'll send you the schedule and let you know if anything changes."

She nodded and slung her mat bag over her shoulder.

When Brila returned home, she found a stout, balding man standing at the top of her stairs. He taped something to her door, unaware that she had pulled up.

"Ms. Landry." The man she now recognized as the head of their homeowner's association turned around, appearing flustered. "Is it correct that you have started some sort of bakery business?"

She rarely saw or spoke to him. Although, from their handful of interactions she'd decided he took great pride in enforcing rules on the condo owners and delighted in the misery of others.

"It's not a business." Not yet, anyway. "But, yes, I've been baking for some friends recently."

He crossed his arms. "You do remember that according to the bylaws of our association, you are not allowed to operate a business out of your condo?"

She'd skimmed the agreement when she first moved in. If she had read that section, she certainly hadn't paid attention at the time and had long forgotten about it now. "Yes, sir. I understand. Like I said, I'd just helped out a few friends and baked for a few events."

He removed the folded paper from the door and handed it to her. "Well, here is a copy of section five of the bylaws. You may want to reconsider your ... generosity." He stomped down the stairs.

"Have a great day!" she called after him in an excessively cheerful voice.

Inside the comfort of her home, the fake smile faded from her face. She sighed deeply and opened the paper. Sure enough, spelled out in more detail than she cared to read, the bylaws prohibited any business from operating inside of any condo as well as on the premises of their complex.

That seemed about right. Just as she committed to starting this business and started pulling things together, a wrench would get thrown into her plans. She opened the growing list on her phone and added "find storefront" to the top of it. After brief consideration, she also added "research out of home requirements" and "look into larger loan possibilities". She threw the copy of the bylaws into the garbage and headed to the bathroom to rinse off. One thing at a time. Whether it took her six months or six years, she would find a way to make this dream a reality.

TWENTY-NINE

While at her parents' house for brunch the next day, Brila's right leg bounced under the table as she cut up and chewed her pancakes. She had rehearsed everything she wanted to tell her parents on the drive over, but finding the right time to begin that conversation proved to be more challenging.

Her dad broke the silence in between bites. "How's the business plan coming along? Are you ready to share any details yet, or are you still keeping everything a secret?"

She took a drink from her champagne flute to buy her a couple of extra seconds. "I think I have most of it done. Maybe we can wait and talk about it after we eat and clean up."

Her parents exchanged a look, then her mom answered. "Sounds great, honey. We can't wait to hear all about it."

Brila couldn't decide if she wanted to shovel the food into her mouth to finish as fast as possible or pick it apart and stall for time. Somehow, she managed to alternate between the two and finished at the same time as her parents.

Her heart pounded while she filled the dishwasher and cleaned the remaining pans by hand. Reminding herself to breathe, she inhaled slowly as she turned off the faucet. She wrapped her hands in the kitchen towel, rubbing them together long after they were dry.

Taking another deep breath, she pushed herself to join her parents in the living room.

She sat cross-legged on the loveseat like she had done so often in high school. It was also how she and Angelle had sat to have so many conversations about anything from classes to boyfriends to career choices. She only sat this way to meditate and to have conversations with her family.

Rubbing her hands on her knees, she began to share the details they had been waiting to hear. "You already know I want to start a cupcake business. It's all I plan to sell. I've done a lot of research to learn about running a home business, especially home bakeries. I've planned out my ingredient costs, pricing strategy, and other investments I need to make. I'm going to start marketing on Facebook and Instagram. I think my past experience with digital marketing already puts me ahead of the game with knowing how to navigate the different platforms. I've also looked into licensing, taxes, and regulations. That's probably been the most challenging part so far."

"It sounds like you've made a lot of progress." Brian leaned forward, resting his forearms on his thighs. "So why would people want to buy your cupcakes over the dozens of bakeries and who knows how many other home bakers around Houston?"

She might as well have been presenting to a room full of suited-up investors. "All of my products and the kitchen I work in will be nut-free, so anyone with those allergies can buy from me. And my signature cupcake is one I haven't seen yet anywhere else in the city." She paused, realizing the hardest part of the conversation was still to come. "It's an angel food cupcake with a berry filling." She swallowed the lump in her throat. "And I'll have ten other flavors: vanilla, chocolate, lemon, strawberry, mint chocolate chip, mocha, cookies and cream, red velvet, s'mores, and orange creamsicle."

Lyla smiled softly. "They all sound delicious. So what do you have left to do?"

"Well, I found out that the condo bylaws prohibit home businesses, and I'm not ready to move. So, if you know of any cheap places for rent or anyone with a second kitchen to loan out, I'm taking suggestions."

"What about our shed?" Brian was referring to their storage building they had converted into a party room. He turned to Lyla then back to Brila. "It's not like we're hosting parties much these days. There's already a kitchen. It probably needs some fixing up, and you'll have to see what kind of equipment and appliances you need to put in it."

"Are you sure?" A flutter floated through her chest. "I mean, that'd be great, but I don't want to impose. But I could take out a smaller loan if I don't have to fund a full rebuild of a place or open a storefront."

"Actually, we wanted to talk to you about that." Lyla shifted to the edge of the couch and placed her hand on Brian's knee. "We know how important this is to you, and it sounds like you've really thought it through. So we'd like to fund your initial investment. Whatever equipment you need, your first stock of ingredients and packaging," she looked to Brian, who nodded in agreement, "and now any repairs we need to make to the shed. We don't want you to be delayed due to the strain of the business loan process."

A tear trickled down Brila's cheek. She had worked throughout high school and college to alleviate the financial burden on her parents. She would have never considered asking them for money or to use their property. "I promise I'll pay you back as soon as I can." She pushed herself off the couch and threw her arms around her mom then her dad. "Thank you so much," she whispered.

"So what are we calling this business?" her mom asked.

She returned to the loveseat and dried her cheeks, even though more tears were on the way. "Angelle's Cupcakes." Another lump lodged itself in her throat, causing pressure to build in her ears. "This was her dream long before it became mine. This is all for her and because of her. She deserves her name on every cupcake I bake."

Her dad's chin quivered, and her mom's cheeks streaked with tears.

"There's one more thing." Brila took a deep breath. This would be even more difficult than she had imagined. "I'd lied when I told you she was coming over that night because D.T. and I had a fight." She searched their eyes and willed the words to come out of her mouth. "I'd had a miscarriage. No one else knew. She was coming to comfort me and help me figure everything out. I should've told her to stay home, to just stay on the phone. I'm the big sister. I'm supposed to be the one taking care of her, not the other way around. And because of me, because I needed her more, she's gone." She hung her head, letting the tears drip onto her legs.

"Oh, honey," Lyla said and moved to the loveseat and put her arm around Brila. "You cannot keep blaming yourself for Angelle's accident. And for you to suffer through a miscarriage alone on top of that. Why didn't you tell us?"

She melted into the comfort only her parents could offer. "I was going to, but after the accident, I didn't want to take anything away from Angelle. It didn't seem right. Then as time went on, I didn't know how to bring it up. But now, I just need you to know the whole story, the real reason Angelle was on the road that night, the reason I have to do this for her."

Lyla squeezed her then retreated upstairs, as she often did when she became overwhelmed. Brila had seen her mom cry just a handful of times. She had always put immense pressure on herself to hold it together in front of others, a trait she had passed onto

Angelle. There'd been multiple times when Brila had overheard her sister crying in the bathroom. When she'd emerge a few minutes later, she'd reappear with a smile and act as if nothing had been wrong.

Brian took his wife's seat next to their daughter. "Sweetie, you should never have to go through anything alone. You could've told us." His eyes filled with tears, and he clenched his jaw as he swallowed hard.

Brila felt him take a slow, deep breath as she rested against his arm. She, too, breathed in deeply, her shoulders relaxing as she exhaled. Her chest opened with the next breath as if she had removed a twenty-pound boulder she didn't know she'd been carrying for the past ten months.

THIRTY

With her parents' emotional and financial support, Brila grew more determined to set her plan into action. She took Cameron's suggestion to look into work-from-home opportunities. She updated her résumé, scoured job websites and listings, and researched eight companies. In the end, she applied for five different positions and received interview requests for three.

Two weeks had passed since her movie night with Cameron. She'd been trying to avoid him since that night but hadn't been very successful. They continually saw one another at work. However, she had done a particularly good job of acting as if nothing out of the ordinary had happened that night, as if she hadn't agonized over every detail day after day.

Did she really have feelings for him, or had she just been caught up in the moment? He was kind, caring, and so easy to be around. Maybe she misinterpreted his friendship for that kind of intimate support she craved. Did Cameron notice something, too, or had it just been her? She wanted to say something but didn't want to make him uncomfortable or make things awkward. Most of all, she didn't want to jeopardize their friendship.

"I'm getting out of here," she whispered as they crossed paths in the hallway Monday morning.

Cameron's eyes followed hers, searching the halls. "For lunch? Where are you going?"

"No. I mean I'm getting out. I have one last interview this afternoon. I should have offers by the end of next week. Thanks again for telling me about your cousin."

"No problem. But I'm going to miss having you around here to keep me sane and help break up the day."

A knot twisted in her stomach. Was there a deeper meaning behind that? "I think you're about the only thing I'm going to miss around here." Her cheeks warmed as she continued to avoid making eye contact.

"Well, don't say it like we're never going to see each other."

She smiled. "True. I guess things just go back to how they were before I worked here. Still, I've gotten used to running into you every day. Kind of like high school and the first couple years of college." What was she doing? She needed to stop talking and get back to her desk.

"Then I guess we can try to do better than before. After all, you still owe me another movie night."

"I know. I've just been busy trying to get everything going." It was partially true. She had been piecing together the final details of her business plan. She'd also been dodging nearly all social activity, especially when it came to spending time with Cameron, but she couldn't avoid him forever. Continuing to put off movie night would eventually become suspicious. At least she had a good excuse to buy her some time.

"Are you sure I can't help? I don't know much about baking or starting a business, but I can research and take notes with the best of them." He locked his eyes on hers. Did he really want to spend time with her that desperately?

She could get lost in those brown eyes if she let herself. She shook her head, partially to answer his question, partially to break his gaze. "I think it's something I need to do on my own but thanks for the offer. And I promise we'll do movie night soon. Maybe after I get those job offers, we can grab lunch, and you can help me decide which one to take."

"Sounds like a plan. Let me know how it goes today."

They both hesitated for a moment before continuing in separate directions. Brila fought the urge to turn around. She had been caught up in her emotions in recent weeks. Confusing his friendship and support with intimate feelings made that clear. She needed to refocus. After all, she had an interview to prepare for. She couldn't compromise her chances of getting out of her current toxic work environment by worrying about her feelings for Cameron or his feelings for her.

Leaving the cafeteria with her coffee in hand, she spotted D.T. walking straight toward her. She surveyed her surroundings, praying she'd find someone to chat with until he disappeared. No such luck.

She had seen him from a distance a few times but had avoided conversation with him until that point. Could she continue walking past him without saying a word?

Before she could decide, he spoke first. "Hey. I'm surprised you're still here. Thought you'd be off running your bakery by now."

She exhaled slowly, choosing her words carefully. Getting upset or fighting his snide comment would do no good. "Yeah, well those things take time. But I have some things in the works. If you're lucky, this will be the last time you see me."

"What's that supposed to mean?" His eyes scanned from her head to her feet and back again.

She continued past him and down the hall. "Whatever you think it means. Take care." A grin spread across her face, and her steps gained a slight bounce. She found a simple joy in leaving him to mull over her words.

That Friday, Brila met Shanna for lunch at a new farm-to-table café. "Pretty soon, I'll be able to set my own schedule, and we'll be able to do this more often." She placed their ticket number in the holder at the edge of the table and slid into a pale blue wooden seat.

"Does that mean you heard back from the last interview?" Shanna sipped her raspberry iced tea.

Brila nodded and sighed. "Didn't get this one either. So I guess the decision is pretty easy."

She had been confident she'd get multiple offers. At least she could avoid time with Cameron for a little longer. With only one job offer, she didn't need to take him out to lunch to help her decide which one to accept. Of course, that brought on mixed emotions. A part of her longed to spend time with him beyond a few minutes passing in the hallway. However, the internal debate about whether or not she saw him as someone more than a friend still waged on. If she couldn't settle that for herself, she certainly wasn't prepared to burden him with it.

"One offer is still better than none. And I thought you liked that one."

"All three were good companies. I just liked this last one a little more."

Over the past week, she had listed out the pros and cons of each opportunity and ranked them based on everything from benefits to their websites to how nice the interviewers were. Angelle would have been proud.

"And the good news is their headquarters are in Dallas, so if I do have to travel for training or anything, it won't be far. Although, I didn't hate the possibility of visiting San Francisco."

Shanna grinned. "Good. We can't have you running off too far when you have a business to run and will soon have a little niece or nephew to love on."

Brila's chest tightened. As excited as she was for Shanna and Tony's hopes for adoption, each time she heard the words niece, nephew, or aunt, it reminded her that she would never have the opportunity to be a biological aunt. She took a deep breath and forced a tight-lipped smile. "How's the adoption process coming along?"

"We have our home visit next week, so I've been cleaning like crazy and reorganizing the nursery."

"Your house is already perfect and baby-ready. I doubt there'll be any issues."

Their conversation paused as the waiter arrived with their food. There was no one more prepared for parenthood than Shanna. Brila hoped her friends would be matched with a child soon. She couldn't stand the thought of watching them endure any further heartache.

"I'm still holding out hope," Shanna continued, "that I'll have a full-term pregnancy one day, but I'm so grateful to have the opportunity to love a child who needs us just as much as we need them."

"You're going to be great. Any child would be lucky to be welcomed into your family."

After lunch, Brila returned to work with a smile on her face but a knot in her stomach. She had delighted in the prospect of giving her notice since she had started looking for other jobs. However, as she walked toward Kathryn's office, her palms began to sweat and the words she had rehearsed for weeks slipped from her mind. She knocked on the door frame and walked in, only to find her boss's seat empty.

Exhaling in relief, she returned to her desk, thankful for more time to prepare herself. She decided to email her acceptance letter to her new employer to make it official. Then she opened her calendar to count out her last two weeks at Halltown. Her last day would be October second. However, her eyes drifted to the eleventh. She couldn't help it. These days, she seemed to seek out elevens nearly as often as they appeared on their own. She looked at Angelle's picture, admiring her smile. Her sister's laugh echoed in her head.

Every sighting of the number eleven had become a reminder of her sister's love and the wise-beyond-her-years guidance she had always provided. Some days it still seemed impossible to believe she was no longer alive. Brila's longing to spend even one more day with Angelle knotted her stomach and tightened her throat in a way that threatened to cut off her air supply.

Some days were easier than others. But on the difficult days, the days when she'd pick up the phone to call her sister, the days when she'd thought about all the future had to hold but would never deliver for her sister, the pain felt like it may never get better.

In an empty Word document, she picked a large, curly font, colored it deep purple, and typed the words Angelle's Cupcakes. She leaned back in her chair, placed her hand under her chin, and studied her creation. As her head tilted slightly to the right, a wide grin pushed her cheeks up under her eyes. She sprang forward and pecked at the keyboard, deleting the Ls and replacing them with ones. She reclined again, folding her arms over her chest and reveling in the adjustment. It was perfect. Most people wouldn't even notice the nuance, but the subtle nod to her special connection with her sister soothed her soul. It no longer mattered how her resignation would go. She was ready to go home and continue working on her business. Their business.

Brila returned to Kathryn's office fifteen minutes later. She knocked on the door frame and peaked in to find her typing an email. "Do you have a few minutes?"

Kathryn checked the clock in the bottom corner of her monitor. "I have a little time before my one-thirty."

Brila closed the door, which pulled her boss's attention away from the computer. She sat down and took a deep breath. "I think we're both aware that I've struggled the past couple months to find my footing within our team. I've enjoyed learning the job, and Halltown is a great company. But I don't think it's a great fit for me." She paused, but Kathryn didn't argue with this. "So for those and other personal reasons, I have accepted a job elsewhere. This is my two-week's notice."

Kathryn leaned forward, resting her arms on the desk between them. "Well, I'm a little surprised you're leaving us so soon, but I can't say I'm shocked. I think if you would have given it some more time, you could have found your place on our team and possibly found a better opportunity in another area within the company. You're a hard worker and a good employee."

Brila felt her face flush. She had received little encouragement or praise in her time at Halltown. Kathryn's words offered her a glimmer of hope that her efforts hadn't been completely wasted.

"It sounds like you've made up your mind, and if you've already accepted another job, I suppose there's not much I can do about it." She offered a soft smile. "It's been great working with you. I'll give it some thought over the weekend, and Monday morning we can plan out your last two weeks here."

"Thank you." Brila slid forward in her seat. "I appreciate all you've done for me."

"Let me know if you need anything, and be sure to let me know if you ever change your mind about PR or Halltown." She rolled her chair back closer to her computer and turned back to Brila. "And remind me to get your contact information before you leave us. I'm going to need you to bake cupcakes for my daughter's birthday in December."

Brila smiled. "Not a problem. I'd be happy to do that." She opened the door and left, pretending she didn't notice her coworkers' stares and whispers as she returned to her desk.

THIRTY-ONE

Over the next month, Brila's plans began taking shape. She had purchased a commercial-grade mixer along with a variety of new utensils and tools to stock her baking kitchen. Minor renovations had begun in Brian and Lyla's shed. They added storage shelving and upgraded to a double oven, which required a new countertop stove. Pieces of her list fused together to slowly shape her dreams into reality.

Brila sat on her couch with her laptop to create a new Instagram account and Facebook page for Angelle's Cupcakes. The mere act of typing the business name sent a mixture of excitement and pain surging through her. She scrolled through the pictures she had saved of her recent cupcakes, choosing a few to share with the caption "Grand Opening Wednesday, November 11. Join us for free samples and discounts on your first order." She scheduled it as her second post for later in the day. The first post for Facebook would take a little more thought, so she could find the right words to share her sister's story. She twisted her mouth to the side as she typed.

Since high school, my sister and I loved to bake cupcakes together. We experimented with flavors and decorations. Angelle always said one day we would open a bakery together. On November 11 last year, she was suddenly taken from us in a car accident. After that, I had no desire to ever bake again.

However, in an unexpected turn of events this past May, I found a renewed love for creating delicious, beautifully decorated cupcakes for others to celebrate significant life events, as well as adding a little sweetness to their day. I started Angelle's Cupcakes in my sister's honor and would find great joy in fulfilling your cupcake needs.

She read it over and over, her mouse hovering over the post button. The realization of this dream was so close that she could reach out and touch it. With each day, new life expanded in her, transforming her into a happier, more confident version of herself. She couldn't think of anywhere she'd rather be or anything she'd rather be doing.

Her phone dinged with the alert of a new text message. She closed her eyes as she clicked the post button on the computer. Her heart fluttered for a moment after she reopened her eyes and verified it had gone live. She selected names from her list of followers to invite them to like her business page. There was no turning back now.

She picked up the phone as a second alert chimed. She sighed in relief at the sight of Shanna's name. Her last day at Halltown the day before had been rather uneventful, with the exception of her final hallway conversation with Cameron. He had again told her how much he would miss having her around before calling her out for still not accepting his invitations for another movie night.

"I'm just really busy," she'd told him. "Once everything comes together. I promise."

Truth be told, she could spare a couple of hours to watch a movie and spend time with her friend. However, her heart and her mind were still debating whether she had romantic feelings for him or simply found comfort in his friendship. They'd known each other for so long. Just because he happened to help her on one of her most vulnerable nights didn't change things between them. Enjoying his company and feeling valued in his presence didn't mean she wanted to date him. Once she could get control of those feelings, she would find plenty of time for movie night.

Girls' night?
Tony's with his brothers and it's too quiet around here

Brila stared at Shanna's messages. She had plenty of items on her to-do list that needed to get done. On the other hand, she certainly deserved a break and a chance to get out of her own head. Tapping the screen to keep it from going black, she debated back and forth with herself. She nearly suggested they watch a movie, but guilt lodged itself in the pit of her stomach.

Dinner and drinks? I'm game as long as it's not a late one.

She closed her laptop, catching a glimpse of the likes and follows that had started coming in. She didn't dare check who or how many.

Brila spent most of October continuing to renovate the kitchen in her parents' shed, stocking ingredients, practicing recipes, filing paperwork, surviving inspections and interrogations, and building her social media following. She also continued to take a couple of orders each weekend. It was good practice and helped build her reputation as well as fund her new business.

On top of that, she'd started her new job creating digital marketing and social media content for a variety of businesses and organizations. After two days of face-to-face training in Dallas to familiarize herself with the company's software programs, policies, and expectations, she began a mostly independent and self-managed work structure.

She quickly learned to create a detailed schedule for herself to stay disciplined throughout the day. It had been an adjustment to not only learn her job tasks but also to work from home and no longer be micromanaged.

Of course, Angelle had been with her through it all. Elevens constantly showed up on the clock, license plates, and TV. With each passing day, she felt closer to her sister. For months after the accident, her greatest fear had been that a day would come when she didn't think about Angelle. It had happened before she had died; certainly, that norm would eventually return. Yet, a year later, in some strange way, she felt closer to her than when Angelle had been alive.

November eleventh rolled in like a thunderstorm of emotions. Brila woke up that morning, tears already welling in her eyes. She pushed them away. "We're not going to be sad today," she told herself as she sat up. She had a feeling a lot of self-talk would be needed throughout the day. With another deep breath to suck up her emotions and put them back in her heart, she pushed herself out of bed and prepared herself for the day.

She grabbed her laptop and the business cards that finally came in the mail two days earlier and scanned her condo for anything else she might need for the day. She didn't spot anything but still hesitated. As much as she had tried to convince herself it was just another day, it couldn't have been further from the truth. Not only would it forever be the day she lost a child and her sister, but it would also now be the day she officially opened her own business.

Angelle made her presence known on Brila's drive to her parents' house. The number eleven appeared on three different license plates and a billboard with the phone number 1-800-416-1111, not to mention the date glaring on the media dashboard. "That's right. You better be here today." She glanced to the passenger seat, almost expecting to find her sister riding along to their grand opening.

Inside her bakery, beautifully boxed cupcakes were on the display shelves and in the refrigerated case. A smile pushed up her cheeks and a flutter danced from her chest down into her gut. She had been there for the transformation. She had been the one putting all of these pieces together. Standing there now, though, it seemed to have transformed again overnight. A real bakery kitchen. A real business. Her business.

She swept her hands across the countertop, breathing in the sugary sweet smell of the frosting stored in the corner. She sat on one of the wooden stools, pulled her laptop out of the bag, and checked her task list for the day. Her boss had given her the okay to take the day off, but having started her job just a month earlier, she wanted to accomplish as much as she could in the morning before shifting gears.

At noon, her dad walked through the door. "Come eat. We have leftover spaghetti and chicken wings. Which do you want?"

"I just need to finish this one project. I'll come in and find something when I'm done."

"Don't push yourself too hard. You want to give yourself enough time before you open these doors to the mobs."

She chuckled. "I'll be happy if five people show up."

"Come on now. It'll be great." Brian smiled, lingering for a moment before returning to the house.

After lunch, Brila mixed together a batch of chocolate batter. She breathed in the sweet scent that escaped the oven and filled the room. She scooped the pale blue buttercream frosting into a piping bag and decorated two dozen vanilla cupcakes with large roses. She boxed them up and placed labels on the boxes she'd missed the day before. Her business cards and menu printouts were set in small holders at the front corner of the counter.

Satisfied with the inside, she went outside to hang the sign Shanna had given her. "Angelle's Cupcakes," written in eggplant purple, curled elegantly and popped in contrast to the dark wood. Her dad had secured the iron post to the bakery's outer wall the night before. Now she just needed to attach the hooks from the sign to the pole.

She stepped back off the ladder, folding her arms as she stared at the ones that replaced the Ls in Angelle's name. "I hope you like it," she whispered. "I hope you're happy with all of this. I hope I've made you proud." She tilted her head back and closed her eyes, letting the sunlight break through the cool breeze and wash over her, reaching into her soul.

Before returning to the bakery, she pulled her phone from the back pocket of her jeans to take a picture of the sign. She posted it to Instagram and Facebook with a reminder about the grand opening. She started a mental list of who might show up. Her parents, of course. Her dad had taken a vacation day from work, and her mom would be home after her two o'clock course. Shanna, Tony, and Cameron had all vowed to come. Another dozen or so friends on social media commented that they would show. Whatever happened, it would be okay. Wednesday was an odd day for a bakery grand opening, but she couldn't imagine doing it any other day.

Inside, she divided the white buttercream frosting into three smaller containers, adding yellow food coloring to one, red to another, and orange to the last. She practiced piping leaves on a piece of parchment paper before adding them to the chocolate cupcakes she had baked earlier.

She stepped back to admire her work. Not only did they look beautiful but the delicious scent of chocolate cake mixed with frosting made her mouth water. Debating whether she should eat one, she jumped at the sound of the door opening, then smiled as her mom walked in.

Lyla surveyed the kitchen. "It looks like you're ready to go."

"I have a few things left to finish up, but I'm almost there." She began packaging the chocolate cupcakes.

"Your sister would be so proud."

Brila stopped in her tracks and looked up to find her mom clenching her jaw and fighting back tears. She swallowed the lump in her throat as she walked around the counter and hugged her. She rested her chin on her mom's shoulder and took a deep breath. "I hope so. I wish she was here."

"All right." Lyla stepped back and smoothed her blouse. "I'm going to freshen up, then we'll be out to help with anything you need."

After her mom left, Brila started preparing trays of samples to set out around the bakery. In just thirty minutes, the door would be open for the grand-opening event. Would anyone care that yet another bakery was opening around town? Was she too arrogant in having a big event in the first place? And would her location in one of the western neighborhoods instead of being near the heart of the city hurt her chances at success?

She wanted to succeed. She wanted her business to mean something. Still, just turning her sister's dream into reality felt like a win. No matter what happened going forward, she would never consider it a failure.

THIRTY-TWO

Everything was set up and ready by 4:15 p.m. She paced around, nudging the packages and sample trays one way, then back again. Checking her phone, she watched the minutes crawl by until 4:30 p.m. came without any vehicles. She knew her friends would come later based on their work schedules. Maybe she shouldn't have started it so early, but she'd wanted to put a decent time span without staying too late.

At 4:45 p.m., the first car arrived. Then two others. By 5:00 p.m., the bakery was bustling with the energy of about a dozen people. Brila walked around, answered questions, graciously accepted compliments, and even took a few orders.

After processing payment for a half dozen red velvet cupcakes, she saw Shanna and Tony taking samples of the s'mores and angel food cupcakes. She hurried over and hugged each of them. "Thanks for coming."

Shanna squeezed her plastic sample cup. "Are you kidding? We wouldn't miss it. And we may become your top customers. How have you not shared these s'mores with us? Do you have any left?"

Brila laughed. "I knew you'd like them. I thought I'd told you when I made them for someone's camping-themed party." She glanced at the shelving on the front wall. "It looks like there's a couple boxes left."

Tony followed her eyes and walked over to inspect the inventory for himself. He returned a minute later with a box. "Will this do?"

Shanna peered around him. "Maybe. Not that I need anything, but I'll go check it out." She turned back to Brila. "We'll be around. Go mingle and make sales. It looks like you have a great turnout, and it's still early." Her smile was infectious, sending a flutter through Brila's stomach.

She continued through the crowd, greeting those she knew and introducing herself to those she didn't. She lost count of the number of people who had come in. It no longer mattered. Excitement surged through the bakery and into her veins. She took a moment to step back and watch people trying samples, looking at each of the flavors, scanning through the menu, and talking amongst themselves.

"This is incredible." Kathryn's voice behind her caught her attention.

She turned with a smile. "I'm glad you made it."

"Free cupcake samples? I wouldn't miss it." She looked around. "I can see why you left. You're going to do great things."

Brila looked to the floor.

"How much for a half dozen?"

Brila reached across the counter and grabbed a menu printout. "It's eleven dollars for a half dozen and twenty-two for a dozen." She handed her the menu. "Here are the flavor options. And I'm pretty flexible when it comes to decorations."

Maybe one day Brila would share the reason behind all of the elevens in her business, but for now, the secret nods to her connection with Angelle remained hers.

"My husband won't let me come home without some. I'll definitely have to get some for my anniversary next month."

"Absolutely. Just give me a call or reach out through social media, and I'd be happy to make whatever you need." Brila stood by and smiled as Kathryn grabbed a sample of the red velvet cupcakes before heading toward the display shelves. She crossed her arms then quickly uncrossed them, not wanting to appear unapproachable.

"Looks like quite the success," a voice called from her right.

She whirled around to find Cameron with an empty sample cup in his hand. She reached up and hugged him, then quickly stepped back and scanned the room. "I didn't see you come in. Have you been here long?"

He shook his head. "Just long enough to snag the last orange cupcake. Everything is perfect, as always." His eyes squinted a bit as he smiled.

"I don't know about that, but I can't complain. It's been greater than I ever could've imagined."

"That's because you're your own worst critic. I knew it'd all work out for you." He shifted his weight from one foot to the other and somehow ended up a half step closer to her.

Brila's heart beat faster. "Well, I appreciate your confidence. I may need to borrow some of it." She looked around, spotting a couple she hadn't met yet. "Are you sticking around, or do you have to leave?"

"I'm not going anywhere until you shut it down."

"All right. Well, I need to go mingle, but I'll see you later." She paused and lost herself in one of those gold flecks in his eyes for another moment, before moving on.

The flow of people through the bakery remained steady. It was never packed, but it also never felt empty. Brila moved effortlessly through the crowd, allowing herself to share Angelle's story with anyone who asked and credited her for the inspiration to start the business. A familiar rollercoaster of emotions accompanied these conversations, but it didn't overwhelm her. It didn't stop her in her tracks or force her to retreat like it had done so many times before.

As the number of new arrivals slowed to the point where she had talked to everyone, she found Cameron resting his forearms on the countertop. The tapping of his fingers on the stainless steel drummed in her head. "Can you stop?" She swatted her hand, flattening his against the counter.

He flipped his hand, wrapped his fingers around hers, and motioned toward the door behind them. "Come with me for a minute." His eyes focused intently on hers.

"I can't." Her heart pounded as she looked around the room. "What if someone wants to buy something or place an order? I can't just walk out of my own bakery."

"We won't be long. No one is going to just leave because you're gone for a minute or two. You can say you went to the restroom if anyone asks. Come on." He lightly tugged her hand again, which was still entangled with his.

She scanned the room again, hoping no one would see them as they snuck through the side door. Once outside, she shivered. Her purple t-shirt was no longer sufficient for the temperature, which had dropped into the fifties with the setting sun. "What's so important you had to literally pull me away from potential customers?" She asked playfully. Her heartbeat felt like it was visible outside of her chest. Why had he grabbed her hand and not let go? Why couldn't he say whatever he needed to say inside?

He finally released her hand, shoving his hands in his pockets as he shuffled his feet. "I needed to make sure you didn't have another excuse to avoid me."

She looked toward the shed and chuckled. "And you thought I wouldn't be distracted by my own grand opening?"

"I know. I just didn't want to wait anymore. And you've been avoiding me ever since that night at your place."

She looked to the ground. "I've been all over the place between starting a new job, trying to figure out how to run a business, figuring out who the heck I am anymore. Sorry if I've been a little distant."

"That's a lot of excuses, but none of them are the real reason you're hiding, are they?"

She couldn't meet his eyes. "I'm not hiding."

"Don't do that. We both know you're lying." He stooped down until she had no choice but to look at him. "You do realize that not all of our run-ins at Halltown were a coincidence, right?"

She furrowed her brow. "What are you talking about?"

"I wandered over to the PR group and took water breaks about twenty times a day in hopes of running into you." A small smile appeared.

"Yeah, I'm sure you spent half your day looking for me." She rolled her eyes.

"Not half the day, but I got up from my desk and spent more time on that side of the floor in those few months than I have at any point in my career."

Brila swallowed hard, daring now to search his eyes for what she should say next.

Instead, he continued, "I can relax and be myself around you more than I can with anyone else. It's always been that way, but something I've noticed a little more lately. Being around you is the highlight of any day. Believe me, I've tried convincing myself that it's just our friendship, that you don't feel the same way about me. But that night at your place, I think you felt something too."

Here he was, vocalizing the thoughts and feelings she'd agonized over for weeks, and she couldn't open her mouth to tell him.

"I know it's weird and scary." He placed a hand on her arm, sending a tingling surge of warmth throughout her body. "I don't want to ruin our friendship, but I miss seeing you. I miss making you smile. I'm just asking to take you out. Not as a group. Not as an accidental meet-up. I want to take you on a real date. Dinner, a live band, and dancing. Let's just see what happens."

She scanned her mental schedule and ran through a list of excuses to give him. "I don't know when—"

"I know you're busy, but I also know you can find time if you want to."

Her head and her heart continued their debate with one another. Honestly, she was tired of letting her head win. With a deep sigh and a smile, she answered, "You're right about ... everything. I don't want to get hurt. I don't want to hurt you. But something happened that night for me, and I guess before then, for you. It's worth seeing if maybe there's something more to it. What about Saturday?"

Cameron pulled his mouth to one side. "Saturday? I don't know if that'll work for me."

She narrowed her eyes and shoved his arm as he laughed. "Shut up. I'm going back in."

He grabbed her hand. "Wait. There's one more thing." He stepped close enough for her to breathe in his cologne.

She looked up to meet his eyes, her heart racing again. Their embrace in her apartment flashed in her mind. She wanted to lean against his chest, be wrapped up in his arms. "What's that?"

As if he read her mind, he pulled her into his warm body. She could've stayed there all night. Then he pulled away just enough to lean his head down to kiss her cheek. Every part of her was electrified. The glow of the shed beckoned her.

His eyes followed hers. "I know you have to get back. Just a little something to hold you over until our real first kiss." He smirked as she slipped out of his arms.

Before turning the knob she looked back. "Are you still staying?"

"I told you I'm not leaving until you shut it down. I'll be there in a little while."

She watched as he pulled out his phone and walked toward the driveway. As she stepped inside, her dad approached. "Where'd you go? Is everything okay?"

She smiled. "I'm great. I just needed a couple minutes. Did I miss anything while I was gone?"

"I think you have a couple of people interested in taking home some cupcakes." He put his arm around her shoulders. "It looks like you have a real sweet business here. I'm so proud of you."

She leaned into his side hug, watching out of the corner of her eye as Cameron returned through the front door. "Thanks, Dad. I guess I should go make those sales."

THIRTY-THREE

A little over a month had passed since the grand opening of Angelle's Cupcakes. Orders continued to trickle in at a steady pace. Brila still struggled from time to time with adhering to her daily schedule, but it was getting easier.

Monday through Wednesday, Brila completed the majority of her digital marketing work. On Thursday and Friday mornings, she also worked from home. Then she spent those afternoons at the bakery. With her laptop set up on the back counter in case any urgent work came up, she prepared that weekend's orders. Depending on the week, she would have pick-ups or deliveries Friday evening, Saturday morning, and Sunday morning. On Sunday evenings, she would prepare her own business's social media posts and create her schedule for the following week.

Her heart swelled with joy—something she hadn't felt since before Angelle's accident. While there were still difficult days, she found it easier to pull herself out of her depression when it struck. All she had to do was look around her. Without fail, an eleven would show up at some point in her day to remind her that Angelle was by her side through it all. It didn't replace her sister's smile, words of encouragement, or shoulder to lean on. Still, it gave Brila something to hold on to, something to ease her pain and warm her soul.

Most days she couldn't believe she'd made this dream a reality. She found fulfillment in her digital marketing work and enjoyed working from home more than she thought she would. She still faced challenges and fought her self-doubt, but most days, she grinned from ear to ear out of sheer joy in this new life she'd built for herself.

Keeping their tradition, Shanna and Tony were hosting their "Friends-mas" party the Friday before Christmas. Brila hadn't accounted for clean-up time when she had planned her schedule for the evening. She weaved through traffic to get back home. She should have brought a change of clothes and makeup with her so she could have gotten ready at her parents' house.

She sighed in relief as she parked and jumped out of her car, thankful Cameron hadn't arrived yet. She hurried inside and began to change. While pulling a red cable knit sweater over her head, a knock on the door caused her to freeze momentarily. Still in the black leggings she had worn all day, she jogged through the living room.

Cameron walked in and softly kissed her lips. "Ready to go?"

Brila inhaled deeply, trying to return her breathing to normal. "I actually just got here. I still need to finish changing and fix my hair and makeup."

"Why? You look perfect already. And we're just going to Tony and Shanna's."

She looked down then back at him. "I just need five minutes." She knew it was a lie as it came out of her mouth, but she would try to be as close to it as possible. Maybe she could get away with the black leggings and some boots. Then she only needed to add a little makeup and check her hair.

Since the grand opening, she and Cameron had transitioned seamlessly from friends to dating, almost as if they had always been together. They skipped the getting-to-know-you phase of a new relationship. There was no holding back parts of her personality and no awkward explanations about her past. Cameron knew it all. The only things that had changed were that they spent more time alone than they had in recent years and the added physicality to their relationship. And even the latter felt surprisingly natural.

Everything about being with Cameron was easy. As much as she had wanted D.T. to commit to a future with her, she hadn't worried about that with Cameron. First of all, she already knew his views on marriage, kids, and the future (or his vision of it). Besides, they were both working on their own personal development and discovering their own goals and ambitions. Supporting one another and navigating the recent change in their relationship was enough for now. They had the rest of their lives to build their future together.

Brila returned to the living room ten minutes later, slinging the strap of her purse over her head. "Okay, I'm ready."

Cameron slid off a kitchen stool with the box of s'mores cupcakes in hand. "Good. I was about to come pull you away from that mirror." He interlaced his fingers in hers, pulled her toward him, and kissed her—slowly, intently, passionately.

Her knees nearly buckled. Pulling away, she brushed her thumb along his bottom lip. "I don't think that's your shade."

"I disagree." He reached for the light switch while she opened the door. "I think it suits me just fine."

For most of the drive, Brila outlined the orders she had for the next two days, her busiest weekend yet. She had even agreed to complete a couple of orders for the day before Christmas Eve. She hadn't thought about developing a holiday schedule in her business plan, but doing so quickly went to the top of her priority list. As much as she loved the thought of filling others' dessert tables for the holidays, she didn't want to compromise her time with her own family.

"Sorry, that's enough about me. Tell me about your day." She glanced at their hands, still intertwined on the center console. The corners of her lips curled up.

"Nothing too exciting to report. I'm still relearning to not wander down to PR or fill up my water bottle when it's half full."

She studied the creases at the corner of his eyes. "So you're saying you've had to learn how to actually get your work done again?"

"I always got my work done. It's just not the same without you around."

"Well, then it's a good thing you get to visit me after work and basically whenever you want." She shifted her weight, leaning closer to him.

He lifted her hand and kissed it. "You're right about that."

"Hello?" Brila called as they stepped inside Shanna and Tony's house.

"We're out here," Tony called through the open door leading to the back patio.

Brila set the cupcake box on the kitchen counter and made her way to the living room, where she froze in front of their Christmas tree and nativity scene. She inspected the vast array of silver and blue decorations, from the glistening angel at the top of the nine-foot tree to the beautifully sculpted baby Jesus in the center of the wooden manger on the shelf beside it. Shanna's holiday spirit and eye for decoration were exquisite. "When I finally get a house, can you come decorate for me?" Brila called toward the patio.

"No need." Cameron walked up behind her, wrapping his arms around her waist. "I could do all this if I wanted."

A flutter tickled her stomach as she crossed her arms on top of his. "But you don't keep your place half as clean as this."

Shanna and Tony joined them. "Cam, are you challenging me to a decorating competition?" Shanna asked. "Because I'll definitely take you down."

"I wouldn't be so sure about that." He let go of Brila and took the wine glasses from Tony, handing one to her. "Besides, you'll have to start childproofing your tree soon. Any news on the adoption?"

Shanna narrowed her eyes at Brila. "You told him?"

"Tony told me," Cameron answered. "I figured you knew."

Tony looked apologetically toward Shanna. "In my defense, I figured Brila had already slipped up." He swirled the wine in his glass. "I can't believe she actually lasted longer than me."

"Wait. Why is everyone assuming I was the one to spill this secret?" Brila folded her arms.

"Does anyone else know?" Shanna continued to question Tony, who shook his head. She sighed and turned back to Cameron. "Nothing new yet. The mom who chose us could still back out at any time. That's why we're not telling anyone until everything's final." She looked at her husband then back to him. "So don't say anything."

"No problem. Sorry I brought it up." Cameron looked to Brila, who shrugged. "Did I mention we brought cupcakes?"

"Cupcakes aren't going to make it better." Shanna's shoulders relaxed as she glanced toward the kitchen. "How's business these days?"

"Busy, but I guess that's a good thing." She sipped her wine, holding back the urge to scrunch her face. There were few wines she enjoyed, and this bitter selection was not going to join that list.

"So what's next?" Tony asked. "Are you going to bake full-time? Open a storefront? Do more than cupcakes?"

She chuckled. "I haven't been doing this long enough to make any of those decisions. Let me figure out how to grow my client list and actually keep them coming back first." She looked around, feeling her cheeks warm. Her voice lowered, "Although, I do have an idea."

Cameron raised his eyebrow. "What's that?"

"I ..." Maybe she shouldn't have said anything. After all, it didn't seem very logical. "I thought it might be cool to have a food truck to deliver and sell individual cupcakes at lunchtime or something." She searched her friends' eyes, waiting for them to laugh.

Shanna spoke first. "You'd make a killing at the hospital. Around campuses. Downtown. Anywhere, really. I think you're on to something."

"Absolutely," Cameron chimed in. "But you'd probably have to work on the weekends too. There'd be some serious money to make on Fridays and Saturdays."

Brila hadn't considered that. "Well, it's not something I need to figure out for a while. It's not like I have money to buy and convert a truck right now. And I still need my day job."

"It might be worth taking out a loan for," Shanna said. "Food trucks are trendy right now. It could be a good way to get your name out there and build your business." She checked her watch. "Let me go check on the enchiladas."

Brila scrunched her eyebrows. "Yeah, well, I'll start with what I'm doing and think about it later." She took a drink but immediately regretted it. "I'm not sure why you're the one cooking enchiladas, but I'll come with you." She followed her friend into the kitchen. "Are you trying to prove yourself to Tony or his family or something?"

"I want to be able to cook the food Tony grew up with, and his mom gave me this super simple recipe." Shanna slipped on her red oven mitts and pulled the door open. "By the way, it's still weird seeing you two together." She looked over her shoulder as she lifted the casserole dish to the stovetop.

"Weird like you don't think we belong together?" She took another sip, making a face this time. Why was she still drinking the wine?

"No, you actually look happier than you have in a long time. It's just that we've all been friends for so long. I never really thought about y'all as anything else." She grabbed a pitcher of margaritas from the fridge and poured it into two glasses, handing one to Brila. "Stop drinking that stuff."

She gladly exchanged glasses. "I get it, but it's actually been a natural transition like it should've always been this way. So you better get used to it. I don't think I'm letting this one go." She caught a glimpse of the clock on the oven: 7:11 p.m.

She smiled as she sipped her margarita. She looked from Shanna to Cameron and Tony in the living room. Life wasn't perfect. Her heart still ached with the losses she had faced in the past year. And she certainly didn't know what the future would hold. Yet, Brila couldn't have been more excited about the path she was on, surrounded by people who loved her, and to have a connection with Angelle that no one could take away. What more could she hope for.

ACKNOWLEDGEMENTS

First, I want to thank my husband Troy. You have always stood by my side and believed in me. Thank you for your understanding as I put every extra bit of energy I had into this project and for entertaining the kids when I desperately needed to finish "one more chapter" on the weekends. To my kids, I hope that in chasing my dreams you will be inspired to never stop chasing your own. And to my parents, sisters, and all those in my small circle who have cheered me on throughout this journey, please know that your encouragement has meant the world to me.

Thank you to my friends, Audy, Raechele, and Amber, and fellow author, Mackenzie Littledale, for reading early drafts of my novel. Your honest feedback led to some much-needed improvements and encouraged me to keep going at a time when I started to doubt if this story was worth publishing. A special thank you to Kimberly Macasevich and Trish Rios, who made the daunting tasks of editing and proofing absolutely painless. Your expertise helped shape *What We Hope For* into what it is today.

Finally, none of this would be possible without my heavenly Father. After a lot of soul searching, He reignited my passion for writing and spoke this dream into my heart. I am beyond blessed and so grateful to have such wonderful people in my life and to have this opportunity to share a little piece of my heart with you, the readers.

ABOUT THE AUTHOR

Kirsten Usé grew up in Iowa but now resides in southern Louisiana with her husband and their two kids. She works in the world of finance by day and pursues her writing dreams by night. Her short stories have been published in the anthologies *Behind Closed Doors: Best of Writers Assembled 2017* and *Person(s) of Interest: Best of Writers Assembled 2018*. In addition to spending time with her family, writing, and reading, she enjoys football and music. *What We Hope For* is her first novel. Learn more at www.kirstenuseauthor.com.

Facebook @kirstenuseauthor
Instagram @kirstenuse

Made in the USA
Monee, IL
13 January 2022

88762300R00163